HER
COLD
EYES

HER
COLD
EYES

TONY BLACK

BLACK & WHITE PUBLISHING

First published 2018
by Black & White Publishing Ltd
Nautical House, 104 Commercial Street
Edinburgh EH6 6NF

1 3 5 7 9 10 8 6 4 2   18 19 20 21

ISBN: 978 1 78530 190 2

A CIP catalogue record for this book is available
from the British Library.

Typeset by Iolaire, Newtonmore
Printed and bound by CPI Group (UK) Ltd. Croydon, CR0 4YY

For John McCormack

'Our struggle is not against flesh and blood, but against the rulers, against the authorities, against the powers of this dark world and against the spiritual forces of evil in the heavenly realms.'

– Ephesians 6:12

Prologue

'Don't cry,' I tell myself. 'Don't cry, don't give them that.'

So, I try not to cry. I always try not to cry, but sometimes there's nothing can stop it.

There's nothing else I can do, because they have this control over me. They always have that, their power. All I have is the one last piece of myself they can never reach.

'Don't ... Don't do it,' I say inside.

I go deeper, to the place they can't follow. Though sometimes they try, and I lose my way. I should be able to shut them out, to push them back, but I'm weaker now, weaker than I was.

'Don't let them, Abbie, don't.'

They've taken everything else, everything I had, and everything I was. I have nothing left except the one place I can go to hide from them: my heart.

Mum's there, and my little brother. Sometimes it's Papa's place, with the paddling pool and the playhouse out back on a hot summer's day. Tyler's soaking me with the hose and laughing, smiling. Little Maxie's barking, jumping away from the spray, and there's ice lollies and blue skies and smiles and ... and I know I've let them in.

A tear.

Small.

Rolling from my eye onto my cheek. As insignificant as an ant, it seems, but carrying the world I hold inside me.

'No,' I say.

They see the tear now. Him, the one that's on me now, is angry.

I feel him going deeper, pressing harder. He wants to hurt me; they all want to hurt me because they know I'm not broken.

A hand presses my face and a thumb pushes my eyelid open. It's him; he wants me to watch what they're all doing to me, to see their staring eyes. They want me to understand just what it is they are, and why they have to hurt me.

'No.' I turn away.

'Yes!' He comes closer, his face touching mine. He's sweating, his heart pounding faster on top of me. 'You belong to us now.'

I say nothing. The tears stop because he has me in their grip now. They are my focus again, and I can't find my way back inside myself.

I can't escape any more.

He grits his teeth. Dirty teeth, decayed and grey, cracked at the edges. His skin is waxy and lined, old. He wheezes and is angry because he's done this a thousand times before, to a thousand other girls like me, and he knows I'm not broken.

But, soon I will be.

I'll be broken.

I know I will be.

Or I'll be dead.

1

As he turned into King Street station, Detective Chief Inspector Bob Valentine braced himself for the usual rigmarole of locating a parking space. The sighing, followed by head-shaking at vehicles overlapping the white lines. But today it didn't happen. He dropped into first, feeling the front tyres negotiate the small kerb between road and car park. At once Valentine realised he wasn't driving the old Vectra with the bloodstains on the back seat. It was gone, even if the memories of his near-fatal stabbing were still very much with him.

He put the car into his allotted space near the entrance and stepped out. It had been a routine of his, an almost masochistic one, to look in the back window of the Vectra at the dark mark made by his spilled blood and remember he was lucky to be alive. Did it keep him alert? Sharpen his guard? He doubted it; people were strange, they did things for lots of reasons but rarely did they understand any of them.

In the foyer Jim Prentice looked up from his copy of the *Mirror* and tucked it below the front desk. He stood up, made a display of brushing his epaulettes and stood to attention. It would have been an impressive piece of theatrical mockery if he hadn't betrayed himself with a snigger.

'Give it a rest, Jim,' said Valentine.

A salute worthy of Benny Hill followed. 'Aye aye, sir.'

'Is she in?'

'Dino, you're kidding, aren't you? Monday mornings are for the hoi polloi, the huddled masses ... which makes me surprised to see you.'

His recent promotion had come as a surprise to Valentine, like most of the big happenings in his life, so it made sense that the ranks would be equally shocked. The desk sergeant's jokes masked a deeper truth, however, and Valentine knew there was no justice attached to his promotion. If there were, a decent, hard-working copper like Jim wouldn't be sitting behind the front desk of the station. There was no way to balm over the injustice – he couldn't give his promotion away or share it around; all he could do was his best.

'I'll have to bear that in mind, Jim. I'm still getting used to this malarkey,' said Valentine.

'I hear it's heady air up there, Bob. Watch it doesn't bend your head.'

'There's no danger of that.' Valentine headed for the stairs. 'Anything in for me to look at by the way?'

'All quiet on the western front, Chief.'

'It won't stay that way.'

'No. It never does.'

At the top of the stairs Valentine glanced into the Murder Squad's open-plan office. DS Phil Donnelly was sitting at his desk, on an early phone call. He seemed to be the first detective in this morning; it would have been an ideal moment to have the chat about the DI's job going to Sylvia

McCormack, but it could wait. Valentine had forgotten about the hidden consequences of taking a promotion, and the ripples of resentment it could cause in the squad. Donnelly was a fine operator but he wasn't ready; of course that was not something a committed professional with a family to support ever wanted to hear.

The DCI went into his office and turned on the lights. It was a small room, larger than the bare cubicle with windows which he usually occupied at the far end of the main incident room, but no bigger than an average bedroom. There was a desk and chair, a set of shelves with glass doors, and a wire coat-stand that had probably been put in when the building went up.

Clare would want to decorate if she saw the grey walls, but in her current mood a visit was some way off. He raised his briefcase, placed it on the desk and removed a picture of his daughters. Valentine held the picture for a moment; in it, Chloe and Fiona were a couple of years younger. It was a favourite image; they looked so happy, smiling and laughing like they didn't have a single care in their heads. He laid down the picture frame and stared. Family was treasure, he thought, there really was nothing else.

After setting up his PC and finding himself locked out of his email he was distracted by a knock on the door. He turned to face the entrance, wondering if he should yell 'come' like the CS but instead rose and turned the handle himself. A woman in a black trouser-suit stood in the hallway, clutching a blue folder.

'Detective Chief Inspector Valentine?' she said.

'Yes.'

'I'm Dr Carter, we spoke on the phone.'

'Oh, yes. The assessment, you better come in.'

She walked to the middle of the room and looked around. 'Oh, dear ...'

'Is something wrong?'

'You appear to have only one chair.'

Valentine nodded. 'You're right, leave it with me. Take off your coat, you can hang it on the stand – I have one of those. I'll be back in a minute.'

He crossed the hall to the Murder Squad's office. DI McCormack had turned up now and was sitting with her back to DS Donnelly, who was staring at his computer screen. The mood was tense, and lacking in industry.

'Morning, Sylvia.'

'Ah, morning, boss.'

Valentine tipped his head in Donnelly's direction. 'How's he getting on?'

'Search me, hasn't said a dicky bird.'

'I should have a word, y'know, the talk. But, I have a meeting ... and I need to pinch a chair.'

'Take your pick.' McCormack waved a hand over the room.

When he returned to his office, wheeling a newly claimed chair, the doctor was standing with her arms folded, peering through the venetian blinds.

'Found one,' said Valentine.

'It's not the most fabulous view you have here, a car park and a block of council flats.'

'We have our sights in Auld Ayr too, beautiful Burns Country, don't you know.'

'I've seen the West of Scotland crime stats; if there's sights out there they're window dressing.'

'You might be right.' Valentine positioned himself behind the desk and made an apse of his fingers. 'So, what do you want from me?'

Dr Carter sat opposite, opening an A4 pad and tapping the nib of a pen on the desk. 'It's pretty straightforward, a standard psych assessment. I'm sure you've been through this sort of thing before.'

'Yes, after the ...' he ran fingertips over his chest ... 'stabbing.'

'I saw that in your file.' Her tone rose. 'Must have been horrific for you.'

'It wasn't a high point of my career, let's put it that way.'

The doctor turned to her notes. 'You had fifty pints of blood ... Fifty!'

'That sounds about right.'

She continued reading from her notes. 'Entry below the diaphragm into left ventricle. Angiography. Thoracotomy. Heart–lung bypass ... And you officially *died* on the operating table.'

'That happened, too.'

The doctor withdrew her pen and used it to flick her fringe. 'I'm amazed you survived, and appear so blasé about the whole incident.'

'I try not to dwell on it.'

She turned back to her notes. 'You had some therapy, I see.'

'Yes.'

'I've been over the notes and, well, you're obviously in possession of some advanced coping mechanisms by this stage. But I will need to delve a little deeper to write my report. It's a standard thing, you understand.'

7

Valentine eased himself back in his chair and crossed his arms; it felt like an unusually defensive posture for him so he corrected it, placing his hands, palms down, in front of him. 'What would you like to know, doctor?'

'Well, let's start at the start, shall we? Can you tell me something about your childhood?'

'My childhood? Are you serious, you really want to delve that far back?'

'Just a little, yes,' she said. 'Do you have any childhood memories that you can recall? Perhaps if you could give me one memory that you can call your oldest memory, most people have one like that. Do you have one?'

Valentine's gaze wandered, settling in the corner of the room. An indistinct patch where the grey walls met the white ceiling tiles. He was searching for something in his clutch of memories that he knew was there, but was very rarely accessed. There were memories he returned to but few from childhood that he dwelled on. It wasn't that he couldn't face those memories, it wasn't a hard time for him, but because he never felt the need. Valentine was a practical man, a police officer, a father. He had no place in his life for the days of his childhood.

'Inspector ... Do you have one?'

'I'm sorry, I was just thinking.'

'Just go on, when you're ready.'

Valentine brought his gaze down from the corner of the room and looked at the doctor. 'Well, I must have been about three or four, it was before school.'

'Carry on.'

'It's summer, one of those burning hot days of summer, in the seventies. And I'm playing in the back garden.'

8

'Are you alone?'

'Yes. Well, no, not really. I'm alone but I'm aware my parents are nearby.'

'Do you see them?'

'I don't. But I know they're there. I'm running about, I'm in swimming trunks and bare feet; it's very sunny, very hot. I don't know what happens, or how, but I end up being lifted onto a stool and I'm reaching up to the whirly where we dry the clothes – it's one of those old spinning ones.'

'I know the type, yes.'

'And I'm laughing, having the most joyous time. Spinning on the arms of the whirly. I think Dad's turning the thing, it's great fun for me. I do a full loop and come to rest on the stool.'

Dr Carter stopped writing and looked up. 'How does it end?'

'Dad goes in, probably a match on or something.'

'Are you alone now?'

'No, Mum's still there but she's pottering about, pulling weeds and so on. The stool's been moved to the path but I put it back under the whirly and start to swing round myself. Nobody sees me, I'm being sneaky.'

'Do you think you're doing wrong?'

'Yes. Definitely. But I don't care, it's too much fun.'

'What happens next?' She returned to her notepad and continued writing down his memory of the event.

'Everything changes. It's not a sunny day any more, I'm screaming, hurt.'

'What is it?'

'I've come off the whirly. My feet reach the stool but it

9

topples and I fall. I land on the concrete flags and I'm hurt. My knees bleed, my chin too, blood everywhere. I see Dad come running from the back door and Mum calls out to me. It all turns to chaos, to horror, very quickly.'

Dr Carter stopped writing and put down her pen. She looked at the picture of Chloe and Fiona. 'Are they your daughters?'

'Yes.'

'They're lovely.'

'Thank you.' The mood in the office had shifted, and Valentine sensed it. 'Did I say something wrong?'

'No,' she smiled thinly, 'no, not at all.'

'What does my memory tell you?'

'A memory like that, at that age, tells me that you're a man who understands the security family provides.' She leaned forward, touching the rim of the desk. 'But what does it tell you, Inspector?'

'Don't operate without proper backup.'

The doctor laughed. 'Well, I suppose that too.'

Valentine rose. 'I'm sorry, I haven't even offered you a coffee.'

'Coffee would be lovely, thanks.'

2

The vending machine wheezed and returned to rest in its low-power mode. It was still dispensing coffee from the nozzle when Valentine reached in to rescue the flimsy, overloaded plastic cup.

'Bugger.'

Two concentric drips landed in the middle of his shoe. It wouldn't have been a problem if he'd worn the black Oxfords, but the favoured option earlier that morning had been the tan brogues. He knelt down to dab the offending area with a handkerchief, something that did nothing for the shoe, except perhaps spread the damage to a wider area and make him grind his back teeth.

'I don't expect genuflection on arrival every morning, Bob, but if this is your new thing I'm flattered.' The chief superintendent descended into bellicose laughter as the lash of her joke reached Valentine.

He rose to face her. 'The machine's bust; it sprayed my bloody shoes.'

CS Martin glanced downward. 'Nasty business, they'll stain, y'know. Try talcum powder, might lift the moisture out. But on your own time, we've got a lot on today.' She edged past him, shuffling a rolled-up newspaper under her

11

arm as she went. 'Come into my office, I need to brief you.'

'But I've got the psychologist assessing me, for the promotion board.'

'Forget that, the paperwork's already done. My office, right away.'

'Can you give me five minutes?'

'Five minutes. And I'm counting.'

Valentine wiped the base of the coffee cup and delivered it back to Dr Carter with an apology for having to leave in a hurry. She seemed resigned, and familiar with the drill, like someone who had grown used to seeing their work being taken less seriously than it ought to be.

On the way past the Murder Squad's office Valentine peeked round the door and called over DI McCormack. 'What's occurring?'

'Sorry, boss?' she said.

'Anything on the wire?' said Valentine. 'I just had Dino shout me down the hall in a hurry.'

'I haven't heard anything, I'm afraid. I could ask Jim, if you like.'

'No, it's fine. I'm on my way in to see her now.'

'Good luck. Always feels like going on *Dragon's Den* to me.'

Valentine smiled. 'As long as it's not like *The Apprentice*. I've only just got this job, I don't want to hear "you're fired!" quite yet.'

Walking down the hall, the DCI couldn't resist a glance at his shoes, followed by a grimace at the darkening patch on the pale leather. He wasn't a superstitious man, despite being the son of a miner with a habit of quoting folklore, but there was something in his programming that occasionally managed to push him that way. Perhaps it was recent events, the sea change that had occurred in him since the stabbing, or the niggling voices that had been with him since.

There had been a row with Clare this morning too, of course, there had to be one of those. Even after the extended holiday to New Zealand, which hadn't worked, a farce really, that was no more than a sop to his wife's conscience, but had managed to double his credit card debt. That row wasn't over either, it had only just begun.

Valentine stood outside the chief super's office and tried to empty his thoughts. The skin on the back of his neck started prickling – he felt like he was being watched, but when he turned around the hallway was empty. He flushed out the emotion and knocked on the door.

'Come.'

'Is now a good time?' Valentine said.

'As good a time as any, Bob. In you come.'

Valentine stepped into the office and made his way towards CS Martin's desk. He settled into the vacant chair and scanned the grey skyline of Ayr in the window behind her. The jagged zigzag of the buildings butted a bleak, cloudless expanse that promised rainfall before the morning's end. He crossed his legs and felt the muscles in his neck stiffen.

'Right, so here we are,' said Martin. She was leaning forward, lacing her fingers and twiddling her thumbs.

'Yes, that we are.' Valentine detected a change in mood since he'd met Martin at the vending machine. 'You mentioned a briefing.'

'In a minute, Bob.' The thumbs stopped moving. 'How did the holiday go?'

'Fine.'

'That's it? Fine?'

'No, it was good. It was a holiday, what can you say?'

'Didn't you go all the bloody way to Australia?'

'It was New Zealand. It was Clare's call, I'm not that much of a traveller.'

The chief super pinched her lips. Valentine had told her about his wife's opposition to him remaining on the force after the stabbing, but she clearly didn't want to delve into the subject again, not least since he had accepted her offer of a new job. 'And now you're back to the grind,' she said.

'I am.'

'Good. Have you touched base with your squad?'

'Briefly.'

'And?'

'DI McCormack seems to be settling in.'

'I'm not interested in Sylvia settling in, Bob. I should think she would be over the moon with being bumped up to DI. It's whether or not there's any tremors I'm interested in.'

'Tremors?'

'Yes, y'know, like tremors that might lead to an earthquake.'

Valentine shifted in his chair. 'Well, DS Donnelly's nose is obviously going to be a bit out of joint, but he'll get over it.'

'He won't have any choice, Bob.'

'No.'

'Certainly not with our workload and the rapidly dwindling pot of resources we have to work with. I need Sylvia to be up to the DI role right away and, if necessary, I want you to spoon-feed her at every step. Do you understand?'

Valentine got the message clearly. 'You want me to do my new job and also my old job, but bring DS McCormack along for the show.'

'Not quite how I'd put it, certainly not if HR was in the room, but I suppose we're on the same page, Bob.'

The CS eased back in her chair and exhaled. She moved from the desk and retrieved a blue folder from the filing cabinet by the window. The sound of the drawer rolling back into place was the high-pitched screech of metal on metal and forced a wince onto her face.

'That bloody drawer drives me nuts. I swear it's getting like Communist Russia around here,' said Martin. 'We'll be re-using teabags next... Austerity? For everyone but the bastards in Parliament who are writing the rules as they go along.'

Valentine let the CS rant and watched a starling swooping outside the window. Rain was starting to spatter softly on the glass.

'Right, here we are.' Martin settled back into her chair and opened the folder; she was flicking pages as she spoke again. 'I take it you know about the Abbie McGarvie case?'

'Just what I've heard, and what I've seen on the news. Missing teenager, isn't she?'

'Yes, it's an interesting case.'

'Interesting?'

'Very.' Martin looked up from the folder. 'I'll give you DI Davis's file, you can take a look for yourself.'

Valentine caught the file as it was flung at him. 'Why are you giving me this? She's not been found. Are you telling me you suspect murder?'

15

'No, or should that be, I don't know. There's some very unusual circumstances surrounding this one. It was the mother who reported the girl missing without the father's knowledge. The parents have separated and the father has custody. When you get into the file, Bob, you'll see it's a total viper's nest of accusation and counter-accusation. Horrific, almost creepily so, and the kind of details that don't make for pleasant bedtime reading. Just some of the most vile character assassination going on, and that's on behalf of both parents as well. Have a shufti at the file and tell me what you think.'

Valentine leaned forward and started to rise. 'Okay, will do.'

'No, don't take it away. I mean just now, Bob … Sorry, I should have said, we found a dead girl's body last night.'

3

The Murder Squad sat facing their screens in almost complete silence, the only sound being the occasional clicking of a computer mouse. As Valentine entered the room he put his hands on his hips and cleared his throat, the sound of which was enough to force DI McCormack to look in his direction.

'Oh, didn't see you come in there, boss,' she said.

'I'm not surprised, it's like a calculus exam in here. What the hell's the matter with you all?'

DS Donnelly eased round in his chair, his fingers hovered above the keyboard on the desk for a moment and then he withdrew them to his pockets and spoke, 'We're waiting for the bell.'

'Well, it's not the bloody bell you were hoping for, Phil, it's the fire bell,' said Valentine. 'Grab your coats and follow me downstairs – home time is going to be a little later today.'

As DI McCormack eased into her jacket she juggled her bag from hand to hand in a practised, well-coordinated move. She was sufficiently speedy to catch the door that was closing in the wake of Valentine's departure from the room.

'Boss, what's the SP?' she said.

He tossed her a set of car keys. 'You're driving. Consider yourself flattered, by the way, it's my new motor.'

Sylvia looked at the key ring. 'Audi, very swish.'

'It's not all it's cracked up to be. The Vectra had a bigger boot.'

'How very practical, and Scottish, of you.'

The DCI sneered at her. 'If you say I'm starting to sound like my old man I'll bust you back to DS.'

The remark was picked up by Donnelly, who'd caught up with the front-runners in the dash to the car park. 'Will that vacancy be thrown open to the floor, boss, or will somebody just be parachuted in?'

Donnelly's remark was pointed enough to register a double bullseye, one on Valentine and one on the new DI, but neither responded, opting for a knowing exchange of glances instead. In an effort to change the subject quickly Valentine removed the blue folder from under his arm and held it aloft as he proceeded to descend the stairs.

'Abbie McGarvie,' he said. 'Are any of you familiar with the case?'

'Missing teen, sir,' said McCormack.

'Has she turned up, then?' said Donnelly.

'That we don't know,' said Valentine. 'We have a fatality, victim of an RTA, which is looking suspicious. That's where we're headed now, a B-road out by Monkton, near enough to Prestwick Airport.'

At the front desk Jim Prentice stood up and saluted, then promptly crumpled into peals of laughter. His hacking laugh could still be heard as the officers reached the swing doors. Valentine stepped aside to hold the handle so the others could pass through, then dispensed a single-digit salute to the desk sergeant.

'Come on, Bob, that's just unseemly behaviour for a man of your position,' said Prentice. 'I expected better.'

'You're right, Jim, we could all do a little better on that front. And you can start by binning that copy of the *Mirror* you have under the counter – you're inspiring me to make sure things are a bit more shipshape around here!'

On the road to Monkton, Valentine opened the file on Abbie McGarvie. The note-taking by DI Davis was extensive but the subject matter, even to an officer with Valentine's experience, made for difficult reading. He had dealt with child abuse cases in the past, but allegations of ritualistic and occultic paedophilia was something entirely new to him.

'Holy Christ,' he said.

'What is it?' said McCormack.

'This woman, the mother of Abbie, she's alleged all kinds of stuff happening to her daughter.'

'Are you on about what I think you are?'

'No. I don't think you could imagine, Sylvia. I'm talking about gang rape and bloody rituals with sacrificial animals and men in robes.'

DS Donnelly leaned in, placing his elbows on the back of the two front seats. 'Sounds very Aleister Crowley to me.'

'Who?' said Valentine.

'The nutcase that they called the Wickedest Man in the World. He was into all that sort of stuff, magic rituals, summoning the Devil and so on.'

'You know about this kind of thing?'

'No, not really. I read a book or two, watched a documentary once. It tends to be discredited, not that I'm saying it doesn't exist but that maybe those who do it have better PR than their accusers.'

'Well, that makes some sense. When Dino briefed me she told me to keep the investigation on the down-low; with all these paedophile politicians and grooming gangs on the loose she definitely won't want any press attention. Tell me more about this Crowley character.'

'Well, I don't know that much. I did a stint in Northern when I was in uniform and it was there that I heard rumours about him. Crowley had a house in Inverness-shire, on the banks of Loch Ness – I think it was called Boleskine or something – this was years back, mind you. I think some rock star bought it and then sold it on again. I believe it was burned down.'

'What rumours did you hear about Crowley?'

'There was talk of him exhuming bodies from a nearby cemetery for occult rituals. I did hear that Crowley had an underground passage from his house leading to the cemetery where late-night sacrifices were held, but I don't know if anything was ever actually proven. That's the problem with a lot of this stuff, it all seems so fanciful to the man in the street that it gets dismissed, but I've no doubt it goes on up there in the hills. Northern's books are full of weirdos arrested with sheds full of decapitated domestic pets and vats of blood.'

Valentine handed Donnelly the file. 'Here, have a look what DI Davis has turned up. You might be able to make more sense of it than I can because I'm reading it like a Hollywood movie script.'

20

'That's because Hollywood's the home of sin, boss. That place would be my first port of call if I was looking for the real truth on what goes on in these circles.'

The Audi pulled into a side-verge ahead of the police cordon. The HGV was blocking the road in one direction where the accident had occurred. It was a quiet road, not one that was used to so much traffic and the police Land Rover, assorted uniforms and SOCOs looked alien in the setting.

Valentine rubbed the back of his neck as he walked from the car towards the SOCOs. The ache in his neck that had started outside CS Martin's office was intensifying, like a niggling, prickling conscience that was trying to tell him something.

'Everything okay, boss?' said McCormack.

'Yes, why shouldn't it be?'

'You have that *look*.'

'What look?'

'You know, *that* look.' She tilted her head and winked.

Valentine took his hand from his neck and stomped towards the officer with the most stripes.

'What's the story?' said the DCI.

The uniform, a sergeant in a dirty yellow hi-vis vest, took his attention away from a radio call and addressed the senior officer. 'Oh, good morning, sir. It's an RTA.'

'I guessed as much, I am a detective.'

'Sorry, I didn't mean ...'

'Can you talk me through the scene, sergeant?'

The sergeant pointed to a wall skirting the side of the road; the grass verge at its base was almost a foot high. 'Well, apparently, the deceased was on the top of the wall

21

when the vehicle came over the brow of the hill. She was descending the wall, on our side, when she jumped down and ran across the road. That's when she came into contact with the lorry.'

Valentine followed the sergeant's line of sight towards the white tarpaulin covering the road. There was a distance of a few yards between the front grille of the lorry and the white covering. On either side of the tarpaulin thick black tyre marks were burned into the road.

The collection of SOCOs seemed fewer than usual and they were being assisted by a smattering of uniforms. It appeared that the scene was being treated more like a standard road traffic accident, and Valentine bemoaned DI McAlister's absence.

'We're missing our advance party,' he said.

'Ally would certainly have been useful to us, very bad timing by those inconsiderate gallstones,' said DI McCormack. She turned towards the sergeant. 'Has the fiscal been on site?'

'Yes, he has.' The sergeant removed a notebook and read aloud. 'Colin Scott was the fiscal depute on the scene and he's been and gone. Along with the doctor.'

Valentine was circling the road markings. 'When did the driver back up the vehicle?'

'Before we arrived, sir. He said his instinct was to apply first aid but it obviously wasn't an option.'

'And where is the driver?'

'The paramedics removed him to hospital. He's in a state of shock.'

'Did he offer any explanation, any reasoning as to what happened?'

'None, sir. Although he did say she looked like she was running from something.'

'Running?'

'He said she seemed scared.' The notebook was referred to again – '*The girl looked terrified. She wasn't watching her steps, she was bloody running for her life . . .* That's his words, sir.'

Valentine watched the sergeant return the notebook to a pocket beneath his dirty hi-vis vest; it seemed to be a final indicator of his knowledge on the matter. He stood silently, facing the detectives for a moment and then made an apologetic shrug.

The DCI turned to McCormack. 'Check in with the hospital. When the driver's over the shock, go and have a word and see if he can tell us any more.'

She nodded. 'Will do, boss.'

There wasn't much to go on from the initial findings and it infuriated Valentine. As he turned away a sharp pain struck his neck, causing him to wince. He massaged the spot quickly and tried to distract himself by drawing his gaze into the distance.

'What's over that wall, Donnelly?'

'No idea, boss. But I'll get on that now.'

'Do that and let me know right away.'

'Yes, sir.'

Valentine dropped his hand and set out on the road. 'Come on, let's take a look at our victim.'

4

The sky settled in to a grey-purple wash. In the distance, hovering over the town of Prestwick, black clouds were gathering. Further out at sea, the skies seemed calmer and brighter, but Valentine knew that didn't count for much. Ayrshire summers were well known to touch all points on the barometer, sometimes all in one day.

As the officers moved towards the crime scene, long grass and overhanging branches were moving in tresses. The side road had been allowed to overgrow and Valentine knew it wouldn't make his job any easier. He cursed the local council for skimping on essential services and the knock-on effect for his murder investigation.

'Does that bloody council do anything other than take my bins away?' said the DCI.

DI McCormack was ducking under a branch as she responded. 'They're probably too busy closing libraries and public toilets to trim verges, sir.'

'And kiddies' parks, they're onto those now,' said Donnelly. 'Did you see that story in the paper about the woman who got caught short and couldn't find a public toilet? She took a dump on the lawn of the Grosvenor Hotel and had all the diners chucking up in their soup!'

Valentine shook his head. 'Stories like that should make us all proud we spent all that money bailing out the banks.' He held up a branch for the officers to walk under. 'Let's try and get this done before the rain starts again.'

A white-suited SOCO was leaning over the tarpaulin on the road, one hand raising the weighted edge to peer underneath. Behind him, two uniforms were wrestling with a larger piece of canvas that appeared to be the main portion of a tent. When the crouched SOCO spotted the approaching officers he released the tarpaulin and stood up.

'Good morning, sir,' he addressed Valentine, but his attention was on the uniforms unravelling the canvas.

'Can you take the face mask off,' said Valentine, 'we'd like to hear you properly.'

'Sorry, sir.' He tugged down the pale blue mask, revealing a simpering smile. 'I have some more masks and gloves for you.'

The detectives plucked latex gloves from the cardboard box on offer, as they did so a black Lexus pulled alongside them on the road. The front side window was already lowering as the car slowed to a halt. When Valentine caught sight of the driver – a broad-faced man in his forties – leaning out, he wondered if there were any officers controlling traffic further down the road.

'Has there been some kind of accident?' asked the man.

Valentine formed a fist around his gloves; he was more than vaguely irritated by the interruption. 'You realise this is a crime scene, don't you?'

The man offered a hand through the window. 'I'm sorry, I work in the Sutherland estate.'

The detective stared at the man's hand, toying with the idea of slapping a handcuff on it, but it was sharply raised to point beyond the road. 'Over that wall is David Sutherland's property. I'm his head of security ... hang on, I've a card somewhere.'

When the card was presented Valentine read the man's name, Ray Coulter, and then he questioned another one of the details. 'It says Laverock Holdings here. I presumed you meant a private estate?'

'Yes, well, both really. Mr Sutherland has his business on the estate, works from home so to speak. Look, this is a main access route for the estate, is there going to be a lengthy disruption here?'

Valentine was growing tired of the man's officious tone. He handed the business card to DS Donnelly and ordered the Lexus be removed from the crime scene. 'And tell him we want full access over that wall. Set up a fingertip search right away and let me worry about the overtime budget.'

'Yes, sir.'

As the DCI walked off he could hear the estate's head of security continuing to question him, then DS Donnelly's gruff voice drowned everything out – 'Shift your vehicle now!'

DS McCormack smirked. 'I don't think the "I want to see the manager" shtick works with Phil.'

'It works better with Phil than it does with me. Remind me to send Phil if we have any more dealings with his lordship.'

The officers circled the corpse as the covering was removed. Beneath was the naked body of a young girl, her head pushed westwards at an unnatural angle. As

Valentine looked at the pitifully contorted figure he was drawn to her eyes – bulging, staring front – which seemed to beg him for sympathy. For a second the pain in his neck, which he had felt all morning, started to intensify and then it promptly vanished.

'This is how we found her,' said the SOCO. 'The driver was certain that she was dead before he could do anything.'

'Did he move her?' said Valentine.

'No, sir. He said he checked for a pulse, but that was all.'

The DCI knelt down and took a closer look at the girl's face, three quarters of which was covered in blood and dirt. He tensed up when he realised the severity the impact had on her pathetically delicate body.

'Is it Abbie?' said DI McCormack.

'I've no idea. She's in some state; we'll have to get her face cleaned up before we can ID her properly.'

Valentine removed the remainder of the tarpaulin, which was covering the lower portion of the girl's legs. He expected to find her legs bare, in line with the rest of her, but found instead a pair of white sports shoes covering her feet.

DI McCormack leaned in to get a better view. 'Tennis shoes?'

'Yes. A pair of Dunlop Green Flash, didn't even know you could still buy them.'

'They look brand new,' said McCormack.

'She couldn't have been running very far, then.'

'No. It makes me wonder about her clothes. If it was a sex assault you'd expect to see some clothes, but with nothing on at all, I don't know, it doesn't fit.'

Valentine had moved on from the shoes and was eyeing

some markings on the torso. He removed a pencil from his inside pocket and pointed the end towards the marks.

'What's this?' he said.

The SOCO turned around. 'It looks like bruising.'

'With flesh tearing?'

'Yes, sir. I know how sinister that sounds.'

Valentine rebutted the remark with a look his wife called his 'stink eye' and got up to face the SOCO. 'What else is there? Markings, abrasions, bruising?'

'Oh, well, there's abrasions on the knees, a fall likely, and there's some grass staining on the elbows which would indicate that, too. There's also a lot of scratches.'

'Scratches?'

The SOCO indicated a set of seriatim lines criss-crossing the girl's forearms. 'Looks like she was running through heavy foliage; they're not defensive, they're not deep enough to indicate a weapon was used. There's a couple of sets of contusions on the upper wrists that look suspicious but I wouldn't like to hazard a guess as to their cause, sorry, above my pay-grade that one.'

Valentine rose and looked at the girl lying prone and exposed on the cold tarmac. 'Cover her up. I've seen enough.'

As the officers grouped again, the DCI edged away from the tarpaulin towards the grass verge. He was forcing the edge of his blunt thumbnail into his chin as he spoke again, 'The doc's been and gone so let's get her on the slab right away, Sylvia. I want to know what we're missing because none of this makes any sense out here.'

'Yes, boss. Do you want me to call Pathology now?' said the DI.

28

'Now. And you can tell Wrighty to bump everything else. This is our priority.'

'Will do.' McCormack removed a mobile phone from her pocket and pressed it to her ear. 'It's ringing. What do you think the cause of death will be, sir?'

'I don't need to think, I know. Her neck was broken.'

'Is that an educated guess?'

'Call it a feeling I have,' said Valentine.

A stray gale whipped down the road and raised a corner of the white tarpaulin, exposing again the girl's lower legs. The sight of the tennis shoes poked at Valentine's thoughts once more and he turned away to feel the brunt of the wind lashing at his face. As he turned he spotted three young uniformed officers wrestling with the skeletal structure of a scenes of crime tent, moving it tentatively towards the victim's resting place.

'They're not much older than that girl themselves,' said Valentine as McCormack rejoined him.

'I don't remember being that green at their age.'

'They say each generation gets softer, makes you fret for the future.'

McCormack nodded. She held up her phone before dropping it in her bag. 'Wrighty's ready and waiting. He'll dig in when the SOCOs are finished later today and suggests we go over first thing in the morning.'

'Well, there's nothing to see here now. You can chase up the HGV driver once his nerves have settled.'

'Will do.'

'Come on then, let's get back to the station before Dino starts calling.'

In the car Valentine fiddled with the position of the

29

driver's seat as he pulled into the road. He trailed the wall, which looked to be about three metres high and was made with interlocking concrete sheets. Every six metres or so was a solid concrete stanchion with an outward-facing lip which could hold barbed wire, though that option had been left out.

'It's some size of wall,' said McCormack. 'It looks like the kind of thing Trump's been pushing for.'

'Seems to be covering almost the same distance as the Mexican border as well.'

Approaching the side road to the village of Monkton, Valentine spotted what looked like an entrance. On the opposite side of the road was farmland, all the way to the bypass. He scanned for a property, farmstead or similar, but couldn't see any in the immediate view.

'I think we'll just take a look in here.' He pulled into the thick, grassy verge and parked with two tyres on the road, stilling the engine.

The officers got out of the car and walked towards a gate that was wide enough for two cars to pass side by side. The gate was an imposing statement, made of thick steel and painted black. There were no markings on the front panels aside from the rows of rivets, set in two parallel lines all the way around the edges.

Valentine pressed a hand on the front of the black panel. 'Solid.'

'And not even an intercom,' said McCormack.

'Nothing. Very strange, don't you think?'

'It could just be a service entrance, where they have the rubbish collected.'

'Maybe.'

A low rumbling like the sound of a two-stroke engine from an old lawnmower started behind them, and as they turned a slow-moving scooter passed by. The whiny engine noise carried on, accompanied by a silvery smoke-line, towards the town when the hardier noise of a tractor engine came in to block it out altogether.

Inside the tractor's cab, a man in a plaid shirt looked startled as he eyed the officers. He slowed the vehicle and drew up beside the Audi at the verge. The driver was removing a set of orange ear-guards as he spoke from the open window of the cab.

'You won't get anyone to let you in there,' he yelled.

'Why not?' said Valentine.

'Well, for a start, you don't have a Range Rover with blacked-out windows.'

Valentine glanced at McCormack, he could almost sense the DI's brains itching. 'What do you mean by that?'

The driver switched off the engine and leaned out the window. 'Down the pub they call it Area 51 in there.'

The DCI turned around to see if McCormack was able to decipher this conundrum.

'Erm, I think he's referring to a spot in Nevada they call Dreamland, it's some kind of covert government facility.'

Now it was Valentine's turn for his brain to itch. He started to walk towards the man in the tractor; by the time he reached him, the detective was starting to sense a shift in the man's demeanour. He was settling back in his seat, withdrawing his elbow from the window.

'What do you mean by that?' said the DCI.

The man's voice grew nervy. 'Who are you?'

'We're police officers.' He presented his warrant card

31

and immediately regretted it. It had been an instinctual response, but there were times when instincts had to be resisted and this was one of them.

The man turned away and started the engine of the tractor once again. He had one hand on the wheel and another engaged in closing the cab's window as he spoke. 'I think I've said too much already.'

The tractor pulled away, scrunching gravel beneath its heavy tyres, and proceeded effortlessly up the road. 'Everyone's a bloody conspiracy theorist these days,' said Valentine.

'If only they actually wore those tinfoil hats we'd be able to pick them out a lot better,' said McCormack.

'It would save on time wasting, I suppose. Right, c'mon, let's get back to the station.'

McCormack followed Valentine's steps to the car. 'Boss, do you want me to call Abbie McGarvie's father to come and ID the body?'

'No. Contact the mother.'

'But the father has legal custody, sir.'

'I know, but looking at DI Davis's file I'd say the mother might tell us more. We can get the father in afterwards, when we'll hopefully have more to challenge him with. There's some old wounds I want to pick with him.'

2009

Mummy leans down beside me. Her eyes are wide and shiny and her voice doesn't sound like it used to. Her words are all wobbly and some even get trapped inside and don't come out at all. I watch her gulp down something, but she hasn't eaten a thing and that's when I see the little tear rolling.

'Now,' she says, 'what a big girl you've become today. Six, how big a girl is that?'

'Very big! Huge!'

Mummy smiles again and I see her eyes are red too, red and shiny because of all the water inside. She has a white tissue in her hand and she turns away and touches her eye with it. I don't know what she's looking at because she's staring at the carpet, and I wonder if she doesn't want to look at me any more.

I don't like to watch Mummy, it feels wrong, and I start to look at the purple and pink streamers behind her, hanging from the fireplace. Some of the streamers, the blue and red ones, have fallen on the floor. The fallen streamers make me sad because it makes me think that my birthday party is over now.

The party had been so nice. All my friends from school

were there. Mummy was there, and Daddy too. And Tyler was a good boy, but now he's gone to Gran and Papa's and the party is all finished. It makes me sad to think that my birthday party is finished and I don't like to feel sad, not ever.

'Have you had a nice time, darling?' says Mummy.

'Yes, thanks.' I watch Mummy tuck her tissue in her sleeve.

'It's been a lovely party, I think your friends enjoyed themselves.'

I nod and smile, and try to look happy. The big sign in the living-room window says *Happy Birthday*. My Mr Happy card sings 'happy birthday' when you open it up and you're supposed to be happy on your birthday. I'm only six and even I know that.

'But, Mummy. It makes me feel sad.' The words just came out, I don't know from where.

Mummy's face changes again; her words come out clearer. 'Why does it make you feel sad?'

I don't know what to say. I think being sad is just something that happens now. 'Now I'm a big girl I have to be sad.'

Mummy's mouth opens and closes very slowly. Her eyes aren't so big and bulgy now, but go all narrow. I can tell I've said something that I shouldn't and I wonder what will happen.

'Abbie, who told you big girls have to be sad?' says Mummy.

'Nobody.'

'Come on, you can tell me. You won't get into trouble.'

'Nobody said anything.' I feel like I am going to get a row and my lip starts to curl up.

'Okay, darling ... that's okay. Don't upset yourself.'

I'm a big girl now. I'm six. I shouldn't cry, but the tears come anyway. I start to cry and my hands cover my face and my shoulders start to shake. I'm crying and crying and I don't want my Mummy to go away ever again. I'm crying and I can't stop shaking and I want to say about the box and the spiders and how scared I get, but I know if I tell it will be worse.

'Now, Abbie, what's the matter? What is it? Why the tears?' Mummy grabs me close and lifts me. I grip tight and I know I've done wrong because I could be found out and that would be the worst thing ever.

'What's happened?' says Dad. He's come through from the kitchen with bubbles on his hands and his arms from the washing-up. He has an orange dishtowel tucked into his trousers like he does when he can't find an apron.

'You tell me, Brian. She's upset out of nowhere.' Mum has her grumpy voice on now.

'What's that supposed to mean?' says Dad.

'It means what it means. Look at the state of her.'

'Perfect. Is this what you had in mind all along? Disrupt the peace and quiet, even on your daughter's birthday.'

I don't want to hear them rowing. I don't want to hear any more shouting. 'Can you stay, Mummy?'

Mum looks at me and her lips go into a little line.

'Can you? Can you stay?' I know she has to go, but I don't want her to go anywhere ever again. I want her to stay here with me and play with my new toys and games and put face-paints on. I want to be a tiger. 'Can you paint a tiger face on me, Mummy?'

'Mummy can't stay, Abbie,' says Dad.

'I'm sorry, darling. I have to go.'

'But ...' I want her to stay. I want her to do the face-paints with me. I want to cuddle up with Mummy and watch *Toy Story* on the television all night and in the morning for her still to be there and everything to be like it used to be, but it can't be like that any more and it makes me sad.

'Now, now, Abbie.' Dad starts to peel my arms away from Mummy's neck. 'Mummy has to go. Don't you?'

'I'm sorry, darling.'

'Say goodbye to Mummy.'

I know not to make a scene, that's what he always says, 'don't make a scene', and so I stay at the window and wave to Mummy. She gets into her little white car and smiles. There's a wave as she drives away and then I watch her car until it's out of sight. I feel cold on the windowsill, there's a chilly bit here, but I don't want to get down. I still want to hope that Mum will drive back in her little white car and we'll do the face-paints I got for my birthday and have chocolate milkshakes and watch *Toy Story*, but she never comes back and I have to get down.

Dad is standing there in the middle of the floor and his face is very hard, like he's angry but hasn't said so yet.

I wonder what will happen next. It's my birthday and you are supposed to be happy on your birthday, but I know from Dad's face that my birthday doesn't matter.

'You know what you've done,' he says.

'I'm sorry.'

'I don't care if you're sorry.'

'I'm sorry.' I feel warm tears again.

Dad lunges out and grabs my hair. He drags me into the hall and opens the door to the cupboard under the stairs.

I'm screaming and screaming as he opens the box and forces me in. I can see the spiders wriggling about in the bottom of the box and I'm terrified, but then everything is dark and I'm alone in the place I fear most in the whole, wide world. I kick and scratch and try to get away from the spiders but I can't, there isn't anywhere to go.

I'm alone and scared and I scream and scream until I have no screams left.

5

CS Martin stood in the main incident room of King Street station, waiting for the Murder Squad's return. She appeared to be slowly edging herself in front of the window that overlooked the streetscape. But when Valentine got closer he gathered that she was actually following the progression of the pedestrian traffic towards the town centre.

King Street had become an intersection where the flotsam and jetsam of the Whitletts estates met the residents of Tam's Brig and a host of drifting, shiftless figures from the town of Ayr. It was a fascinating vantage point, one Valentine utilised himself, to glimpse just how dramatically the town had changed, and continued on its steep, downward trajectory.

'Don't get too comfy there,' said Valentine, entering the glassed-off corner office they called the greenhouse.

Martin glanced over, a half-turn that couldn't be confused with actually disengaging from the goings-on in front of her. 'I've watched a drunk woman rattle down the street with a bottle of Buckie, all the way to the bus shelter, where she's now sitting on the ground in a pool of her own piss.'

'It's quite a window on the world, isn't it?' said Valentine.

'No one's even batting an eyelid at a woman sitting in piss-soaked joggies. What in the name of Christ have we come to as a society? Have people lost all respect for themselves?'

'Don't do that – questioning how far we've fallen. You'll start to question why we're doing the job next and then we'll all be in serious trouble.'

The CS shook her head and left the window. 'No danger on that front. I get a monthly reminder in the form of my mortgage payment about why I do the job.' She crossed the floor towards the desk that Valentine was now sitting behind, booting up the PC. 'Right, what have we got on the girl's body?'

'No ID, I'm afraid.'

'It's not the McGarvie girl?'

'We can't confirm or deny. Her face is bashed; she took the full impact of an eighteen-wheeler and it shows.'

Martin curled down her lower lip. 'Poor bloody girl.'

'Everything else about the victim is a tick: age, height, build and so on. I'm hoping for a lot from the post-mortem, which Wrighty is taking on as soon as the SOCOs get through. When she's been made a little more presentable I'm going to try for a parental ID.'

As the talk lulled, DI McCormack stuck her head round the open door of the office. She paused for a moment, making sure she had their attention, then addressed the DCI. 'Boss, that's some of the crime scene images just in.'

'Stick them up, Sylvia.'

'So, what are you thinking, Bob?' said the CS.

Valentine got up from behind the desk and walked to the

other end of the tiny office. As he looked through the blinds into the incident room, he watched McCormack starting to stick up the photographs from the crime scene they'd all just left. CS Martin stood beside him, arms folded, and took in the static picture-show that was unfolding.

'It's an unusual case,' said the DCI. 'Davis's file is either riddled with hyperbolic distraction or we're delving into the belly of the beast.'

'The courts didn't buy it – they dismissed the mother's accusations of ritual abuse and left the kids with the father.'

'Yeah, I saw that in the file.'

'And social services were in full agreement with the court's verdict.'

'I saw that, too. But I have some lingering doubts, some unanswered questions.' Valentine pointed to one of the pictures McCormack had stuck on the board. 'See that? Tennis shoes; she was naked except for a pair of trainers. This wasn't a normal RTA, or a straightforward sexual assault after chasing down a victim. There's nothing normal or straightforward about this.'

Martin turned from the board and walked back to the desk, easing herself onto the corner. 'I was worried you might say that.'

Valentine detected an unusual hint of self-doubt in the chief super's voice. 'You were?'

'Ian Davis came to pretty much the same conclusions.'

'Go on.'

'He didn't buy the court verdict, and at the time he predicted we'd be in exactly the predicament we find ourselves in now.'

'You mean DI Davis thought Abbie McGarvie was actually being abused.'

'Worse than that. He believed she was likely being systematically abused by a broad spectrum of people, and he guessed that she wasn't the first and wouldn't be the last.'

The DCI loosened his tie and removed his jacket, placing it over the back of his chair. As he sat down he clawed the blue folder containing DI Davis's notes towards him. For a moment he sat silently, drumming his fingertips on the cover of the file. He had that familiar feeling, which always gripped him at the start of an investigation. Humans were pre-programmed to recognise patterns and Valentine's speciality, carefully honed over the years, was in identifying the patterns of criminality.

'This isn't the whole picture,' said the DCI. 'Davis only took on the missing person's case. Who handled the abuse allegations?'

'Kevin Rickards from Glasgow. He's retired now.'

'Retired? Kev's younger than me, did he have a lottery win?'

The CS's gaze seemed to have receded, like she was looking inside herself. Her mouth widened and hung open for a second or two longer than seemed natural. 'Look, I'll draw down the original case files and you have my authority to re-investigate the original allegations, but only if this latest victim appears to be connected and only if you do it quietly. And I mean very quietly.'

'Softly, softly, you have my word.'

'I mean it, Bob. I don't want anyone to get wind of it if you find anything.'

Their conversation was interrupted by a rapid knocking on the office door.

'Can I come in?' said DI Davis, pushing his head beyond the jamb.

'Yes, Ian, in you come,' said Martin.

Davis was wearing olive-green Farah trousers and a short-sleeved yellow shirt. In the top pocket of the shirt was a packet of Benson & Hedges. He had a thin, boyish frame, but wore a heavy moustache that made Valentine think of a former gym instructor from his time in basic training who bellowed so close to him that he could feel the man's bristles on his ear.

'We've been discussing the Abbie McGarvie case,' said the CS.

'Oh,' said Davis. 'I've not had much to report on that lately.'

'Well, that's why you're here.'

'Okay.' He glanced over to Valentine and then back to the CS. He was clearly eager to hear more.

'We've had a development overnight.'

'Another girl's body?'

Valentine leaned forward in his chair, balancing elbows on the desktop. 'What do you mean another one?'

'I don't think Abbie McGarvie is the only missing girl. I think there's others.'

'Others? How many are we talking about?'

Davis shrugged. 'I wouldn't like to put a number on it. But, I'll say this, I think my investigation is just the start. We're just scratching the surface here.'

CS Martin's back stiffened. She looked tense as she pointed towards the door and directed DI Davis to the whiteboard where DI McCormack was still sticking up the crime scene photographs. 'Ian, can you take a look at the pictures DI McCormack's putting up? She can fill you in on the rest, while I have a quick word with Bob.'

'Sure. But, didn't you want me to brief Bob on my case? I thought that was why you called me down here.'

'Of course, just give us a minute.'

As DI Davis went over to the board, Valentine waited for the CS to close the door and come back to where he was sitting. She eased herself onto the corner of the desk again. 'What do you think, Bob?'

'I think there's more than enough crossover for us to link the two cases together. Even if it turns out to be an ongoing missing persons and a fresh suspicious death, there's still plenty of common ground.'

'Do you think we have a murder investigation on our hands?'

'It's not as clean cut as "did she jump or was she pushed?", but if she was pursued to her death that's murder in my book. We have enough suspicion about the circumstances to pursue a murder investigation and if there's links to Davis's case, or any other cases he has on the back burner, then I think we should be pooling resources.'

She eased herself off the desk. 'Funny. I was thinking just the same thing.'

Valentine rose. 'If this investigation turns out to be as far-reaching as Davis suggests then the squad's going to need all the help we can get, especially with McAlister on sick leave.'

'Ally's sick? Nothing too serious, is it?'

'Gallstones. Going to put him out of action for a bit.'

'Well, the budget impact will be minimal.'

'Almost imperceptible, I would have thought.'

Martin opened the door and called out to DI Davis. As he began walking over, the CS turned back to Valentine. 'This could be a win/win for everyone. But don't get carried away with the overtime. Resources are stretched tight.'

Davis approached the CS. 'You called?'

'Meet your new boss!' She flagged in the DI and stepped out of the door.

6

There was something about the image of the girl's tennis shoes that haunted DCI Valentine as he drove home. It shouldn't have been like that; the girl was naked, her head and face crushed and bloodied: that was surely what he should have recalled. But, inexplicably, it was the innocuous shoes at the end of those pale, white legs that had stuck with him.

As he turned the steering wheel and took the roundabout past the Market Inn, Valentine tried to channel some new thoughts. There had been a persistent pain in his neck that had started outside the chief super's office in the morning. It had been a sign, he knew that now. He was beginning to read the indicators that came to him from God knows where. McCormack's contact, the Crosbie fella she called a precognitive, had told him that this would come. But the returning focus on the tennis shoes continued to elude him and was beginning to irritate.

There'd been a time when Chloe and Fiona had taken an interest in tennis, was it last year or the year before? Some time in the summer, when Wimbledon was never off the telly, and they'd joined a kids' tennis club in Seafield. He remembered buying the racquets with the huge heads that weighed next to nothing. They were a long way from the heavy wooden jobs he'd played with at their age when Björn Borg was all the rage.

It was a funny mix of memories to have in his head. His own distant childhood, which seemed so far away as to have existed in another world entirely, and his daughters' ever-mutable march to adulthood. His thoughts were getting too close to home; he couldn't afford to mix up how he felt about his family with the emotional shock of seeing a young girl lying dead on the road. Focus was everything to the detective, and getting to the root of this young girl's death would depend on it.

As Valentine pulled into his street he waved at a passing neighbour who was being tugged along the street by an obstreperous Cairn terrier. The area he lived in always felt like a haven, a sanctuary that supplied the reason he spent his days poking about in strangers' murders. His home was the small island of sanity where he was allowed to be an actual human being, and not just the cold automaton that spent his days weighing people's ability to succumb to or resist evil.

In the hall, Valentine called out but got no response. He put down his briefcase and walked towards the kitchen, which seemed like the best bet to locate members of his family.

'Oh, you're back.' Valentine's father was stooped over the cooker, prodding a frying pan with a wooden spatula.

'Where's Clare and the girls?'

'Well, there's a story attached to that.'

'I thought there might be.' Clare always cooked dinner, except on those occasions where she wanted her husband to know she was displeased with him. It was her way of initiating a wildcat strike action – withdrawing labour to highlight a grievance.

'Yes, well, the girls fancied pizza, so they were going on and on about that, and eventually Clare gave in and took them out to that hut place over at the big Asda.'

Valentine knew his father was covering for his wife. Since the old man had moved into the extension he'd appointed himself shop steward in these disputes. His father, by nature, had always followed the path of least resistance. Valentine had never known his dad to seek conflict; he'd always been a peacemaker. As he watched his father at the cooker, frying pan in hand, the detective's first instinct was to point out that he knew Clare was protesting about him taking the new job but he resisted.

'So, what are we having?'

'I thought I'd do us a wee mixed grill. Is that okay?' His father turned round and circled a finger over the centre of his chest. 'I know you watch the fried food, what with your ... heart.'

'My heart's fine, Dad. Everyone should learn to stop trying to wrap me up in cotton wool.'

Valentine walked through to the dining room and sat down. He was drawn to glance back into the kitchen, where he caught his father's grim expression, and instantly realised he'd made a harsh comment that was actually directed at Clare.

'Sorry, Dad.'

His father stepped into the doorway. 'What for?'

'Biting your head off. I don't want you to feel like you're living in no man's land with Clare and I taking pot-shots over your head.'

47

'I don't feel like that, son.'

'I know she's not happy about me taking this job. I'm just annoyed that she's being so pig-headed and now she's dragged you into it too.'

'She's angry because she's worried about you.'

Valentine looked at his father. He was an old man, at the end of his days, and he didn't need these worries that weren't really his. He should have been pottering in the garden and enjoying having his granddaughters around him. 'Dad, my heart's almost fully recovered. Clare's worrying about nothing. She might like the idea of me packing in the force but it's not going to happen because there's people that rely on me to do my job.'

His father stepped back from the cooker and came to sit down beside him. 'I understand,' he rested a bony hand on his son's forearm, 'you have a family to provide for; everybody gets that.'

Valentine tapped the back of his father's hand. 'I didn't mean it that way. You're right, of course, but I meant there's people you never see that rely on me. I have to do what I do because I sometimes think that, after all I've seen, I couldn't live with myself if I didn't.'

'You sound like you've had a hard day.'

'They're all hard days, Dad. Though, these days, it seems like they're getting harder. It's like I'm discovering that there's worlds within worlds and each one is darker than the last.'

'I've told you before that I don't know how you can do what you do. I'd be round the bend if I had to spend a day in your shoes.'

'You learn to compartmentalise, to put the bad stuff in a

box.' Valentine looked into his father's concerned eyes and didn't want to burden him any more. 'It's just that today the box is pretty full, Dad; you're best to ignore me while I'm trying to close the lid on it.'

'And that works, does it? Hiding things, like that.'

'Up till now, yes. But if I find that it stops working, I'll let you know.'

His father made a sideways glance that indicated he only half believed what his son was telling him, then pushed out his chair and headed back to the kitchen. 'Right, let's get some grub together. Everything feels better with a full belly.'

When Clare came back from Pizza Hut she gave the girls an hour to get ready for bed and promptly disappeared upstairs to run a bath, without even acknowledging her husband. Valentine had a five-minute chat with Chloe about her newfound distaste for garlic bread with cheese and then a message appeared on her phone and she was lost in cyberspace. For a minute, Valentine thought about trying to extract his other daughter from her iPhone, perhaps engaging her in conversation about her day or even his, but viewing her level of concentration, opted instead to retreat to the dining room with DI Davis's case files.

As Valentine delved into the Abbie McGarvie file, and closely examined the allegations of her mother, Caroline Simpson, he began to feel his consciousness drifting into an unwholesome place. In interviews she had talked about a death cult that preyed on children. She called them a coven of evil that operated in the shadows by night, but by day lived openly among us.

In one of her outlandish statements Caroline had described her own understanding as slow, progressing from outright disbelief to a stage of actively ignoring the evidence. Eventually, however, the facts had become too strong to ignore and she claimed the awakening was like having scales fall from her eyes.

Everything Caroline once believed about the situation had turned out to be completely wrong and irrelevant now, because reality had shocked her into accepting what she could no longer dismiss as implausible. Child grooming, blood sacrifices and ritualistic abuse became believable then. But hadn't the police investigation and the court ruling concluded that none of it was real?

Valentine knew he wasn't going to be able to contain his curiosity until the morning and so picked up his phone to call DI Davis.

'Hello, Ian, sorry to cut into your family time,' he said.

'It's okay, I live alone, sir.'

'Oh, right. I just wanted to pick your brains about the case notes you gave me.'

There was the sound of sofa springs wheezing. 'Fire away.'

'I've been reading Caroline Simpson's statements and there's a lot of detail I've never come across before.'

'Yes, I suppose it's quite grisly, sir.'

'I'm not just talking about the grisly details, there's some technical jargon she references frequently to back up her allegations,' said Valentine. 'What's this term "trauma-based mind control" she keeps parroting?'

Davis exhaled loudly. 'Okay, that's a tricky one to put into a pithy summary.'

'Try hard, Ian.'

'Well, basically it's about subjecting a child to terrifying abuse – locking them in cages with dead animals is one way, finding their worst fears and forcing them into contact with them is another. It's done in order to cause a split in the child's personality.'

'That sounds sadistic. And why would you want to split a child's personality?'

'That's a more difficult question to answer, but the short reply would be so that undesirable, or what might be thought of as weak, personalities can be suppressed or whither, and a new stronger personality can be encouraged.'

Valentine closed the file and pushed it away from him; he was beginning to summon revulsion. 'Ian, I'm really, really struggling to understand why any of this bloody torture of children would be deemed desirable.'

'Boss, can I speak frankly?' Davis's speech pattern had softened, from initially sounding eager to help he was now becoming more cautious with his words.

'Of course you can be frank. I'm trying to grasp the reality of the situation we're up against here.'

'There's a former detective that I'd like you to meet as soon as possible, sir. I think he could help you understand a lot of the murkier aspects. His name's Kevin Rickards.'

'The Glasgow DI, I've met him once or twice; we did some of our basic training together. Didn't he handle the early abuse allegations?'

'He had the Caroline Simpson case, yes. But he's taken

51

early retirement now. Rickards gave me some advice at the outset that I have sworn by since. He said, when you investigate these crimes you have to abandon all your reference points for morality – government, the courts, the police, social services, education – they have no moral authority. They are all your enemies.'

'That doesn't leave us with many on our side, Ian.'

'It leaves us with precisely ... one.'

7

It wasn't dreaming, it was never like dreaming. DCI Bob Valentine sat on the edge of the bed watching his wife sleep. She seemed perfectly content, deep in her unconscious slumber. In the room's half-light Clare looked different, much more at ease than when she was awake. She did her battles in the day, thought Valentine, though didn't we all? He felt like it was him alone who also battled during the night.

The whispering started again. Low at first, like a sound coming from another room that he couldn't quite make out. After a few more seconds the whispering became decipherable; the words were a girl's and it was the same voice he had heard before.

Earlier, when he went to bed, Clare was already asleep. He went over the usual replay of the day's events and found fatigue creeping over him. When the voice appeared he thought at first that it was Clare, that she'd woken up and was trying to talk to him. However, as he turned to face her he found he was paralysed by sleep. It wasn't like a dream, because he was passive in the dreams he participated in – he felt awake and able to influence his surroundings.

'Who is it?' he said.

The reply was too quiet to make out.

He looked at Clare again and got off the edge of the bed. As he grabbed his dressing gown from the back of the door Valentine heard the whispering again.

'Listen to me, *please.*'

He moved into the hallway; the curtains were still open and the street light outside the window was shining in. He had a compulsion to look at his hands, to make sure he wasn't in another dream. He drew fists, opened and closed his fingers, and confirmed he was in full control of his movements.

'I need you, *please* listen.'

He stopped still in the hallway and looked around him. He was alone. As he stared to the front he saw the mirror and moved a few steps closer to the reflection. As he stared ahead Valentine's first instinct was one of confusion, a reaction which was quickly replaced by a strange fear: the face staring back at him wasn't his.

The young girl in the mirror was pale but her image was clear. Her blue eyes were bright and alive, her soft mouth was moving slowly but with a passion to impart something. Valentine watched the girl speaking to him but the words failed to register. There was a message, told in whispers, but he could only hear the loud thumping inside his chest.

He started to grow dizzy and reached a hand out to steady himself on the wall.

'What do you want?' he said. He was closer to the girl's image, she spoke faster, but the words were so quiet.

'Help them, please.'

'What?' Valentine's arm was seized with pain, forcing

him to jerk his hand from the wall. His shoulder slammed into the plaster and he slipped to the ground.

He didn't remember landing face down on the hall carpet, or have any idea how long he'd been lying there, but the first signs of daylight and the stirring of birdsong told Valentine he'd been out cold for some time. He raised himself onto his haunches and dragged himself up.

He was cold and had a dull ache in his back and neck, probably from a night spent on the floor, but he was relieved to be in familiar surroundings. As he pulled the cord on his dressing gown, Valentine moved towards the mirror. It seemed an entirely different object from the one he'd looked in earlier, but the reflection, at least, was his.

'Oh, it's you?' Clare was emerging from the bedroom. 'What are you hanging about out here for?'

'I had a bit of a rough night. Is it breakfast time already?'

Clare eyed her husband cautiously, like she was surveying him for signs of insanity. 'Are you all right, Bob?'

'Yes, fine.' It was an instinctive parrying of her remark. Any hint of an increase in his stress would lead to a row about the job. 'I'm not a morning person, you know that.'

Clare gave Valentine a knowing look and, heading down the stairs, left him standing in the hallway, with his back to the mirror.

He took a long shower, letting the warm jets beat into his crown as he tried to make sense of what he had seen. As the steam rose he touched the thick seam of scar tissue that ran down the centre of his chest. The fleshy ridge, as thick as a man's index finger, was his reminder that his life had been seared in two. There was the man he was before

55

the long-bladed knife cut into his heart and there was the man who came after. Neither seemed related now.

Valentine struggled with the changes he'd been through since the attack. There had been a time of denial, a time when he'd told himself that this just wasn't happening to him. And there'd been a time of trying to understand, when he'd sought answers to the problem like it was a new case he was working on. He wasn't quite at the third stage yet, but he knew some kind of acceptance was going to be inevitable if he was to move on.

He dressed slowly, in the sort of ruminative mood that he would have to snap out of soon. The people around him were as wise to his changes as he was, and they spotted the signs. That was another stage of his development: hiding the signs. It wasn't always easy, though, especially when he was taken unaware by strange new phenomena. And girls talking to him from mirrors was as out-there as he could imagine; he wondered what might be next.

Clare was sitting in the kitchen with a copy of the morning paper and a cigarette burning before her when he went down. Valentine could hear his father moving about in the extension, and presumed it wouldn't be long before he appeared, so chose his moment to confront his wife.

'Can I expect the silent treatment to last much longer, Clare?' he said.

She picked up the cigarette and inhaled deeply, blowing smoke towards the ceiling. 'I'm speaking to you now.'

'You weren't last night.'

'I was tired, Bob.' It was only a half-truth. She may have been tired but the trip to Pizza Hut and subsequently ignoring him on her return was designed to isolate him:

to cut him off from the family with only his decisions to consider.

'I'm tired too. I'm tired of rowing and I'm tired of explaining why I have to go out to work. Who's going to pay for the New Zealand jaunt if I don't?'

She reached over to stub her cigarette in the ashtray. 'You said you'd come away from frontline policing and go back to the training academy.'

'I asked for a transfer, you know that.'

'You obviously didn't ask loudly enough, or persistently enough.'

'Clare, the force is under a lot of constraints right now. Government wants savings everywhere, there isn't the latitude there used to be.'

'You're not the only officer on the force, Bob. Don't they need people to train at the academy, too?'

'Not so much, obviously. Look, I tried but they need me where I am because there just isn't a lot of experienced personnel.'

Clare rose and picked up the ashtray. She walked to the sink and ran water over the dishes. 'It sounds to me like it's a situation that you're completely happy with, Bob. That's what galls me the most.'

'There was a time when you used to say what got to you the most was seeing me put in danger. Isn't that what it used to be about?' Valentine wanted to withdraw the words as soon as they left his mouth. Clare's reaction, flaring her eyes at him and smacking the tap back off, only confirmed his regret.

'I'm sorry, I've had a sleepless night.'

'Stop making excuses for yourself.' She raised her index

finger to a point only a few inches from her husband's nose, but before she had time to load her second barrage the door from the conservatory creaked open.

'Oh, good morning,' said Valentine's father.

Clare dropped her finger and headed back upstairs.

'Was it something I said?'

'No, Dad. It was something I said.'

'Oh, I see.'

'Yes. Mostly, it's something I said.'

'You should work on that, son.'

Valentine nodded. 'That and one or two other things.' He retrieved his briefcase and headed for the front door.

DI McCormack was waiting in her navy-blue Megane at the top of the drive. She waved when she saw Valentine and started the engine. The DCI wondered how long she had been sitting there, and whether or not she might have been better ringing the bell and coming inside, but when he gave the idea further consideration he conceded she was probably wiser to wait at the top of the drive.

'How long have you been here?' he said.

'Oh, maybe ten minutes.'

Valentine fastened his seat belt and put his briefcase on the back seat. 'You're probably safer out here, it feels like crossing enemy lines going over my doorstep these days.'

'I take it Clare's still not happy about you taking the new job.'

'No, she's not.' He tried to steer the conversation away from his wife, because he still remembered McCormack overhearing one of Clare's earlier tirades about himself and the new DI having to spend a night in a hotel on Arran when a case caused them to miss the last ferry. It hadn't been pretty then and he doubted it would be any prettier now.

'Where's Donnelly today?'

'Chasing up a few angles on the Laverock Group. They appear to have more arms than that Indian statue.'

'Shiva, the God of Destruction.'

'Sorry?'

'The statue you mentioned. Let's hope this Laverock lot are easier to handle.'

The road from Masonhill was relatively free of traffic, for the time of day, but when they reached the bypass there was a line of cars sitting at a standstill. Valentine looked out on the green Ayrshire fields and the rapidly encroaching new-build housing estates and wondered where the urban creep might end. It seemed entirely possible to him that the village of Mossblown might soon be swallowed by a procession of McMansions.

'Sir, can I ask what you think the post-mortem will tell us?' said McCormack. She pulled on the handbrake as the traffic stalled completely.

'I don't need to think, I know.'

'What?'

Valentine turned away from the window. 'You remember that wink you gave me yesterday?'

'Ah, I see where this is going. You got a sign?' Her remark seemed so matter-of-fact that Valentine contemplated asking her when they had both became so blasé with such matters.

'Yes and no. Sylvia, you know you're the only person I've ever talked to about any of this ...'

'Except for Hugh Crosbie.'

'Well, yes. After last night I think I'm going to have to have another talk with him.'

'What happened last night?'

Valentine looked out on the line of traffic and lowered the window a few inches; the temperature inside the car seemed to be rising. 'I saw her.'

'What?'

'The girl.'

'Abbie McGarvie?'

He nodded slowly. 'I'm afraid so.'

'Jesus.'

'Why bring him into it? I'm pretty sure she's beyond even his help.'

McCormack leaned forward in her seat and folded her arms over the wheel. She seemed to be contemplating the information, or at least filing it away for future retrieval. Her expression was dipping into solemnity when a lopsided grin sprung up. 'She spoke to you, didn't she?'

Valentine turned away from the window, his stomach cramping. 'They've never done that before. This time was very different. In the past they just showed and were subtle, but this time she just spoke out ... like I'm doing with you now.'

'What did she say?'

'*Help them*, I think. I had some trouble hearing her, and accepting it all. And then I passed out.'

'You passed out! Are you all right?'

'Yes, I'm fine. But I've realised that I can't just bury this, like before. I can't just ignore it. Like Hugh said, I need to understand this.'

'Didn't he say that acceptance was the first step?'

'Yeah, he did. And maybe I'm getting there.'

'We need to set up another meeting for you with Hugh.'

Valentine nodded. The traffic had started to move and McCormack released the handbrake and engaged the clutch.

'I'll get Hugh on the phone once we get to the morgue, sir.'

'Do that, Sylvia.'

She glanced over. 'I never thought I'd see the day when you'd actually embrace the idea.'

'Maybe embrace is too strong a word. But I'm ready to get to the bottom of all this.'

8

By the time the officers reached the city, DI McCormack had adjusted her driving pattern. It was immediately obvious that Glasgow roads demanded more attention than Ayr's. There had already been a near miss with an erratically driven white van on the Kingston Bridge, which had seen Valentine pumping an imaginary brake pedal in the footwell of the passenger seat. He might once have suggested the road conditions stemmed from an issue with the locals' temperament, but jokes about the Dear Green Place were now wearing thin on McCormack. As she aggressively rode the gears and pounded the horn, it seemed almost inevitable that her warrant card would soon be produced and shoved in the face of an unsuspecting city driver.

'Caw canny,' said Valentine.

'What? Is that some red-neck jargon?'

'Don't they speak Scots in the Smoke?'

'Not like that, we don't.' She flicked on the blinkers and changed lanes, prompting a roar from the motoring horn section. 'I'm almost losing patience for my old home town.'

Valentine grinned and turned on the radio. The airwaves were full of crackling interruptions, a staccato rendition of 'Wonderwall' being the clearest offering. After trying a few more stations he found an FM broadcast that, on the surface, was a gardening programme but seemed almost entirely composed of adverts for products aimed at retired Boomers. He'd need the hip replacement surgery and the indoor stairlift soon enough and definitely didn't need reminding of the fact; he flicked off the radio and settled on the view, grim as it was.

The traffic, and tension, thinned as they neared the morgue, but McCormack didn't look like she was enjoying being back on home soil. There were advantages to living in a big city, that's what everyone kept telling him, but Valentine couldn't fathom them. In Ayr things were simpler, the lines of behaviour rooted in a more stable past, and it took longer for the latest politically correct dogma to be adopted. In Glasgow, he never quite knew if he were using an outmoded term that would have him judged as a clog-wearing rural Luddite. None of it bothered him, not beyond a superficial irritation anyway, because he knew who he was and what he stood for. What was the line? Above all else, be true to yourself. It was something like that – the poet might have put it in a prettier fashion but the sentiment was what mattered. He knew who he was, where his people came from, and why he did what he did. Nothing else mattered to him.

'Sylvia, I spoke to Davis last night on the phone, but I forgot to ask if he was meeting us today?' said Valentine.

'Well, your guess is as good as mine. To be honest, I find him a bit of a queer fish.'

'Ah, that'll be why he doesn't have a wife and kids.'

'I didn't mean *queer*, not that way.'

'So he just likes living alone, then. I always find that odd, perhaps I shouldn't.'

'I live alone.'

'That's different. You're a career woman, you're expected to forgo all happiness in pursuit of the glass ceiling.'

'Isn't that a bit sexist?'

The DCI made a show of looking at his watch. 'Under five minutes, I think that's a record!'

'What are you on about?'

'It usually takes me at least an hour in the city to be tripped up by my Ayrshire upbringing. I haven't been called sexist in a long time though, perhaps the programming's wearing off. I should ask Dino for a course or something in case I embarrass the squad on these trips.' He was dipping into the familiar territory of teasing; it was time to change the subject before McCormack put him in his place. 'But, perhaps you're right, Davis might just be a bit of a queer fish. In all seriousness, we'll have to keep an eye on him.'

'Well, I agree that might be a good idea. Do you want me to flag it up with Donnelly and the others?'

'No. I don't want to start a whispering campaign – that might do more harm than good. Just keep your antennae up when he's around.'

'Okay, boss. It's not like we haven't had cuckoos in the nest before.'

As they pulled into the morgue car park, Valentine scanned the rows of vehicles but couldn't see Davis's car. It wasn't essential that the DI was there to hear the post-mortem findings, but Valentine had hoped to question

64

him some more about the Abbie McGarvie file, which he had continued to read after their call the night before. The file's contents had been shocking, even for an officer of his rank with more than twenty years' experience, but he worried about the rest of the team.

It had taken Valentine a long time to build up his outer armour. He had trained himself to ignore the emotional pulls a case made on a detective. It wasn't because he wanted to become more brutal or harder, but because to give in to such instincts hindered an investigation. There was only room for the rational, for reasoning and judgement. All else was distraction, including the very parts that made him human.

He was a hunter, he continued to tell himself, and the hunt demanded a level of commitment that had taken him a long time to accomplish. He'd paid a dear price to operate the way he did, and he couldn't expect others to understand that, or even appreciate the results, but that didn't matter because he understood perfectly.

There would have to be some sort of briefing for the squad, he decided; the subject matter of Davis's file had the potential to disturb those who weren't warned what they were dealing with. Not everyone had his armour, after all. In fact, very few were even in the process of acquiring any protection.

In the pathology-department building Valentine and McCormack made their way to the morgue and suited up with gowns and gloves. It always seemed over the top to the DI – he wasn't going to start poking about with a scalpel – but he abided anyway, for the sake of tradition more than anything. Wrighty was waiting in the centre of the room, arms folded over his green plastic apron, when they went in. 'Morning, Bob.'

'What have you got for us?'

He turned back to the slab, where the body of the girl was lying. In the bright overhead lights she seemed even paler than the DCI remembered her. Every point of her anatomy was stripped of shadow, revealing a new image of a girl that had previously been no more than an anonymous victim, lying prone on the dark, wet bitumen. Her face had been cleaned up now, the blood and dirt wiped away. Here was someone who had lived and breathed, whose delicate facial features had once animated a teenager's joys and woes. A mother and father had gazed into those cold eyes – had their hearts filled with hope?

Valentine took in the Y-shaped incision running from her shoulders, joining over the sternum and running down in straight lines to the pubic bone. Neat black stitches looped over the red incision wounds.

'You've been busy, I see,' he said.

'We never rest in here,' said Wrighty. 'There's time enough for that when you're dead.'

'Touché,' said Valentine. 'Come on then, get your notes out.'

The pathologist reached behind him and withdrew a manila folder from the stark steel shelf. He took a pair of horn-rimmed glasses from the top of his head and balanced them on his shiny nose. 'Right, some very interesting findings, Bob.'

'Go on ...'

'Well, I'll start with the cause of death, which was a catastrophic cervical fracture.'

Valentine raised a gloved hand. 'For the cheap seats, please.'

'She broke her neck. The X-ray indicates a base fracture and there's spinal cord injury too.'

McCormack coughed into her fist. 'Just what we thought, sir.'

'Girl versus HGV only has one winner.' Valentine shook his head.

'She wouldn't have suffered, if it's of any consolation to her family,' said Wrighty. 'There'd have been immediate loss of sensation, paralysis ... instant death, in other words.'

The DCI started to walk around the table, gazing at the victim he was now tasked with finding justice for. She was so young and delicate that her loss seemed even more grievous than he'd previously thought. He tried to omit the thought but found it forming with another: sympathy for the girl's mother. He allowed himself these mental wanderings for a moment – they were natural; he was a father too – but then he banished them to the vault where he stored such interruptions to his detective's reasoning.

The girl's bruising and scratches were more visible after the clean-up, as were some other marks.

Valentine moved on. 'Any other indications of wrong-doing?'

The pathologist started to leaf through the pages of the file. 'Ah, here we are ... I need to draw your attention to the lab report on the stomach contents. We have a positive reading for something quite unusual: barbiturates.'

'Barbiturates are a sedative, right?'

'They're used to suppress the nervous system and, as

they're a heavy sedative, you very rarely see them used these days because most doctors won't prescribe them.'

'Why not?'

'They're a serious overdose risk.'

'Perhaps that wasn't a consideration.'

'Well, indeed.'

Valentine walked back round to the other side of the table. His mind was already working on a new range of possibilities. 'Was there anything else?'

'Yes, I'm afraid so.' Wrighty pushed his glasses up his nose. 'There's some signs of sexual assault. Serious bruising and tearing to the vagina and vulva, and also rectal damage. It's the kind of thing you'd expect to encounter with a vicious gang rape. We're talking about a prolonged and serious sexual assault of the most grievous nature.'

Valentine drew a deep breath. 'Holy God. What the hell am I dealing with here?'

'I'm sorry, Bob, but I'm not finished.'

'You're not?'

'No.' The pathologist paused. 'I need to point out that you're dealing with two victims.'

'What do you mean?'

'This girl was pregnant.'

9

'Chapel of Rest' didn't seem an appropriate name for the pathetically small room with a dais at one end and some plastic-backed chairs at the other. The pale walls might once have been beige, or perhaps butter, but could now be mistaken for bare plaster. Without a wall-mount or a single pane of coloured glass in the window the overall effect was soul-crushing dullness. It reminded Valentine of an old British Rail waiting room: a place with a purely utilitarian purpose. Surely the deceased deserved better, but then they weren't the main consideration here. The room was designed to cause no offence to the living, because of course, causing offence is the greatest crime we are capable of.

'Could they have done a worse job on this place?' said Valentine.

'It's a bit grim. But then, a glitter-ball would only look out of place,' said McCormack. She caught Valentine's hard stare and retreated. 'Sorry, I'm lowering the tone.'

'Makes a change from me, I suppose.' He crossed his legs and pinched the crease in his trousers. 'What kind of contact have you had with the parents so far?'

'I spoke to them yesterday. Alex McGarvie's due in an

hour or so, and Caroline Simpson should be here by now.'

'How was she?'

'Honest appraisal? She was broken.'

'She'll be a lot worse when she hears about the post-mortem.'

McCormack lowered her head, her face darkening. 'God, how do we break something like that?'

'Gently, Sylvia.'

'I can't imagine how it must feel to lose a child, but to be told you had a grandchild-to-be you didn't know about and ...' She halted and turned to the window. 'I shouldn't let the job get to me like this.'

'No, you shouldn't.'

McCormack took her gaze from the window and focused on the DCI again. 'How do you do that? I mean, how do you shut out the personal stuff that affects you so much.'

Valentine waited for the right words to form in his mind and after a few seconds realised they weren't coming. The perfect response wasn't coming because it wasn't there, not in him anyway. 'There was a DS I worked under years ago, a good copper but not one of those rank chasers. He told me that the best you can do is let the job wash over you, never let your outside become your inside.'

'Wise words.'

'Really? You think so? I tried to do that but found it only made me put off the introspection, to pile it up into one great heap that left you with a mountain of hurt to deal with in the end.'

'Oh, right ...'

'I suppose the only advice I can give you, Sylvia, is that you learn to cope.' He paused, gathering his thoughts. 'I

70

don't know how, or why. We're resilient creatures, with enough exposure to the job and with a long enough passage of time, we learn to cope. I'm not saying we cease to be shocked or even appalled, but the impact lessens. The initial damage can only be done once, we heal, and the scar tissue is much stronger than the original wound ever was.'

'I don't want to be one of those cops that keeps their feelings behind a wall,' Sylvia said, meeting his gaze. 'I don't want to become desensitised.'

'Those cops were born that way; they always had walls around them. There's millimetres between some cops and criminals on the same spectrum.'

'You mean like the difference between a genius and a lunatic?'

'Exactly, there's only a cigarette paper between them.'

The chapel attendants entered the room, rolling a trolley from the morgue. They raised the trolley level with the dais before delicately lifting the victim's corpse onto the platform. Valentine had asked for the body to be taken to the chapel for the purposes of formal identification, but after last night's visitation he already knew he had found Abbie McGarvie.

It was all just another procedure, a legal requirement. He was sure the girl's mother could do without the rigmarole, but the investigation could not.

As the DCI waited with DI McCormack, watching the chapel attendants adjust the over-bright lighting, he became aware of a mood change in the room. He got to his feet and turned to face the door, where he met Caroline Simpson's gaze.

The woman was clutching a blue paisley scarf, twisting

71

it between her fingers. There was a faraway glare in her eyes, like the look of a woman who had already received enough shocks in her life. She stood still, unmoving except for the fidgeting of her fingers around the scarf, and then she made her way towards the detective.

Caroline's instinct was to offer a hand to shake but her nerves betrayed her and she snatched her hand away to her mouth instead. She seemed perched on the edge of tears.

'Mrs Simpson, I'm Inspector Valentine and this is DI McCormack.'

'It's *Miss*...' She sucked in her lips and quickly released them again. 'I'm not married any more.'

'I'm sorry, Miss Simpson,' said Valentine. 'Can I offer you a seat?'

'No. I'm fine. Thank you.' Her gaze had settled on the other end of the room, beyond the plastic-backed chairs, where the morgue attendants had laid out the corpse, beneath a blue-green covering. 'Is that her?'

Valentine motioned to the dais. 'I believe you spoke to DI McCormack on the telephone. Our information is very limited at the moment, but we found a girl who matched the description of your daughter. We've no means of definitively identifying her, which is why we called you here.'

'What happened to her?'

'It was a road traffic accident.'

She glanced at the detective and started to walk towards the dais. When she reached the other end of the room she touched the cloth covering the corpse and hurriedly withdrew her hand. 'Did she suffer?'

'It was instantaneous.' He saw no reason to burden

her right away with the details of the sexual assault. 'She wouldn't have suffered at all.'

Miss Simpson fiddled in her pockets and, with trembling hands, removed a small white handkerchief. She dabbed at the edges of her eyes as she moved around the prone figure in front of her. Her eyes, though glazed with tears, seemed still and peaceful now, scanning the length of the figure. Occasionally, she bit into her lower lip as if the act was helping her to compose herself, but her overall appearance was of a woman ready to crack open and reveal the misery inside.

'I think I'd like to see her now.'

Valentine moved to the head of the dais and nodded to the chapel assistant standing nearby. He stepped forward and gently peeled back the blue-green covering to reveal the pale features of the dead girl. Her face seemed to have darkened a little, perhaps caused by the lowered lighting, and shadows sat in the hollows of her cheeks and beneath the eyes.

Caroline Simpson stared for only a few seconds before she turned her face away and screwed up her eyes. Her tightened eyelids weren't enough to hold back the tears. She nodded briskly. 'It's Abbie.'

DI McCormack placed an arm around Caroline's shoulders and led her towards the nearest seat. As they went, the chapel assistants took their cue to return Abbie McGarvie's body to the trolley and start to leave the small room.

'I'm sorry I had to put you through that, Miss Simpson,' said Valentine.

'She told me, you know, that she'd die like that. She

73

said they'd kill her in the end because she wasn't like the other girls.'

'Other girls?'

'There were dozens, she told me that. I told the police before, after I'd told the social services, though fat lot of bloody good it did me. No one looked out for my daughter. None of them. And that judge, the one that took her away from me... Oh, God, they still have Tyler. Is my son okay?'

DI McCormack was still comforting Caroline, rubbing her hands with her own. 'Tyler's fine, I'm sure. There's been a weekly social services visit since Abbie went missing.'

'Those idiots! Do you know what I call social services now? I call them the SS. They're as bad as all the rest. They turfed out the only one who ever helped me. Jean Clark believed me and they sacked her.'

Valentine stored away the social worker's name – it wasn't one he had seen in Davis's file. 'Why did they sack her?'

'Jean was the first and last one to believe me. Oh, I think your Davis fella might have been coming round, but he's such a hard man to read, I can never tell. It's not like you people would ever let on, anyway. But Jean knew what they were doing to Abbie; she believed her. It was all so horrific, and nobody else wanted to believe it was true. They just wanted to brush it under the carpet and then when the school got dragged in and some of the prominent names involved started to come out, they just put all their wagons in a circle. It was as if everyone with any power to stop it, to save Abbie, were sworn to do the exact opposite. Poor

Jean didn't stand a chance against them, so what chance did Abbie ever have?' Caroline withdrew her hands from McCormack's grasp and pressed her face into her palms. Her shoulders shook as she sobbed before the officers.

Valentine exchanged looks with McCormack and made to leave, but as he got up, the doors to the chapel of rest opened and a stooped, gaunt man in a navy raincoat stepped in. The man's hair, thinning, was plastered to his crown by the recent downpour and made his head appear like nothing more than a skin-covered skull. It took Valentine a moment or two to realise it was Alex McGarvie standing before him. The DCI turned back to the others to gauge their reaction, which as he expected, wasn't good.

'You bastard!' Caroline stood up and pointed at Alex. 'You did this, you killed your own daughter!'

DI McCormack tried to hold back Caroline, as she clawed the air to get at her ex-husband. She continued firing accusations and insults as Valentine guided Alex back out the door.

In the corridor the DCI was challenged. 'Wait a minute, if that's my daughter in there, I've every right to see her.'

'Of course, but if you'd mind waiting until we've cleared the way,' said Valentine, wondering why the father seemed less interested in the fate of his child than projecting his wounded pride.

'I'm the parent with custody,' said Alex, jerking his arm away from Valentine's grasp. 'Why is my ex-wife in there?'

'Mr McGarvie, you're both parents.'

'I have legal rights.'

'Sir, if you don't mind, please.' The DCI directed Alex into the vacant waiting room, but he objected, instead

75

turning around and heading down the corridor towards the doors. 'I will need to talk to you, Mr McGarvie.'

He spun around. 'What?'

'If now's not a good time, would you like to come in to the station when it's convenient for you?'

'On what charge?'

'There's no charges, sir. I'm conducting an investigation, it's a matter of procedure.'

'Like calling my ex-wife, I suppose.' He stomped back down the corridor and barged through the exit to the car park, leaving the heavy doors swinging noisily on their hinges.

The DCI's thoughts pooled as he wondered what he had just observed and what he was dealing with. He had a dead girl, who had been twelve weeks pregnant, and a mother and father in all-out war.

Outside, Valentine jogged back to the car, dodging the puddles and potholes, only to realise that he didn't have the key to McCormack's vehicle. He tried the handle but it was indeed locked; he was cursing himself and his stupidity when the rain started to fall again.

For a moment, as he stood looking back to the morgue, over the roof of the car, his vision started to blur, pushing the building out of focus. When his eyes cleared and he could see plainly again, he spotted a young girl standing in front of the closed doors of the morgue. She was watching him. Where had she come from? He hadn't passed anyone in the corridor, and there was nobody stupid enough to stand out in the rain, except for him.

Valentine stared at the girl for a few seconds more and noticed that, despite the heavy rain, she appeared to be completely dry. Her hair wasn't even damp, whereas his was sticking to his head. When she spoke, he tried to make out the words but couldn't – he could only follow the movement of her lips.

As the girl raised her arms to him he realised at once who he was staring at. There was an instantaneous connection between them that he had never felt before, and he heard her voice whispering to him, just like she had when he saw her in the mirror.

'Help the girls, please. There's no one else. Please, help them.'

As quickly as the voice came it disappeared. The doors of the mortuary swung open and DI McCormack came running towards the DCI. 'Sorry, boss,' she said, pointing the key at the car, 'you're soaking wet, look at you.'

McCormack got in and dropped her bag on the back seat. As she started the engine she opened the passenger's window and called out to Valentine. 'Boss, the door's open now.'

The DCI clambered in and acknowledged McCormack. 'Sorry, I was miles away.'

'It's bucketing rain!'

'Sorry.'

McCormack switched off the engine and pivoted in her seat to face Valentine. 'Is everything okay?'

'I don't know.'

'Boss?' She tilted her head. 'You're acting very strange.'

'Strange, am I?' He turned to face her.

'Oh, I get it. We've had a moment.' She started the car again. The wipers screeched on the windscreen as the car pulled out. 'Good job I called Hugh Crosbie earlier. I hope 8 p.m. tomorrow night sounds okay for getting to the bottom of this once and for all.'

2011

Paige is my friend. She's a big girl in Primary 7. We walk to school together and, sometimes, Daddy lets her come to our house to play. I like Paige because she's nice to me and lets me be her friend, even though I'm only little. I like people who are nice to me like Paige and Mummy. But lots of people aren't nice, lots of people are wicked.

At school, Paige shows me her diary. There's pictures of men and women in there that she's drawn, all by herself. Paige is good at drawing. The ladies in her pictures all have clear bright skin and long golden hair. Paige says they're her real friends but don't live in the real world like us.

'Where do they live?' I ask her.

'Oh, far away. In another place entirely,' says Paige. I like her voice, she sounds all grown-up.

'But how do you know? If you can't see them.'

'I see them in here.' Paige touches the side of her head and smiles at me. I like her smile; she has very white teeth and very pink gums.

'Do you mean you make them up?'

'No, they're real. They live in another place but they're real.'

I don't understand but I smile and pretend like I do.

There's lots of things I don't understand, but I want Paige to be my friend so I pretend. It's nice to know a big girl – it makes me feel special.

After school Paige is waiting for me outside my classroom. All the other school kids have gone, but Paige is there waiting. When I come out Mrs Thompson comes out too and says it's time for us to go to the chapel.

'But I have to go home now. It's home time,' I say. I don't want Daddy to be upset with me.

Mrs Thompson shakes her head and says, 'No, you must follow us to the chapel hall.'

Paige holds out her hand and says, 'It's okay. I'll be there too. It won't be nearly as frightening.'

I start to feel sad and I wonder what is going to happen and then Mrs Thompson says, 'Your dad will be there. You won't get into any trouble. This is an important time for you, Abbie; you have to understand that.'

We all walk to the chapel hall and it seems strange to be in the school when everyone else has gone home. I start to wonder about Tyler and who will take him home from his school and then I remember that today is his day to go to Mum. I get a little teary when I think of my brother and I want to be with him and Mum, but I try to hold back my tears because I'm not supposed to show things like tears.

In the chapel it's very quiet and dark. All the curtains have been closed and the only light comes from candles on the stage. There's very tall candlesticks with thick black candles burning on top of them that I've never seen before and there's strange pictures with shapes on them, too.

'What are all the funny shapes?' I ask Paige.

'They're glyphs. Shush, you shouldn't speak.'

I feel a little bit scared again when I see the people come out, but Paige holds my hand tight and her eyes say *don't be scared* when she looks down at me. I think of all the pictures she showed me in her little diary and I don't think any of the people here will be nice people like the ones she showed me. The people here wear hoods and walk slowly, back and forth, back and forth, and sometimes hold up silver cups. They all say strange words I can't understand. I start to feel the tears coming down my cheeks and I can't stop them this time.

'You're trembling,' says Paige.

Mrs Thompson hears her and says, 'Stop talking and disrobe.'

We have to take our clothes off and leave them on the ground. It's really cold and I get shivery all over. I discover more girls in the shadows, they're all taking off their clothes.

Paige tells me very quietly, 'Don't be scared, this isn't a scary part like all the others.'

'What others?' I say.

'The rites.'

'What's rites?'

'Never mind. It's not a mass, you just have to say the words and that's all. No one will hurt you today.'

The girls stand in a line in front of the stage and a man in a black hood walks in front of them. He has a dead bird in his hands and it has no head, only a stump where the blood is coming out. Sometimes the blood drips on the floor and leaves a red dot and I can see a line of dots behind him. I hear him say the words and the girls say them back and he wipes blood from the bird on their faces. Some of the girls are crying now and Paige has to go and tell them to stop

80

with a loud, 'Shush.' When they don't stop she shakes their shoulders or pokes them hard with her finger in their chest and then they stop.

When the man in the hood comes to me he stands still. His face is dark inside the hood, hidden under shadows. He looks straight at me, his eyes are angry but his voice is very still and quiet when he says, 'Repeat these words: *I belong mind, body and soul to Lucifer.*'

I do what he tells me and then he says something else. 'Repeat: *I am his and part of him.*'

I say this too, but my voice croaks and he looks into me with his dark, angry eyes as he wipes the bird's blood on my face. When he's gone Paige comes back and says it's time to get dressed.

I run to my clothes but Paige says stop running and walk slowly. My heart is beating faster than ever – I just want to get away as quickly as I can.

When I'm dressed I try to ask Paige all my questions, but she keeps telling me, 'Shush.' I want to know about the bird and the man in the hood and why my teacher was there and will we have to do this every day now?

When we get outside my heart is still beating too fast but I don't feel nearly so scared. I'm almost happy to be away from the chapel and back with Paige – I've never been so glad that she's my friend. I think she's my best friend in the whole world now and I want to hug her tight.

'Go and wash your face,' says Paige, pushing me away.

'Okay.' I'm so glad to be with her I don't even mind being pushed away and I run all the way to the girls' toilet at the other side of the building. I still want to ask my questions and Paige lets me talk now.

81

'Why did that man in the hood have a dead bird?' I say.

'Because sacrifice pleases the Master.'

'Who's the Master?'

'Lucifer, silly.'

I don't know who she means or why I'm silly. I run the water in the sink and start to wash my face. The white sink starts to turn pink with the swirling water and the blood from the black bird.

'Why did we have to say all those words, Paige?'

'It's like a marriage in a big church,' she says, 'but with different words.'

I don't understand. 'Are we married now?'

'Kind of. I don't know, really. Stop asking all these questions. I want to go and play now.'

Paige has stopped smiling, and I don't want to see her stop smiling ever, so I stop with all my questions like she says. She watches me clean my face and pat down my skin with the paper towel and then she says we should go.

'Can I look at your diary again?' I say.

'No. Not today,' says Paige.

'But I like your pictures.'

'Not today.'

'*Please ...*'

'No!' she snaps. Her voice sounds different. I wonder if I've upset her. I won't ask about the pictures ever again. I won't do anything that upsets Paige ever again because now I know I need her more than ever and I can't risk losing her, not ever, not even for a second.

10

Morning sunlight streamed through the window. There was an unusually white glare etching the Town Hall's spire onto a cloudless sky. In such conditions, Ayr – from the rooftops up anyway – made for a pleasant scene. You could ignore the decaying streets below, forget the great unwashed for a while, if not permanently hide from them.

DCI Valentine stood in front of the window, rubbing the back of his neck. A dull steady ache had begun to pester him as he drove over the Fenwick Moors coming back from the mortuary. He knew it was no more than age, a tight compression of seldom-used muscles, but as DI McCormack entered his office he withdrew his hand sharply, lest it be misinterpreted.

'Good morning. I thought you might fancy a coffee, boss.' She skirted the desk briskly and laid the cup down.

Valentine blinked in surprise. 'You didn't need to do that, Sylvia. You're a DI now – fetching coffee's well below your station.'

'Well, I know.' She held up a yellow post-it note and made a show of sticking it on his PC screen. 'A wee reminder. Hugh Crosbie, at eight tomorrow in the Red Lion.'

'Thanks, I think.' The coffee seemed like a deal sweetener now. He moved over to the desk and retrieved the cup.

'The team's ready when you are, sir,' said McCormack.

The DCI gazed over her shoulder and into the incident room. 'Where's DI Davis?'

'He was there a minute ago, I'll go have a look.'

'Good. There's no show without Punch, after all.'

'Yes. His input's kind of essential. I've asked him to spare us the worst of the details at this briefing. I don't want to unnecessarily burden – or do I mean scare – uniform right away.'

'No, keep them on a need-to-know basis. But copy the files from the original Abbie McGarvie case for the squad detectives – they need to know what we're dealing with.'

'Will do.'

'Great. I'll be out in five minutes.' He tapped the side of his head. 'I just need to get a few things straight in here first.'

'I'll let them know you're on the way.'

'Thank you,' he said. 'Oh, and, Sylvia ... thanks for setting me up with Hugh again.'

McCormack smiled thinly as she closed the door. Her actions could be read as conspiratorial, but the DCI knew differently: he needed her help and he was grateful for it.

Valentine stationed himself behind his desk, then retrieved a pile of paperwork sitting adjacent to his office phone. He kept expecting the phone to ring, and the little bulb beside the chief super's line to light up, but so far he'd been spared; when she found out about the victim's

ID, and Wrighty's other discoveries, there'd be all kinds of bells ringing.

He tried to process the morning's events. Confirmation that the victim was the same girl as in DI Davis's missing person's case grated on his mind. He wanted to know why the girl hadn't been found, and why her murder wasn't prevented. Both were achievable, even with the suffocating budget cuts and staff shortages.

Abbie McGarvie had been the subject of two previous investigations: one dismissed – wrongly it had been confirmed by the post-mortem – and one now terminated by her violent death. Valentine felt a deepening guilt for how badly she had been failed by the police force. As he held these thoughts he saw again the young girl's mother, sobbing in the chapel of rest. Lives had been ruined, and it was down to him to make sure those responsible faced consequences.

McCormack knocked on the door. 'Davis is back. We're all ready when you are, sir.'

Valentine got up and headed through to the incident room. McCormack had gathered the troops, and he was greeted by a semicircle of bodies that he had to separate to reach the board. When he faced the team his mind was still sunk in sympathy with the deceased, but he abruptly threw off that thought pattern and engaged the role of leader.

'Right, here we are again,' said the DCI, his voice rising. He pointed to a photograph on the board, a headshot of Abbie McGarvie. 'We know the victim to be a 15-year-old schoolgirl from Troon. An HGV collision on an open road at night might not arouse suspicions at first sight, but then we don't rely on what we encounter at first sight, do we?'

'No, sir,' came in chorus.

'No, we do not.' Valentine collected a pen from the table beside him and pointed to the board again. 'Coming under the "very suspicious indeed" category would be the victim's complete lack of any clothing, except a pair of Dunlops. She was in a frantic disposition, by all accounts, and when examined at the scene we found her body covered in marks and bruising.'

The DCI asked for the SOCOs' photographs to be passed about the group. 'Wrighty's PM has since confirmed she died instantly. Who she was running from we can only speculate on here and now, but once we dig out some suspects we can start narrowing down motives, and perhaps pinpoint some answers. One answer we have been able to furnish already, and this contradicts a previous investigation and court ruling, is that Abbie McGarvie was the victim of serious sexual abuse. It doesn't end there, though. This young girl was pregnant too, which means we're dealing with the loss of two lives.'

Valentine wanted to impress the squad with the seriousness of the crime – this wasn't everyday criminality they were dealing with. There would be worse to come and they had to be prepared for that. He pulled out a chair and sat down; the movement indicated the end of his introduction, but he folded his arms to press the point. The group remained silent, taking some time to digest the full, shocking nature of the DCI's revelations.

'Now, who wants to be the first usherette at the horror show?' he said.

None of the officers came forward.

'Great, Phil, you start us off,' said Valentine, volunteering the DS. 'What have you got on the crime scene?'

'Oh, right...' DS Donnelly lunged for a blue folder on top of the adjacent filing cabinet, shuffling the contents before him as he spoke. 'The locus of the RTA is interesting, being butted by a walled private estate...'

Valentine cut in, 'The victim was seen clambering over this wall before the crash.'

'That's right, and uniform's been doing a fingertip search there, too.'

'Anything turn up?'

'They've just winding things down now, sir. I'll report any findings as soon as I have them.'

'What about that uppity ponce at the scene – what did you get from him?'

Donnelly grinned. 'You must be referring to Ray Coulter. He's just security. The estate is owned by David Sutherland, a businessman who runs an air freight operation from Prestwick Airport.'

'Handy, being right next door.'

'Yes, the estate actually butts the airport.'

'Have you spoken to this Sutherland?'

'No, sir. He's out of the country on business. He's due back tonight, so I will speak to him then and arrange a meeting in person. I did run him through the system and he's not even got a parking ticket to his name, perhaps not really that surprising if you're chauffeur-driven everywhere. Interestingly, though, there were a number of complaints to police made by Sutherland's estate about kids trespassing, but they turned out to be nothing more than teenagers larking about, certainly nothing criminal.'

'I can't get my teenagers off their phones,' Valentine said. 'Makes me wonder what the attraction was.'

DI McCormack raised her hand and spoke. 'Sir, that's even more curious in light of the encounter we had with the tractor driver at the estate.'

'That's right, what did he call it – Area 51?' Valentine turned back to Donnelly. 'Take a few officers and do some door to door, Phil. Get the word on the ground about this Sutherland estate. And track down those teenagers who were trespassing, too.'

'Will do.' He closed over his folder.

'Right, let's see what DI McCormack has got for us,' said Valentine.

McCormack took her place in the centre of the board and spoke. 'Well, the lorry driver, Andy Evans, is over the worst of his shock. Though I doubt he'll ever fully escape the memories. He seems a very genuine bloke, dad of three daughters himself, and he's very messed up by this.'

'There's nothing to connect him to the girl, is there?' said Valentine.

'No, sir. He's from Liverpool, straight shooter, and this wasn't his regular route, he was taking an extra shift. He got lost, basically.' McCormack was animating her points with hand gestures. 'Andy Evans will never get behind the wheel of a truck again. He's utterly convinced Abbie McGarvie was running for her life, terrified of something.'

'Okay. Evans clearly can't be thought of as a suspect at this point in the investigation,' said the DCI. 'We have, however, a number of loose threads hanging over from Abbie's missing person's case and also the earlier abuse allegations brought by Abbie's mother against the girl's father, and I'm going to hand over to DI Davis now for a rundown on those two investigations.'

DI McCormack remained in front of the board, turning back to Valentine and lowering her voice. 'Before we hand over to DI Davis, sir, can I just add that I've looked for the social worker that Caroline Simpson mentioned at the chapel of rest; her name's Jean Clark.'

'Oh yes. What was it Caroline called social services? The SS.'

'That's right,' DI McCormack said. 'And I can see why she's not a fan, I can't say they were particularly helpful.'

'Oh, really. You do surprise me.'

'I don't mean in the pious do-gooder kind of way. As far as they're concerned Jean Clark is persona non grata. They won't comment on her, or release any of her work, without a court order.'

'I'll get on that, then. They're obviously hiding something.'

'And they're not alone, sir.'

'They're not?'

'Jean Clark's missing too. Either that or she's opted to live off the grid because I can't find hide nor hair of her.'

11

'What do you mean, missing?' Valentine sat up stiffly, his expression changed from someone passively recording information to a look of consternation.

'I mean I've been unable to find a fixed abode for her. No telephone number, nothing. Her last known address is vacant and her neighbours say it's been like that since Clark moved out about six months ago.'

'What about her family? Friends?'

'Her mother won't speak, she slammed the phone down. She has a brother, but he's working in London apparently, and nobody knows where exactly.'

Valentine creased his brows; it was an action his wife often disapproved of, something about creating lines he could ill afford. 'Well, she hasn't just vanished.' He touched his forehead, a soothing motion, which did little to allay his mounting frustration. 'Try Revenue and Customs. And the DVLC as well. No one just disappears without a trail these days – everyone's keeping tabs on everyone else.'

'Yes, sir. I have put calls out to the utility companies.' McCormack's response sounded like a plea for clemency.

'Good. If you don't get anywhere, let me know. We'll

doorstep her mother and spell out how concerned we are. Surely she'll appreciate the fact that we're investigating a suspected murder.'

'Yes, sir.'

'I'm all for family loyalty but there's a point at which it becomes misplaced. If Jean Clark is missing, there's more than a fair chance she's in danger, or worse.'

'We need to spell that out,' McCormack confirmed.

'Indeed we do.'

Valentine retreated within himself, taking a moment to let what he had just heard sink in. It seemed like all they had uncovered so far kept echoing back to the previous investigations. He had a dead, pregnant teenager who had been the subject of a serious sexual abuse investigation and a missing person's case. After all that had happened already, how was it even possible that this girl had ended up the subject of scrutiny by his murder squad?

'Okay, Davis, you're up,' said the DCI, gruffly.

As his name was called, heads turned to locate DI Davis at the back of the room. He was leaning, one arm draped louchely over the top of a gunmetal-grey filing cabinet. For a moment he hesitated, stood still, and then jerked into motion and walked to the front of the board. The DI's movements were stiff and his bodyshape angular as he went, like an uncomfortable youth in unfamiliar sur-roundings.

When Davis started to talk, he stared ahead unseeing, as though he was waiting for his thoughts to coalesce into a coherent response to what had gone before. It didn't take long for the DI to locate the words he was looking for and his gaze quickly turned from the vague middle-distance to a sharper focus on the expectant group. 'I hope you'll forgive this stuttering start but I'm only just hearing about the post-mortem results myself,' he said.

Valentine interrupted, 'I should probably have mentioned, for those of you that don't already know, DI Davis was involved in the initial investigations and that's why he's joined in now.'

'That and Ally's piles,' said DS Donnelly.

When the laughter subsided, Valentine continued. 'I thought it was gallstones, but I might be wrong. Hope I'm not starting any rumours – that would be terrible for poor Ally.' The DCI waved his hand and implied the floor was Davis's once more.

'I'd like to point out, here and now, that the early investigations I was involved with didn't reach the same conclusions as the courts,' said Davis. 'We felt very strongly that Abbie McGarvie was indeed a victim of abuse, and that consensus was across the board.'

'So what are you saying?' said DI McCormack. 'You were stiffed by the prosecutor?'

'I couldn't possibly comment on that.'

'Oh, go on,' pressed McCormack.

'Let's just say the investigations encountered some shadowy opposition that I don't think it would be appropriate to go into here.' Davis turned to Valentine as he changed tack. 'The post-mortem results do concur with our earlier findings. We had taken evidence from Jean Clark, and medical assessments too, that indicated sexual activity, but obviously the courts took the view that the weight of evidence was insufficient for a conviction.'

'Incredible, isn't it?' said Valentine. He shuffled in his

seat, shrugging heavy shoulders. 'I sometimes wonder whose side they're on.'

'Well, I think it's clear it wasn't Abbie McGarvie's side.'

'No. It definitely bloody wasn't.'

DI Davis leaned over to retrieve a blue folder from the desk beside him, removing a picture and holding it up. The image showed a man in his forties, dark hair receding, leaving only an angular strip up front. He was dressed professionally in a collar and tie. The photograph appeared posed, like a shot taken for a website or newspaper report.

'This is Alex McGarvie, our victim's father. He's a teacher, a deputy head actually, at a public school in Glasgow – I'd call it private, but I'm working class, so what do I know?'

'What's the school called?' said DI McCormack.

'Finlayson, out in the West End.'

'I know it. They boast a couple of former cabinet members among their alma mater.'

'Yes. They tend to dine out on that a bit, even though you have to go back a half-century to find them. More recently they've had a Commonwealth Games sprinter and, I believe, a fairly senior BBC exec.'

'I loathe them already,' said Valentine, the squad agreeing with a chuckle. 'Can we go back to the case, please?'

'Sorry, sir,' said Davis. 'The investigations both experienced a great deal of pushback. There was a lack of cooperation from the outset and we came to the fairly swift conclusion that this was directly attributable to the very specific and controversial nature of the allegations made by Caroline Simpson.'

'Caroline Simpson is the victim's mother, former spouse of Alex McGarvie,' said Valentine.

'That's right. Would you like me to touch on her claims now, sir?'

'Lightly, yes.'

'Okay.' DI Davis paused, and when he resumed speaking his voice sounded wary, like he was unsure how he might be received. 'Miss Simpson reported a number of claims of sexual abuse involving her daughter. These claims were made over a period of some months to police in Troon, where the family lived. The allegations involved a particular kind of ritualised, incessant and depraved abuse that we came to describe as occultic.'

A brittle tension settled into the room as DI Davis drew breath. He stared above the group, towards the back of the room, where the only point of reference was a blank wall. It was as if he was avoiding eye contact for fear of being touched by any kind of human response.

'How did you arrive at that particular definition?' said Valentine.

'When DI Rickards, who was leading the investigation, realised what it looked like we were dealing with, he called in an expert, Dr Stephen Mason, from the University of Glasgow. Mason has a considerable reputation as a researcher in this field and he provided the clarification we needed.'

'Clarification?'

'In Dr Mason's view, it was a clear-cut case of ritualistic child sexual abuse.'

Valentine's rigid features cast hollows in the sides of his face. 'What did he base his findings on?'

'He's interviewed upwards of a hundred similar victims, all exhibiting the same symptoms. Things like being forced into cages, regular beatings, force-feeding of faeces. The abuse escalates towards something like having the soles of their feet cut and being made to watch animal sacrifices. It then moves on to still more serious torture and rape, the details of which I'll spare you here.'

'He's seen more than a hundred similar cases?' said Valentine, outrage seeping into his voice.

'Dr Mason is on record confirming that in every case, and these are his words, "It's the same story, over and over again."'

DI McCormack eased off the desk she was leaning on and moved to the front of the group. Her expression implied she was having difficulty grasping the concept. 'But why, Ian? Why do these people do it? What explanation does this doctor give for such behaviours?'

As Davis turned to face the DI his eyelids twitched. 'He says these people believe in evil, and believe in their right to express evil.'

For a second or two the incident room was soundless. It would have been hard to detect any motion before Valentine got out of his chair and positioned himself in front of DI Davis. 'Right, that's where we are, folks. And I think that's enough for one day.'

A low soughing noise spread through the room and then the squad separated, returning to their desks. There was talk now, but the claver was hushed, like a respectful church gathering that was emptying after the service.

Valentine was facing Davis as he spoke again. 'This doctor, can you call him and arrange a meeting for me?'

'I don't see why not. Are you thinking of asking him for clarification?'

'I don't know what the hell to think to be honest. All I do know is that someone's going to have to interpret this for me because it's nothing like anything I've ever encountered before. There was talk of ley lines and mystic runes in that file for crying out loud.'

'Oh, you missed the goats' heads and pentagrams did you?'

'Don't jest, Ian.'

'I'm not. Wait until you get to the spirit cooking, now that's some seriously messed-up shit.'

Valentine shook his head. 'We're lacking expertise. We don't know what we don't know.'

'I said it before, you need to talk to Kevin Rickards about this. I think you'd find his experiences very enlightening.'

'Are you referring to the shadowy opposition you mentioned earlier?'

DI Davis was smirking as he reached over to the board to pin up a photograph. 'You're going to run into them at some point, boss. It might as well be sooner rather than later.'

12

The Red Lion sat a little shy of Prestwick's ancient cross, at the top end of the main street. When he looked around him, Valentine thought Prestwick was what Ayr had once been: a nice place where people wanted to live and raise families. He hoped the town wasn't, one day, going to suffer the same fate as its larger neighbour, but he knew that was the curse of modernity. Nothing was out of bounds any more, and the world around him was being deconstructed in a way he sometimes felt helpless to even interpret.

He went into the pub and ordered a bottle of still water, taking it to a small seating area with comfortable, well-upholstered chairs. The detective always arrived early, and always slotted himself in the corner. He liked to acclimatise himself, and have a vantage point in any new territory. He put this down to police training but conceded it might just be an intrinsic trait.

Valentine was pouring the bottled water into a tall glass when he heard Hugh Crosbie addressing him.

'Good evening, Bob.' Crosbie draped his jacket over the back of the chair.

'Hugh, thanks for coming.'

Crosbie didn't reply. He sat down, crossed his legs and

started gazing all around him. For a few seconds he seemed lost in reverie and then he spoke softly, 'Hmn, geraniums.'

'What's that?'

'Oh, nothing. Don't mind me.'

A waitress, still in her teens, approached with a bar tray pressed to her hip and drew Crosbie's attention. 'What can I get you?'

'Tell me something first, are there geraniums on display somewhere?'

'Not that I know of.'

'I definitely smell geraniums.'

The girl smiled politely, indicating some bafflement. She glanced at Valentine and then back to Crosbie. 'Can I get you something?'

'Just a lemonade, please. No ice.'

As the waitress retreated to the bar Valentine felt his stomach cramping. Approaching the esoteric with Crosbie had always terrified him, but now it was for a completely different reason. He'd changed since those early days following his stabbing, when he found himself questioning his sanity. If he'd been told then that he would come round to the notion of communing with a spiritual dimension, he would have laughed. But here he was, with Crosbie again, and he didn't even need DI McCormack to give him a push.

'I really appreciate you helping me out like this again, Hugh,' he said.

Crosbie smiled. The waitress returned with his drink, placing the glass and a white napkin on the table in front of them. He nodded his appreciation as she backed away. 'And how can I be of assistance this time, Bob?'

Valentine paused. 'It's hard to know where to begin.'

'I find the start is generally the best place.'

Their last meeting had been a practical one: Valentine had detailed his experiences and his trouble accepting them. He had expected to be told a load of mumbo jumbo but had, in the end, found himself reassured. Something was happening to him that he didn't understand, was beyond his frame of reference, beyond even logic itself. Valentine still couldn't rationalise what he had seen but he had moved beyond questioning it, if only because the questioning nature of his mind changed nothing.

'When we last met, you told me to abandon my scepticism,' said the detective.

'I told you to accept it,' Crosbie corrected him. 'It's not going to go anywhere. You need to let it be and pay no heed to it.'

'I think I found your advice useful. I've stopped looking for answers where there clearly are none.'

'Open-mindedness is the key to understanding this phenomenon, Bob. There is no worldly solution. I know that must be difficult to come to terms with for a man whose life is so clearly wedded to logic and the pursuit of truth.'

Crosbie sipped from his glass and then returned it to the table. There was an assuredness about the man that was calming. He inspired confidence. Valentine imagined Crosbie being able to coolly direct troops while bombs were going off all around him; his strength was a silent presence between them.

'I feel like I've entered a new stage,' Valentine said, 'like I'm quite receptive now. I think I'm ready to hear more of your explanation. Maybe not all, but maybe one day I will be.'

'Sounds to me like you're reaching out to your higher self.'

'I don't understand.'

'Each of us has a part of our being that can act as a link between the spiritual and physical dimensions,' said Crosbie. 'There's a reservoir of higher knowledge beyond our own that can provide guidance to us. The closer you get to your higher self, Bob, the more you'll be able to access this understanding.'

Valentine started to play with his shirt cuff. 'Did Sylvia mention why I wanted to see you?'

'She mentioned the dreams, yes.'

'They're not really dreams, it's like I'm awake. I know I'm dreaming, but I'm within the dream at the same time. Does that make any sense?'

'You're lucid dreaming,' Crosbie said. 'You have freedom of choice to direct the action and outcome of the experience. These states are not uncommon, and they always happen for a reason.'

'Can you explain that?'

Crosbie leaned closer, balancing his elbows on the flat of his thighs. 'Your mind is at its most receptive to intuition in the sleep state. When you receive a communication in this way it's to make an impact on you. You're being shown something important – don't ignore any messages that come to you this way.'

The image of Abbie McGarvie returned to clog Valentine's thoughts. He knew the girl had appeared in his dream on the night she had died, but he had seen her since then too. He knew the girl wanted to be seen, to show herself to him. But it wasn't like the other times he'd had these visions. This time felt different, the girl was anxious, troubled. She wanted him to know something – he didn't know what that was, but he knew she wouldn't stop until he did know.

'Hugh, the girl I saw in that dream showed up in my waking life.'

'Oh, really.'

'Yes.'

'That's very interesting. Can you tell me more?'

'The night she appeared in my dream was the night she died, but then she showed up a short time later when I was at the chapel of rest.'

Crosbie eased back into his chair, his earlier look of irritable distraction replaced with a concentrated scowl. 'It sounds like the girl's spirit is in limbo between worlds.'

Valentine shrugged. 'What does that mean?'

'Well, some more colourful commentators might say she's trapped on the Bridge of Souls, which is the path to the afterlife. A soul can be trapped between worlds because they believe they have unfinished business here.'

'Business with me?'

'That's why she's coming to you, Bob, because you're receptive but also because you can make a change she wants. She knows that, and you should too.'

'So what do I do now?'

Crosbie pinched the tip of his nose to suppress a sneeze. 'I think you should try and engage this girl.'

'What do you mean?'

'Ask her what she wants. Otherwise, you might find she hangs around for a very long time indeed.'

Crosbie was pinching his nose again, a sneeze queuing

behind his fingers, when the waitress reappeared. 'I asked about those geraniums,' she said.

'My boss says we haven't had geraniums in the bar for more than a year, not since his wife passed away. She used to love them.' She leaned closer. 'He got a bit teary thinking about that, so he's off to get some from the florist now to sit on the bar.'

Crosbie smiled at the waitress and patted her on the arm. 'I think she'd like that. No, I know she definitely would.'

13

The last rays of an ebbing sun glinted off the car's roof as Valentine stood in his driveway. He was tired, peering coldly over the lawn towards his front door. His father had had the mower out, something he'd have to caution him on again – the old man was far too infirm to be wrestling a Suffolk Colt over the grass. Though Valentine did have to admit, his father had done a much better job than he ever could in effecting the parallel shadow striping.

It had been a long day, longer still with the Hugh Crosbie meeting tagged on at the end, and it had taken its toll. Valentine wondered if he was getting old himself, too old for the job? The chief super had assured him the promotion would mean a lot more time spent behind a desk – more application of brain than brawn – but that hadn't materialised. Should he have expected anything different? He didn't think so; only an idiot listened to the promises of superiors or politicians. Their priorities were in getting over the next bump in the road, nothing more; if he dropped dead on the job that would just be another bump to be surmounted, as and when, or if, it appeared.

Valentine went in through the front door, placing his briefcase on the floor next to the hallstand. There was some mail, bills mainly, sitting beside the phone on a semi-circular table that he was sure he'd never seen before. A couple of utility reminders and a credit card statement loudly proclaimed the fact that the recent trip to the Antipodes was still four figures in arrears. Abruptly, he put the statement back in the envelope. How would he ever settle that amount? He'd agreed to the expense on the basis that the family badly needed a break. And he'd persuaded himself he could afford it with the popular piece of cognitive dissonance that this was how people lived now – what difference did a few thousand pounds of debt mean when the entire country was virtually bankrupt?

He picked up the credit card bill and put it in his pocket. The idea of his father, who'd never been in debt a day in his life, seeing the statement sickened him. The idea that he wasn't alone, that virtually everyone he met was living in exactly the same way filled him with an altogether different kind of terror. When the credit line ran out, and the comfort everyone was used to vanished, he knew he'd be among those tasked with maintaining order. And that might be impossible given the state of recent resources.

The phone on the little table in front of him started to ring.

'Hello,' said Valentine.

'Hello, boss.' It was DI McCormack.

'Sorry, Sylvia, I had my mobile off while I was in that meeting with Hugh Crosbie.'

'How did it go?'

'About as well as expected.' He shuffled the phone onto his shoulder as he took off his jacket and hung it on the balustrade.

'Did he give you any pointers, or any indication of what you're actually dealing with?'

'Well, yes and no. He told me that this is happening for two reasons; one because I'm able to tune in to it, and two because I can do something about it.'

'And does that make sense to you?'

'I think so. But I need to learn to interpret the signs first, and I'm a long way from that.'

'Everything takes time, boss.'

'I know.' He sat down on the steps and spied a price tag dangling on a piece of string beneath the table. 'Look, Sylvia, I want to thank you for your help. I don't really have anyone else to talk to about this and things with Clare are so tense since I took the new job that ... well, you know what I'm saying.'

'I understand.'

He paused for a moment, grabbing the price tag. 'What was your reason for calling?' The tag revealed the table had cost £200 from TK Maxx. He rolled his gaze towards the ceiling.

'Uniform concluded the search of the Sutherland estate.' McCormack's tone shifted sharply. 'And there's some interesting developments.'

'Tell me more.'

'I haven't seen the full report yet, I presume that'll be coming some time tomorrow, but I had a chat with the sergeant on the site and he says they've found a rope ladder next to where the victim came over the wall.'

'A rope ladder?'

'Yes, erm, wait a minute, I made some notes ...' The sound of pages being turned in a notepad came over the line. 'Yes, here we are. White nylon ropes, either side of interlocking wooden batons, or steps I suppose.'

'Has this been seen by the lab?'

'It's en route now.'

'Any markings or anything we might get DNA from?'

'The batons are filthy; looks like some pretty clear impressions from a running shoe.'

'Fabulous. If we can tie that to the victim we have cause to extend our crime scene into Sutherland's estate. Better yet, if we locate some DNA, then we'll be solid.'

McCormack's words quickened. 'Actually, boss, I was thinking about what Phil said earlier about arranging a meeting with David Sutherland.'

'You must have read my mind. Phil said Sutherland gets back tonight. Let's be there waiting for him. In fact, let's organise a welcoming party.'

'I'm sorry, what do you mean?'

'I'm gambling that the lab confirms our suspicions,' said Valentine, 'but I want you to organise a second search.'

'Do you want me to contact the fiscal for a warrant?'

'No, let's not get ahead of ourselves. I doubt a sheriff would grant one without the lab results. Let's just play to this Sutherland's good side. If he's got nothing to hide then he's got no reason to keep us out of his property.'

'We have permission to be on the land, from the security guy, Coulter.'

'Let's push the boat out and assume it extends to out-buildings, too.'

'If you say so, boss.'

'I do.' Valentine stood up and collected his jacket again.

'Meet me out at Sutherland's estate right away, Sylvia. And don't spare the horses.'

As he put the phone down, Valentine noticed Clare standing at the open kitchen door. Her arms were folded in front of her; her look was confrontational, if not nearing on downright combative.

'So, things between us are tense, are they?' she said.

Valentine opted for the defensive. 'Haven't you heard that people who listen at doors never hear any good of themselves?'

'It's a damn good job I did listen at this door, otherwise I might not know that my husband is conducting a smear campaign against me.'

'Oh, come on, Clare.'

She unfastened herself from the doorjamb and approached him. She seemed to be carrying a tightly controlled bolus of anger inside her. 'And that was her again, wasn't it?'

'What?'

'Don't play the innocent, Bob. You were speaking to that Sylvia woman that you spent the night with on Arran.'

'I told you before, that was work, the last ferry had gone and we were hardly staying in the same room. Look, why am I defending myself when I've done nothing wrong?'

'I could ask you that question myself.' Clare's voice sharpened. 'It's very suspicious, isn't it?'

'No, Clare, it's silly. That's what this is, just silly.' Valentine collected his briefcase from beside the hallstand. 'I have to go back out.'

'You're meeting her, aren't you?'

'You know I am, you were eavesdropping when I said so

on the phone.' Valentine knew he was playing into Clare's hands – she wanted a confrontation and he was giving her one. But he was tired; he'd had too long a day to sensibly resist.

'If you go out that door, Bob, you might as well not come back.'

'Okay, then I'll leave this with you, will I?' He reached inside his jacket and removed the credit card bill, which he slapped down on the new table. As he turned for the door he remembered the price tag he'd pulled from the table earlier and spun round, slapping that down beside the credit card bill.

He didn't look towards his wife as he went, heading straight out the door and down the driveway. He'd had sufficient control of his emotions not to slam the door, and for that he had some pride. But by the time he was sitting in the car he felt enough shame mounting inside him to know that he'd soon regret his other actions.

On the road to Prestwick, Valentine toyed with the idea of calling his wife to apologise. It was a stupid tiff, over nothing. When he examined why Clare had acted the way she had he knew it was just her insecurity, the same insecurity that caused her to impulse shop without thinking about how they were going to pay for it. Whenever the DI rationalised his wife's actions, he knew he couldn't actually fault her – she was only acting out her programming, and that unsettled him.

He should have known better, but the job was taking so much from him just now. Perhaps Clare was right about that too.

14

Valentine felt the blood stiffening in his veins as he drove towards Monkton. It was suppressed anger, the type that tightened in the chest and constricted around the heart muscle. When he had returned to active duty, after a forlorn stint at the police training college in Tulliallan, he had been warned about these episodes by a doctor. All stress was bad, always, in his condition. However there was no way of avoiding stress; it was as much a part of the human experience as breathing, but knowing this only increased his problem. It was like conceding to Clare that the very reason she was confronting him – though he'd rebuffed it – was in fact true.

Clare knew, perhaps even better than he did himself, that Valentine was no longer fit for purpose. When the visions had begun, he'd questioned his sanity and that had remained his overriding preoccupation, until only very recently. However, now that he was beyond the questioning phase and nearing acceptance, his mind was latching onto other issues.

Valentine had started to notice his own deterioration: the grey hairs at his temples, the creeping of the notches on his belt, and a sundry collection of aches and pains that seemed to be multiplying daily. There had been an internet meme he'd spotted a short time ago that showed a middle-aged tradesman holding up a cardboard sign reading: 'Only someone that spent all day in an office could think working past 70 was an option.' Valentine had stared at the picture and wept inwardly because he knew only too well that there were limits to human endurance. He didn't long to be put out to pasture like some old pit pony though, because he knew he wouldn't last long enough to see the green grass. The job had shortened his life, but his life *was* the job. At some unforeseen point on the horizon the two lines would converge and cancel each other out; he just hoped that by then he'd done enough to make a difference to those who mattered.

Bouncing light from a low, receding sun breached the road and put a harsh glare on the windscreen. The buildings of Ayr looked shrunken under the broad and cloudless sky. Huddling together behind a bleached, hazy screen that shimmered along the roadside, stark towers rising and falling, before disappearing as the car sped along.

Driving was like walking, thought Valentine, you picked up and put down thoughts as you went. He made a halfsmile as his thinking began to coalesce around the day's more pressing events. There was a young girl, abused and pregnant, whose life had been taken. That was his priority. Everything else was just unwanted chatter inside his mind; he was the hunter here and that meant keeping his focus on the prey.

As the DCI pulled into the entrance to the Sutherland estate a police Land Rover was slowly crossing the gravel scree that butted a high grass verge. Two uniformed officers in hi-vis vests were sitting in the back of the vehicle, carefully delineating the road's edge by dropping a row of yellow cones.

He spied McCormack's car ahead. She'd parked in front of a grand building that could accurately be described as neoclassical but to Valentine was only ever going to be seen as pretentious at best, intimidating at worst.

A delicate knock sounded on the driver's-side window.

'Hello, sir.' McCormack had a bundle of blue folders under her arm that she was feeding into a black leather satchel. The wind took her hair, which responded by whipping her face.

'Bit blowy out,' said Valentine, exiting the Audi.

McCormack seemed unfazed, clicking the lock on the satchel. 'No sign of Sutherland yet, I'm afraid.' She pointed towards the end of the cone trail, where the gravel driveway ended. 'We're heading this way.'

As they walked, the path petered off into a bridleway that appeared to be well trodden. Deep declivities, filled with water, made their progress difficult, causing them to shimmy round the worst of the muddy pools. By the time the wall was in sight Valentine was cursing the state of his shoes.

'I've got wellies in the boot,' he said. 'You should have told me it was this bad.'

'Sorry, boss. Uniform have been trooping through here all day, it's worse than I expected.'

By the edge of the wall, the detective's attention had shifted again. 'Is it me or does that wall look higher from this side?'

'It is higher, at least five feet or so,' said McCormack,

pointing to the wall's base that was coming into view, though still obscured slightly by the land's incline. 'Look, there's a pit this side.'

'What in the name of Christ?' Valentine halted on the edge of the pit that skirted the wall, running the full length of the perimeter. 'Who digs a pit inside their property?'

'Someone who doesn't want you to get out.'

The DCI peered down the line of the wall, then returned his gaze to McCormack. He shook his head before speaking again. 'When I was a lad they used to have broken glass cemented into the top of the wall at the footy ground.'

'I bet they don't have it now.'

'No, we don't have ducking stools either.' He walked up and down, staring into the steep pit. 'No leaves or twigs, nothing cluttering it up.'

'It looks to be well maintained. Someone's keeping it clear anyway.'

The detective turned back to the route they were walking. 'Lead on, Sylvia.'

'This way, boss.' The sound of a passenger jet drowned out her voice, causing her to shout. 'The ladder was found just up ahead.'

'That plane's low. We must be virtually on the runway.'

'Yes, I discovered there's an access point too – it's a private road between the Laverock depot and the estate.'

'Cuts the morning commute, I suppose,' said Valentine. 'Not so sure I'd be that keen on mixing business with pleasure, though.'

'No, kind of makes you wonder, doesn't it?'

'It does indeed, Sylvia.'

The officers continued walking. Valentine allowed his

new observations room to percolate. 'Is Phil at the scene?'

'No, he's interviewing those teenagers he mentioned at the briefing.'

'The ones that were caught trespassing?'

'That's them, yes.'

'Well, I hope he's not bribing them with a few bottles of Buckie.'

McCormack laughed. 'I looked at the file on them – they all seemed a bit feral – and you just never know with Phil.'

'What about Ian?' Valentine corrected himself, 'Oh, don't answer that, I see him now.'

DI Davis was holding a small, clear plastic bag up to the light. Beside him a stocky man in a hoodie and red Adidas track-pants was furtively talking into a mobile phone. Even as he examined the little bag, Davis seemed to be keeping one eye on the other man.

As the officers approached Davis broke away and stepped towards the others. 'Hello, sir,' he said. 'DI McCormack, good to see you.'

'What's that you've got there?' said Valentine.

Davis handed over the plastic bag. 'Have a look for yourself.'

Valentine took the bag and turned it over in his hand. 'Looks like those things you get on women's dresses, the fancy ones.'

'Sequins, sir,' said Davis.

'I'm impressed,' said McCormack. 'Are you sure you're not married?'

Valentine handed back the bag. 'Where did these come from?'

'Over there.' Davis pointed to a stone outbuilding. As

he did so, the man in the hoodie started to walk away, distancing himself from the others.

'Who's the beat boy?' said Valentine.

'The groundsman, Malcolm Frizzle.'

'Isn't he supposed to be in green and tweed?'

'Says he was just finishing up when we arrived. He's on his way to the gym, but has been trying to rouse his boss. Seems a bit pissed off, to say the least.'

'Well, maybe he's got good reason to be.' The DCI started out for the outbuilding, and as he reached the doorway a white-suited SOCO was emerging with a cardboard box in his hands.

'Hold up, what's in there?'

'Soil sample, sir.' He nodded towards Davis. 'The detective inspector wanted the lot.'

Peering into the box, Valentine pointed. 'What's this white stuff.'

'We think it's salt,' said Davis, answering for the SOCO and nodding him off. 'We found it on the ground, quite a quantity of it, too. That's where we found the sequins as well.'

The DCI turned towards Davis and tilted his head. 'Salt?'

'It's commonly used in purification rituals, sir.'

'In *what*?'

'It's something to do with spirits. Kevin Rickards would be able to tell you more.'

'Bring Rickards down to Ayr as soon as you can, Ian. We need to have a chat.' Davis nodded and the detectives went into the outbuilding. It was a small, unlit chamber with drystone walls. The roof beams were exposed and

114

the ground earthen. At one end two more SOCOs were engaged in bagging evidence by torchlight.

'What have you got there?' said Valentine.

'Looks like blood,' said Davis. 'And lots of it.'

'No splatter marks that I can see. The walls seem clean. It's like a bucket was just emptied.'

'Very strange, sir.'

The DCI asked the SOCO for his torch and shone the beam upwards. A glossy black dampness covered the roof-beams, but there was fresh scoring in the centre of the beam. 'Take a look at this, what do you think?'

'It's something sharp, not rope, more like metal,' said McCormack, stepping forward.

'A chain,' said Davis, 'possibly on a pulley, maybe for lighting? There's a waxy black residue on the floor, too. It looks like drippage, from candles perhaps. We'll need to have that analysed, of course.'

'It certainly looks like the building's been used for something unwholesome.' Valentine turned back to the SOCOs. 'Anything you find, scoop it up and bag it. Fibres, fluids ... anything. This building is a crime scene now; I want the place sealed off.'

'Yes, sir.'

'Ian, get some uniforms on that door, too. Nobody comes in or out without my say-so.'

'Yes, sir.'

The detective headed back to the door and into the open air. Outside, joined by the others, he asked DI McCormack to show him where the rope ladder was found. She indicated a stretch of wall about two hundred metres away and they set off. The ground around the wall was hard packed,

115

too hard to show any footprints or tracks. Valentine was crouching down, pressing the soil with his hands when McCormack spoke. 'The SOCOs have the rope ladder in the lab now, sir, but I have a picture here.' She removed a photograph from a blue folder in her satchel and handed it over.

'Looks expensive, are those mountaineering grips?' Valentine said.

'Hard to say, but it doesn't look run of the mill.'

'No, with any luck it's rare and we can narrow down its origins. There's no doubt something went on here, but I'll be honest I've no idea what.' He handed back the picture and exhaled heavily. 'That old cowshed's been used for something, but I'm not sure the ladder is connected. I'd wager that whoever was responsible for the blood and the salt wouldn't have left a ladder hanging around in the open.'

Davis nodded. 'Certainly not after a young girl was killed a matter of yards away.'

Valentine smoothed the stubble on his chin. 'Something's not right here at all. I get a very bad vibe indeed about the whole place.'

2015

'I know where babies come from, I'm not silly.'

Paige doesn't like to hear the word baby, none of the older girls do. She puts her head down and goes all quiet. I think I've upset her now. I want to go over to her and say sorry or can I take it back but I'm not sure. Sometimes I get things mixed up and the words come out all wrong.

Paige starts to cry.

'What is it?' I say.

'Nothing.'

'No, it's something. Tell me.'

'It's nothing.' She gets off the bed and goes to stand at the window next to my Snoopy curtains. That's when I see her belly. It's bulging, not much, just a little. She turns quickly and catches me staring and that's when she pulls the curtain over her.

'I saw it.' The words come out before I can even think.

'No you didn't.'

'I saw it.' I can't stop, it's like I have to speak.

'You didn't see anything.' She's crying harder now. 'Go away.'

I stand up, the Monopoly cards fall off my lap, but it doesn't matter, nothing matters any more. I walk over the

117

board and the little Scottie dog is crushed under my slip-
per.

'Paige ...'

She buries her head in the curtains. Lucy, the bossy one
who always pulls the football away from Charlie Brown, is
smiling in front of me and I want to rip the curtains down.
But I'm not angry, just confused. I'm all upset to see Paige
crying. She's usually the strong one – she's older than me
and tells me what to do.

'Please, Paige. I want to help you.' I pull the curtain
away and she starts to cry even harder, her face going
all red on her cheeks and the tears slipping onto her
T-shirt.

'Oh, Abbie. If only you knew what it was like.'

I give her a hug and I feel her belly pressing on me. It
feels bigger than it looked. It feels strange too, because I
know there's a little baby growing in there.

I stop cuddling and take Paige back to the bed where I sit
her down. I get some tissues and help her to dry her eyes.
She smiles a little, not a proper smile, just one of those
'thank you' ones that people make sometimes, and I feel
all sad inside. I don't want her to be unhappy, or hurt, or
upset, because she's my friend and I just want things to be
like they were before when we were playing Monopoly and
laughing and joking about the things on telly. But I know
it can't ever be like that again.

'How did it happen?'

'I'm not supposed to say,' Paige says.

'You can tell me.'

She looks up at me, her eyes are still all watery. 'But why
do you want to know?'

'You told me I have to do what you do, so you have to tell me some time.'

Paige's lip goes wobbly then her shoulders shake and she's crying again. I put my hand on her but she pushes it away and can't even look at me. 'Oh, Abbie,' she says.

'Please, Paige. I have to know.'

She lifts her head and looks at the window, I think she doesn't want to look at me, but then I see it's because she can't look at me without the tears starting again.

'When you meet your keeper, you'll know.'

'I don't want to meet my keeper.'

'Oh, Abbie, you don't have any choice. You'll have to start the rites soon, all the girls do.'

'I've done the rites, what do you mean?'

'Not those. I mean the *real* ones.'

I don't understand and when Paige looks at me she realises this too. 'I mean the sex stuff, we all have to do it.'

'What sex stuff?'

'Stuff that pleases the Master. There's a group of girls, all of us have to do it. Oh, Abbie, it's horrible stuff, *horrible*, but we all have to do it.'

My throat starts to go all stiff, like I might cry too. 'Why do we have to do it?'

'The lower you become, the more it pleases Lucifer, and the more power you will be given when you die. Oh, it's horrible, horrible. Sometimes they make us drink stuff or take pills and you get sick. But that's not the worst thing.'

'What's the worst?'

'I can't say.'

'You must.'

Paige whisks her head away, but I grab her chin and pull

her eyes back to face me. 'You must tell me now, Paige. You must.'

She nods slowly and some tears escape from her tight-closed eyes. 'Okay. I'll tell. The thing that really pleases him – is blood.'

'What do you mean?'

'I mean eating flesh and drinking blood.'

I can't make a picture in my mind of her words so I ask again. 'Paige, how do you eat flesh and drink blood?'

'Remember in history class, how they told you about the ancients who did child sacrifices? Well, they never told you that there were still people doing that sort of thing, did they?'

'No.'

'Well, when we go to the groves and do the magic rites, that's what we do. They say it's when what we think is wrong becomes what's right.'

'But where does the blood come from?'

Paige goes all quiet and stares into my eyes. She touches her belly and I wonder what it is she's trying to tell me. For a moment I keep wondering and then it's clear in my mind and I know.

'It can't be true.'

'I had one before. It was already dead when it came. I was on the loo and it just happened. I was afraid they'd take it away, take it away for the rites.'

'What did you do?'

'I took it, but didn't tell anyone. I kept it in a drawer at home and put little flowers around it. I used to just look at it, I'd keep looking at it for the longest time, but then I stopped and put it in a shoebox under my bed.'

'Did they find it?'

Paige nodded. 'They took it away.'

'Where?'

'I don't know.'

Paige reaches out and takes my hands in hers. 'Abbie, they're going to take this baby, too.'

'No, we won't let them.'

'We can't stop them.'

I grip her hands. 'Yes we can.'

'No, there's nothing we can do. Not if it makes the Master happy.'

15

The detectives were descending the path, heading back towards the stone outbuilding, when the groundsman stopped them. His mobile phone was out of sight now, but he was no less animated than he had been at the height of his earlier conversation. As the officers halted, directed by Malcolm Frizzle's flailing arms, they observed his antics unfolding.

'Right, you can't go any further,' he said, putting out his hands and splaying his fingers like he was keeping goal.

The comical scene prompted the officers to laughter. 'Cool your jets, Groundkeeper Willie,' said Valentine.

The man gave them a gummy smile and lowered his arms. 'I'm just doing what I'm told.'

'By whom?' said the DCI.

'My boss, Mr Coulter.'

'Oh yeah, I've met him too. And was equally under-whelmed. Where's the organ grinder? I'm sick of speaking to his monkeys.'

'If you mean Mr Sutherland, he's on his way now.'

Valentine observed Frizzle's twitchiness and made a

connection that he normally associated with a particular type. 'Do I know you, Frizzle?'

'No, not me.'

'Are you sure? I think we might have met before.'

'No we haven't.'

'Well, I never forget a face. I'm annoying that way. I'd hate to be proven wrong, mind you. That might not work out well for you in this current situation.'

Frizzle became noticeably more nervous, scratching his thigh through the pocket of his tracksuit. 'I've never even seen you before in my life.'

Valentine turned to the others. 'Detective Inspector Davis, get on the blower and run this scrote's details through the system. If he's lying to me, then please extend him the great honour of a shot in your nice shiny police car, all the way to the station.'

'Yes, sir.'

As Valentine walked on he listened to Frizzle's protestations and DI Davis's much firmer shut-downs.

'That wasn't very nice of you,' said McCormack as they went.

'Police aren't very nice, Sylvia, haven't you heard?'

McCormack smiled. 'Perhaps it's for the best, when we're sopping up the dregs of society on a daily basis.'

'There can hardly be any doubts about that. It feels like we've descended to the bottom of the barrel.'

'What do you think's gone on here, boss?'

Valentine turned, his eyes narrowing as he took in the DI. 'I've no references for any of this sort of thing, and everything I've gleaned from Davis so far is giving me nightmares.'

'That reminds me.' McCormack looked back towards the track. 'You were going to tell me how things went with Hugh Crosbie.'

'As interesting as ever,' he said, as the pair continued to descend the trail. 'He told me that the girl, Abbie, had something to pass on to me.'

'Like a message?'

'Yeah, something like that. He said she obviously thought I could help her in some way.' Valentine turned to face McCormack again. 'I wish I could believe that, because right now I have more questions than answers.'

As they reached the edge of the gravel path skirting the house, the sound of footfalls crunching in the scree came upon them. Two figures, both male, were approaching.

'Is that who I think it is?' said Valentine.

'I'd bet money on it.'

When the figures neared the officers, and it became clear Ray Coulter had spotted them, their pace dropped and a brief, whispered exchange took place.

'Hello again,' said the DCI.

The security officer nodded and slunk back as his boss stepped forward. 'I'm David Sutherland.'

'I'm sorry for the disturbance to your property, Mr Sutherland,' said Valentine. He wasn't sorry in the slightest, but did his best to disguise the fact.

'It's a bit of a shock to come home to a three-ring circus on your lawn.' Sutherland ran his fingers through a thick crop of unruly hair, but the overlong fringe disobeyed, flopping into his eyes once again.

'I'm sure it must be, but you'll appreciate we have to be thorough in such matters.'

'My understanding is that the girl was knocked down on the public highway – the road doesn't run through my estate, detective.' He seemed pleased with his remark, a slight smile twisting the side of his mouth.

'I'm concerned with what occasioned that event, Mr Sutherland,' said Valentine. 'Which is why we're here.'

'You can't seriously believe that anyone on my property has anything to do with that.'

'It's not about what I believe, sir. It's about the facts, which haven't been established yet.'

Sutherland rolled his eyes towards the sky, his agitation obvious. However, much as this might have enjoined his staff, or a wine waiter, to act in his favour, it had the opposite effect on Valentine.

'I'd like to take a look inside your property, Mr Sutherland,' said the DCI.

'Do you have a warrant?'

'No.'

'Then it doesn't really bother me what you'd like to do, detective.'

'I'm sorry to hear you say that.' Valentine ushered DI McCormack onto the road. 'I'll be leaving a few officers here for now, Mr Sutherland.'

'What?'

'Yes, I'm afraid so. I've declared your outbuilding a crime scene, so they won't be going anywhere. I'd also like to extend an invitation to you to join me down at the station, in your own time of course, as there's a few questions I'd like to ask you.'

'You can't be serious.'

'Oh, I'm very serious indeed, Mr Sutherland. I definitely

do not make jokes about matters of life and death. Shall we say you can make yourself available, within the next forty-eight hours, at King Street station.' He nodded and moved on. 'Call in advance when you have a suitable time in mind and I'll make myself available.'

As Valentine and McCormack made their way to their cars, the DCI felt like a laser sight was being drawn on the back of his head. The encounter with David Sutherland had not gone to plan, or been conducted with any degree of civility, but he had succeeded in setting the ground rules. He was not going to be pushed around or intimidated – any bowing and scraping could be left to the chief super.

DI McCormack was pinching her lips and emitting a low whistle as she removed her car keys. 'We're really winning friends and influencing people today, sir.'

'Is it just me or does that type get up everyone's nose?' said Valentine.

'Comes with the territory.' McCormack waved her hand over the rolling lawns. 'I suppose it's hard not to feel a little superior when you wake up to this view every morning.'

'What happened to preaching that we're all equal?'

'Nobody really believes that nonsense.'

Valentine tipped back his head. 'Well Sutherland certainly doesn't.'

'Why didn't you just pull him in, boss?'

'I want to get the lab reports first, perhaps we'll have something on him by then.'

McCormack's phone pinged, and, as she stared at the screen, her mood seemed to rise. 'Result!'

'What is it?' said Valentine.

'It's Phil. DVLC came up trumps – we've found our missing social worker.'

'Jean Clark?'

'The very same.'

The DCI tapped the roof of his car. 'Good work, Sylvia. Let's pay her a visit first thing in the morning.'

'Yes, boss.'

The detectives were getting into their cars when DI Davis appeared on the path, a distressed Malcolm Frizzle trailing behind him and remonstrating loudly. When they came level with the officers' vehicles on the driveway, Davis placed his hand on Frizzle's chest and halted him. Two others were following on the path behind them, Sutherland and Coulter stopping shy of the commotion to observe.

'What's going on?' said Valentine, stepping out of his car.

'Your suspicions were accurate, sir,' said Davis. 'This is indeed a lying toe-rag. And, not only is he in possession of a list of previous that would make your eyes water, but it looks like he's breached an existing probation order.'

'How the hell did you work that out?' said Valentine.

'Phil ran his details and discovered that the name tallied with the statements from his teenage trespassers. It looks like Malky Frizzle here has some questions to answer.'

'Sounds like Phil's had a busy day all round.' The DCI pointed to the rear of his car. 'Put him in the back, we'll see what he has to say for himself when he gets down the station.'

'I didn't do anything,' said Frizzle.

'Shut up, Malky,' said Davis. 'You can forget about making the gym tonight, mate.'

As the officers pulled out, Sutherland and Coulter stood side by side watching as one of their own was driven away. Coulter seemed the most concerned, peering at his boss and turning down his mouth like a scolded child. Sutherland's expression was harder to decipher, his features being granite-firm and unmoving, only his eyes turned towards the road. He followed the police until they had left his property and then strode briskly in the opposite direction.

'Did you see that?' said Valentine.

'Not chuffed, I'd say.'

'I think you're right.'

16

Jim Prentice was putting on his coat as the squad returned to the station. The desk sergeant took a moment to pause, with one hand half way down the sleeve of his coat, as he eyed the returning officers. There was a moment of complete silence as Prentice stood, frozen, making the surreal shape of a drinking elephant with his coat sleeve. He broke the image by glancing at the clock, and then over to the slouching Malcolm Frizzle, being led briskly towards the front desk by DI Davis.

'You're having a laugh, aren't you?' said Prentice.

'Sorry, call it one for the road.'

'I've been here since seven a.m., that's a twelve-hour shift I've put in and I don't get any bloody overtime!'

Valentine made his way to the front of the desk and, grudgingly, joined in the discourse. 'Haven't you got anyone to replace you?'

'Willkie's not due in for another hour.'

'Well, who's manning the desk?'

'Wee Stevie Sims, but he's only ducking in – he's covering the cells.'

'This place is a joke,' said the DCI.

'I don't see anyone laughing, Bob. Can't be a very funny

joke.' He pulled his arm from his coat sleeve, causing it to turn inside out. The rest of the coat was bunched up, ruffling and sagging, and flung on the chair.

'Right, you ... name?' said Prentice gruffly.

'Thanks, Jim.'

'Aye right. I'll get my reward in heaven, I suppose.'

Davis put his hand on Frizzle's shoulder, forcing him to jerk away and begin another tirade. 'You just can't do this to me.'

'Oh, we can and we are,' said Valentine.

'I know my rights.'

'Good. You'll know we'll bring you a cup of tea in the morning then, which is a damn sight more that you did for that wee girl.'

The DCI's pointed remark passed Frizzle by. 'Morning! You're keeping me in all night?'

'It'll give you some time to sleep on what I said, Malky.'

Valentine nodded towards DI Davis and headed for the stairs. He was ready to head straight back out the door, go home and try to patch things up with Clare again, but there seemed to be little prospect of that looming.

At the top of the stairs the DCI waited for DI McCormack to catch him up. 'Look, Sylvia, it's been a long day for everyone, if you want to get off home no one will blame you.'

'No chance of that, boss. I'm supposed to be shadowing you, remember?'

'I think I can cut you some slack.'

'It's fine, really. All I'm going home to is a microwave lasagne and to catch up on the idiot box.'

Valentine felt a pang of sympathy for her, even with

all his own home problems, he always had Clare and the girls to go home to. The idea of returning to an empty flat after the day they'd just had was almost too painful to contemplate. They continued through to the incident room, where DS Donnelly was standing in front of the board, pinning pictures up.

'What's all this about Jean Clark turning up out of the blue?' said Valentine.

Donnelly turned away from the board and took a few steps towards the others. 'She sure has. DVLC found her; she's been living in a mobile home in Croy.'

'Croy. Not the caravan park on the beach?'

The DS leaned over the desk and retrieved a piece of notepaper. 'Looks like it, is that the wee park right down the front?'

'There's only one. Pretty exposed spot, wouldn't fancy it in the bad weather. Still, it's a quiet place, if that's what you're after.'

'I suppose we'll find out tomorrow,' said DI McCormack.

Valentine pulled a chair out from under a desk and wheeled it into the middle of the floor. Since he looked to be getting settled the others followed suit, forming a semicircle on the worn and faded carpet tiles.

'What about Frizzle,' said Donnelly. 'Is he coming in?'

'We have him downstairs.'

'In the cells?'

'Davis is turning the key now. We'll have a word with him tomorrow,' said the DCI. 'What can you tell us about this bunch of teenage trespassers you've just spoken to.'

Donnelly ran his thumb and forefinger down the length

of his tie, flicking it up as he reached the tip. 'Christ, where to start? I have to say, I thought they were winding me up at first, but I put their stories to the test and they seem completely genuine.'

'Come on then, let's hear what they had to say.'

'Do you remember when you said you'd met the bloke on the tractor who called the Sutherland estate Area 51?'

McCormack cut it, 'Oh yeah, the tinfoil-hat bloke.'

'Yeah, him. Well, I wondered what he was referring to, and now I think I know.'

Valentine leaned back in his chair, crossing his legs. 'This sounds interesting.'

'Well, two of the girls got to know Frizzle at a bus stop in Monkton where they were hanging around at night. It's a small village, there's not much to do and Frizzle was a flashy git with a motor, so they're going to be easy meat to the likes of him.'

'Go on.'

'He started taking the girls for drives, plying them with a bit of grass, a bit of booze; they lapped it up, obviously. But the main part of his shtick was bigging himself up, making himself out to be the big man.'

'I think I see where this is going,' said McCormack.

'Well, yes and no,' said Donnelly, moving his hands like a puppeteer. 'You see, his talk kind of had the opposite effect. It put the girls right off him and put their curiosity and their boredom onto something completely different.'

Valentine's interest started seeping into impatience. 'That's enough build-up, Phil. Get to the point, please.'

'I'm coming to it. Frizzle told the girls about some strange goings-on at his workplace: the Sutherland estate, which already had an air of notoriety in the village, as we know.'

'What did he tell them?'

'A lot of it was quite disjointed. I'm going to go over the notes tonight and write everything up. But, the girls said Frizzle told them about high-rollers being flown in for masked balls and all kinds of freaky events.'

'Back up there – high-rollers?'

'They didn't have names, but the rumours were of rich and powerful types. Elites, celebrities, politicians. The thing is, they were adamant about the masked balls turning into orgies and bizarre rituals. Frizzle spoke about goats being cut up and people running about the grounds naked.'

'Are they for real?'

'I told you, they're one hundred per cent certain. They said that's what took them to the estate in the first place. They couldn't see inside the property though, because all the windows are above the line of the floor to stop you seeing in. Frizzle told them that even the main hall and the dance hall have no windows and the staff can't go there. When these events are going on the staff have to pass drinks through a double hatch so they can't see in.'

'Well, that sort of stuff should be easy enough to check,' said McCormack.

'You think so? Sutherland wouldn't let us in his property today.'

Donnelly interrupted. 'Another thing the girls told me was, and I found this odd, that all the bedrooms are interconnected. What I mean is, there's doors from one to the other. Why on earth would you need all the rooms to be connected?'

133

'If you're changing partners like a game of musical chairs, it's a must, I would imagine,' said the DI.

'My thoughts entirely,' said Valentine. 'And if your property's laid out like a posh knocking shop, the last thing you're going to do is allow a nosy detective in for a look around, just in case it gives him any ideas about poking his nose into your activities.'

McCormack seemed to be deep in thought, but broke their thrall. 'Sir, can I put something out there?'

'Fire away.'

'I don't know if this is relevant, but if you remember the estate opens onto the airport.'

'Oh, I think that's very relevant, Sylvia. If you're a member of this perverted jet set I'd say privacy would be at a premium, wouldn't you?'

17

Every step down the staircase felt real, but he knew he was dreaming. Valentine reached out to the banister, it felt solid. The wall, too, as he ran his fingers along the cold plaster, was as firm as he recalled. Wasn't he asleep, then?

As he opened the living room door he found he wasn't alone. There was someone there; it felt like walking into the kitchen in the morning and discovering the door to the extension closed, but sensing his father was just out of view. It was impossible not to detect familiar souls because he recognised their presence immediately. He recognised this presence too.

For a moment, the girl stood silently, gripping Valentine with her cold eyes. And then she moved. Forward at first, as if she might embrace him. It was a welcoming gesture, but it wasn't directed at the detective. There was another girl too.

The tall, pale girl stood to one side. She seemed older than Abbie, but not old enough to be sufficiently wise. She was in some kind of trance, gazing into the distance behind her. Valentine turned away as Abbie spoke.

'This is Paige, she's lost too.'

'Lost?' He didn't understand.

Abbie nodded, touching Paige's arm. As the older girl turned Valentine saw she was carrying a child, her stomach swollen. She lifted Abbie's hand onto the bump and they both turned back to Valentine, pleading.

'I don't understand,' he said again.

The girls stayed silent, staring at him.

'What do you want from me?'

As he spoke, more figures joined the girls. From behind them, moving slowly from the shadows, appeared a group of children. Their number was small at first but it grew and grew, forcing confusion and panic to crash over Valentine.

'I don't understand. What do you want of me?'

The girls continued to stare as the room filled up with more and more small children. The detective closed his eyes, tried to shut it all out, but the children kept coming.

'Stop! Stop it now.' His voice was a roar.

'Bob ... Bob ...' Clare shook him awake in the bed.

'Christ almighty.' He was trembling, his T-shirt soaked in sweat.

Clare rose and leaned over her husband. 'Bob, what's going on?'

He sat up, easing the duvet back and perching on the edge of the bed. 'Nothing.' He got to his feet and staggered for the bathroom. 'I thought you weren't talking to me, anyway.'

'I don't have any choice when you're shouting in my ear.'

'Let me fix that right away,' he said as he reached for the door. 'I'm going for a shower.'

'Bob, are you OK?'

'I'm fine. Go back to sleep.'

136

'Bob ... Bob ...' She kept calling his name, but the sound of the shower drowned out her voice as Valentine laid his forehead on the cold, wet tiles.

The sound of cups clattering on a tin tray set Valentine's nerves jangling. He looked up from his desk and saw a uniform PC removing the coffee mugs that were piling up beside the photocopier. He wanted to call out, to demand the cups stay where they were and the PC stop annoying him, but he reined himself in. It was pointless taking his tensions out on the squad. He'd been in groups like that himself, where people were too frightened to move for fear of a blast coming from on high. It didn't work, unless your aim was to build resentment and a reputation as a dictator.

He got up and closed his door, to keep the noise to a minimum and his temper in check. As he stood there, resting his back on the flat of the door, he felt cold and alone. Not just alone in the room, but alone in the world. He tried to imagine how those girls had felt, facing the end. No one should ever have to feel like that; he knew those girls had been failed, not only by the police force, but by everyone.

All that life, all that living ahead of them, snuffed out. He'd heard people talk like this about those who had died young, but it wasn't enough. Those girls were the future, our future, everyone's future. The loss of such promise was a greater tragedy than he could begin to contemplate.

The image of Abbie McGarvie's pale corpse lying on the bitumen came back again. It kept reappearing to him, kept flashing up behind his eyes. It was like a reminder of the great wrong that had been done to her and an ominous prediction of much worse to come. What kind of people did this to their own? How had we come to value young life so poorly?

Valentine thought of his own daughters. He imagined Chloe or Fiona fleeing, running for their very life. The image came clearly; he could see the fear on their faces, the anguish and the terror of their hell to come. But, worst of all, was to be a father and know this was just someone's sport. Because he knew without doubt, somewhere off stage, someone was watching the scene unfolding and laughing in perverse enjoyment.

A rattling beyond the door broke his concentration. He snapped into a new state of consciousness and realised he was gripping the doorknob so hard the knuckles of his hand were white. When he stepped aside, wringing his fingers, the door's hinges started to screech.

DI McCormack peered cautiously down at the handle, then stepped inside, closed the door behind her. 'Hello, sir,' she said.

'What is it, Sylvia?' He slumped into his seat and scrunched up his brows, massaging them with his fingertips.

'Everything all right?'

'Yes,' he snapped.

'Are you sure?'

'Yes ... No ... Oh, I don't know.'

'That sounds more like it, going by the look on your face.'

McCormack approached the desk and pulled out the vacant chair. She was holding a blue folder but placed it on the desk, as if to indicate it could wait. To Valentine the room felt suddenly claustrophobic, like he was being cramped into the corner after previously ruling the entire territory.

'Is it that obvious?' he said.

'A little. But then I did notice you haven't been out of your office this morning, which some might interpret as you being antisocial, but I tend to assume you are in a contemplative mood.'

'Oh, really?'

'Yes. And we know what that means, don't we? So, come on, spill the beans.'

Valentine couldn't return McCormack's gaze; it felt like an accusation. He looked up to the ceiling where a dim bulb burned overhead. 'I had another little visit, you might say.'

'The girl again?'

'Yes. But she wasn't alone.' The DCI detailed the encounter with the older girl and the growing swarm of young children. When he was finished, McCormack was covering her mouth with the back of her hand, looking like she was trying hard to suppress her response.

'I've no idea what the message was this time,' said Valentine, 'but I have an idea.'

'There were children?' said McCormack.

'Lots of children.'

'And this new girl was pregnant, too. Just like Abbie.'

'Yes, I made that connection too.'

'Then I bet your thoughts followed mine.'

'In that case, Sylvia, I hope we're both wrong.'

Valentine watched the DI sitting solemnly and silently before him. The sound of cars beyond the window

139

dominated the room for a few moments and then McCormack leaned forward and retrieved the blue folder. As she shuffled through the papers she explained the print-outs as being Malcolm Frizzle's previous convictions.

'I don't need the whole list, only the current conviction for sex below the age of consent, and what was the other, grooming?'

'Grooming, sex with a minor, and indecent assault, sir. In addition to the probation order there's an existing harm order that relates to a historic case of grooming, too.'

'The bloody scum.' Valentine stood up. 'Right, let's put him through the grinder.'

The officers headed for the cells, ready to question Malcolm Frizzle about his involvement in Abbie McGarvie's death. At the top of the stairs Valentine asked McCormack for an update on the SOCOs' findings from the outbuilding on the Sutherland estate.

'Nothing we can tie in to the McGarvie girl, no hair or tissue, and the blood is animal, I'm afraid.'

'Animal?'

'Yes, porcine. That's pig's blood to you and me,' said the DI. 'I spoke to Davis about this and he says it's another one of those weird things that turns up at these occult rituals, like the salt, and the black wax that appears to be candle wax.'

'I suppose sequins from girls' dresses is just another trait, too?'

'No idea, sir. There's a ton of prints, and some match Frizzle's files. There's also a palm-print that's been taken from the ladder, and guess what? It matches Frizzle's file.'

They'd reached the interview rooms. Valentine nodded

to the guard on the table and ordered him to bring in Frizzle. 'Thing is, Sylvia, given he's an employee there, those prints are understandable.'

'And purely circumstantial.'

'Yes, that too.'

The officers entered the room and retrieved chairs from under the one table that was positioned with its end butting the wall. McCormack was looking through the notes in the blue folder when Frizzle was brought in, leaving Valentine to do the greeting.

'Well, well, well...' he said, 'how nice to see you again, Malky. Under such propitious circumstances, as well.' He smiled and crossed his arms as the interviewee was directed to his seat in front of them.

Frizzle, sitting with his shoulders hunched, didn't look comfortable before the officers. When McCormack slapped down the file Frizzle winced and sucked in his thin lips like he was stifling a scream.

'You don't look like you had a good night, Malky,' said the DCI.

'You've got no right. That was a liberty, keeping me in.'

'I think you'll find we've got every right,' said Valentine, leaning over the desk and focusing on Frizzle's eyes. 'Don't you know a young girl died, in perhaps the most unusual circumstances I've ever seen?'

'I don't know anything about that.'

'Are you sure?'

'Well, apart from what you've just told me.'

'Is that all now, Malky? That's not what I hear. Wouldn't you like to tell me how you knew Abbie McGarvie.'

He dropped lower in the chair and seemed shrunken

before the officers, nervously tapping dirty fingernails on the back of his knuckles. 'Never heard that name before.'

Valentine got up from his seat and walked over to McCormack's side of the desk, where he retrieved the folder. He read aloud Frizzle's explanation for his whereabouts on the night Abbie McGarvie died. 'You were on a six-mile run.'

'That's right, keeping fit's my thing.'

'I thought fiddling with teenage girls was your thing, Malky.' Valentine slapped down the file, making the suspect tense in his seat. 'At least, that's what your previous states.'

'Look, I haven't done a thing. I've been as good as gold since that last offence, you can ask anyone.'

'Oh, I have. And I got some interesting answers.'

'I don't know what you're on about. This is police harassment. You've lifted me because you can't find anybody else.'

Valentine tipped back his head, smirking. 'I don't think that's how it works in the real world, Malky.' He passed the file over to DI McCormack. 'Show him the statements we got from those young girls he's been grooming.'

'Yes, sir.' The DI opened the file and retrieved two closely typed pages of statements taken from the teenage girls who had been caught trespassing on the Sutherland estate.

As Frizzle took the pages he leaned over them and started reading the words by following the tip of his dirty fingernail. When he was finished, he pushed away the pages and slouched in his chair with his hands forced beneath his thighs.

'Nothing to say, then?' said Valentine.

'They're lying. You put them up to it.'

'You think so? Well, there's an easy way to check that out. Come on, get your coat and we'll drive out to the Sutherland estate and see if the bedrooms all interconnect. Just like you told the girls.'

Frizzle looked horrified. 'You can't do that.'

'Oh yes I can. I'm the police, Malky. And you'd do well not to forget that.'

'I won't.' The words came so meekly that they prompted a reaction in Valentine that he wasn't expecting.

'Good!' he roared. 'Now tell me what the bloody hell's been going on up there, and I want to know it all. The masks, the bed-hopping, the pig's blood and the little girls running naked in front of heavy goods vehicles.'

'I don't know.'

'Don't give me that.'

'I don't. I just see things. I should have kept my mouth shut.'

'Yes, you should have. But it's too late for that now because a girl's dead and you're the one I'm looking at over a police interview room table, Malcolm Frizzle.'

He gazed up from the desktop. 'It's nothing to do with me. Honestly, it isn't. I just spoke out of turn, that's all.'

'Then why are you so nervy?'

'Because you've got me in here, and you can put me away.'

'Malky, I most definitely can put you away. What you need to decide here and now is whether I put you away for breaching your probation order or for the death of that young girl. Now make your bloody mind up because my patience is running right out with you.'

18

Valentine stood outside the interview room and waited for DI McCormack to join him. He was tapping the edge of the skirting board with the toe of his shoe in a mark of his impatience when she appeared. For a moment the DI seemed confused, unsure of what she'd just witnessed, and then she blew up her cheeks and let out a deflated sigh.

'What was that all about?' she said.

'We've nothing to go on,' said Valentine.

'Not even the stepladder?'

'Not without something else, something more conclusive.'

The DI walked around Valentine and leaned on the wall beside him, gazing down the corridor towards the interview room they'd just left. She seemed to be looking for some answers to escape the room, catch them up and solve the dilemma for them.

'Just the rope ladder, print and all, is pretty lame,' she said, eventually.

'I know. But Malky doesn't know that. Did you see how nervous he was; the bastard knows something.'

'Are you thinking we might be able to goad him, if we get a little more?'

Valentine started to tap the front of his teeth with the knuckles of his fist; he had all the pieces in front of him but none of them were making a recognisable shape. 'Let him go, now.'

'What?' McCormack pushed herself off the wall to face the DCI.

'Let him go. He's no use to us.'

'But, boss, he's all we've got.'

'A flighty little score like that is more likely to find even more trouble for himself when we let him out. Get Phil to follow him around for a few days and make sure he's not too subtle about it. I want Frizzle to think he's more important than he is, and with any luck, he won't disappoint.'

Valentine pushed through the swing doors leading away from the interview room and headed back down the corridor. On the stairs he heard DI McCormack's footsteps following behind. As he turned she was already composing her next enquiry of him.

'So what do we do now, sir?' she said.

'Grab our coats.'

'Come again?'

'We're going out to see some people.'

'Who might that be?'

As they reached the top of the stairs, the DCI paused to hold open the door. 'We'll start with your social worker friend.'

'Jean Clark, out at the caravan park in Croy.'

'Let's hope we get a nice day for a run around Burns Country.'

'I hear there's still some beauty spots. Maybe we'll be lucky.'

'We need a change of luck. I hope you're right.'

Valentine pointed the DI towards DS Donnelly and watched his reaction – hands up to the sky – as he received the news he was going to be shadowing Malcolm Frizzle for the immediate future. The response made Valentine smile, until he remembered that Donnelly was still holding a grudge about missing out on promotion. He didn't want the DS to think he was being unfairly treated, but he also didn't want to let him know that he was carrying the best hope for the investigation. It was one of those moments when Valentine had to keep his intentions to himself – it was lonely in the end office, he concluded.

As he grabbed his jacket the detective caught sight of Malcolm Frizzle walking out the front door – he was moving briskly, almost jogging until he stopped flat. Another man, taller and more agile-looking, was heading in the opposite direction – towards the front door of the station – when he halted too.

Frizzle made eye contact with the man and the two of them seemed to exchange words. As quickly as the incident occurred it had ended, and Valentine found himself perching on his fingernails at the window's ledge. He watched Frizzle continue over the paving flags, towards the bus shelter beyond the King Street roundabout, and then further into the town, and out of view.

Valentine's thoughts were pooling as the door to his office opened and McCormack stood there with her coat over her arm and the long strap of a handbag dangling over the top.

'Well, Phil's less than chuffed, thinks he's being given the jobs nobody else wants,' she said. 'I tried to make it

146

clear that with Ally off we're running at considerably less than full steam, but I think he was just looking for a chance to moan, really.'

'He'll get over it.' Valentine was grinning to himself.

'What are you so happy with?'

'Guess who I just saw Malcolm Frizzle exchanging pleasantries with outside? Alex McGarvie.'

'Really?'

'Yes. I can't be sure there was a genuine connection, maybe they just bumped into each other, but it's something worth checking out.'

'It certainly is.'

'Get DI Davis to conduct the interview with Alex McGarvie, he should be downstairs now.'

'Will do, boss.'

'And make sure he probes him for any knowledge of our good friend Malky Frizzle.'

McCormack nodded and headed back out the door, bunching her bag and coat under her arm like she was unsure whether she was coming or going.

Wind worried at the latch of the gate outside the Croy caravan park where the officers had come to find Jean Clark. There had been a burst of heavy rain on the way out but it had stopped now, and still its effects sat in pools on the pitted road before them. As he went out to open the gate and flag McCormack through, the DCI listened to the loud gurgling in the drain beneath the cattle grid. There was more water issuing from a broken downpipe that was spilling into a barrel-sized water butt, the noise of which echoed round the park and picked up approving replies from its counterparts.

As he returned to the car Valentine massaged his wrist; he wasn't used to lifting heavy wooden barriers in the cold and wet, but there was still something about the setting that appealed to him. Perhaps it was being perched on the Firth of Clyde, or the dramatic granite cliffs, protruding like headstones into the swell. Either way, the view was much more appealing that the King Street roundabout and the contact with nature made him feel strangely renewed.

'It's wild out, sir,' said McCormack.

'It doesn't bother me, when it's just me and the elements.'

'There isn't much else out here.'

'I'm guessing that's why she picked it, for the peace and quiet.'

'You'd think the loneliness would drive her mad.'

'Maybe it has.'

McCormack pointed to a lot at the end of the track where a red camper van was positioned. 'That's the number plate we're after.'

The officers exited the car and headed to the door on the side of the camper. Valentine's knock made a strange tinny noise that was followed by movement inside and the screech of springs below the vehicle.

'Sounds like somebody's home,' said McCormack.

As the door opened there was a waft of smoke and the smell of wood burning. Jean Clark didn't look like she was expecting guests, poking her head round the door and smarting in the daylight.

'Yes, what is it?' She raised the flat of her hand to her forehead, shielding her eyes from the light.

Valentine spoke. 'Hello, we're looking for Jean Clark?'

'Well you've found her.' She widened the door and stepped forward, revealing her full height, which couldn't have been much more than five foot one. She was dressed in torn jeans and an oversized wool sweater. Her hair, long and naturally curly, was dyed the colour of red wine at its ends but had a thick greying wedge either side of a middle parting.

'We're police officers, Jean. Could we come in and talk to you?' said the DCI.

'What on earth for? My tax on the van's up to date.'

'We've come about another matter, I'm afraid.'

'Look, what's this about?' The woman glanced back into her camper van, seeming to be concerned with the smoke escaping out the door and the fire going out. 'I'm not interested in speaking to the police.'

DI McCormack stepped forward, placing her foot on the first rung of a wooden step. 'Jean, it's about Abbie McGarvie, I'm afraid there's been some bad news. I think it would be best if we came in and talked to you.'

After listening to the officers detail the young girl's death, Jean began to make tea on a pot-bellied stove. She stayed silent throughout, only cursing her stupidity when stubbing a toe on the corner of a wrought-iron stove leg.

'I'm sorry, I'm not used to having visitors,' said Jean. 'I came out here to get away from all that.'

'I heard about your run-in with your employers,' said Valentine.

'Huh ... the SS, you mean.'

149

'You call them that as well?'

'They were bastards, all of them. I suppose there's a few of them in your line too.'

'You're not wrong.'

'Oh, I know. I've met those bastards too.'

Valentine watched as Jean poured out the tea, placing the cups on a small tin tray that looked like a charity shop find. The whole place looked to have been put together with the help of charity – a conscious effort was being made to drop all obedience to the pretensions of normality.

'I've been working with one of the officers from the original investigation, and if it's any consolation to you, Jean, I think the police force failed Abbie in the most unforgivable way,' said Valentine.

'It doesn't console me in the slightest. I'm sorry if that sounds harsh, but you must have no idea what you're really dealing with, chief inspector.'

'That's why I'm here, to find out. I want to know everything you know. This is a clean slate from here, a new investigation.'

Jean put down her cup, grinning. 'Do you think that will make any difference? Do you really think the powers that be will allow you to take this investigation anywhere near the truth of the matter? If you do, you're living in a dream world.'

'And what is the truth of the matter?'

'I'm not sure you want to go down that particular rabbit hole. If you do, you'll not get out again, and you can't unsee anything shown to you there.' Jean put up a hand and waved towards the room. 'Look at how I'm living. Do you really want to know, or even begin to understand why

I cannot contemplate returning to the real world? I know what evil lurks there, Mr Valentine.'

'I got a court order to see the case files you submitted. I read all your allegations and I know you believed every word that Abbie McGarvie told you about her abusers. But there's a lot I don't get yet, that's why I've come to see you.'

'Those files don't tell you the half of it, they wouldn't let me put any of the real truth in there.' Jean put her head in her hands and groaned. For a moment she sat in that position, head in hands, and then she forced herself to sit up.

'Please, we're here to help. You can trust us,' said Valentine.

Jean's face seemed calmer than before, her eyes no longer searching for answers to anything. She was resigned to a fate that would not let her escape what she knew. 'I'll tell you what I know,' she said. 'But you need to understand that there is a reality within your reality which you cannot fully comprehend. It's a reality so evil, so corrupt and so inhuman, that if you were to fully comprehend it then your own fragile reality might begin to shatter.'

Valentine turned to McCormack and when she nodded her assent he returned back to Jean. 'We understand.'

'We're talking about the worst, the most heinous evil imaginable – the ritualistic torture, abuse and murder of children by an elite group of psychopaths.' Jean's composure altered as she spoke, tears welling in her eyes. 'These girls are trapped by Luciferians that use them to breed more children for sacrifice. But it's not just the children who are sacrificed, sometimes it's the breeders too. Women at various stages of the reproductive cycle are sacrificed and sometimes their aborted foetuses. All the rituals have different requirements but they all need flesh and blood. I told you it was sick, but this is the truth nobody will ever talk about.'

DI McCormack was still, perched on the edge of her chair, knees pressing tight to the table. She looked tense and uneasy, her gaze roving the room for something to alight on. 'But why? That's what I can't get my head around. Why kill children, for what possible reason?'

'They believe there's a veil between the worlds – our world and Lucifer's – and that all the evil we create here provides almighty energy on the other side of the veil. To do evil here is to honour their god.'

'But that just sounds absurd,' said McCormack.

'It doesn't matter what you believe,' said Jean, her eyes widening. 'It doesn't even matter that you think it sounds absurd, it's what they believe and that's what matters here. Don't you see that? They're the ones in control. It's their beliefs that are behind all of this, and it's their beliefs that killed Abbie.'

Valentine spoke, his voice calm and reflective. 'I don't quite get what you're saying, Jean. Who are these people? Who killed Abbie?'

Jean turned to face the detective, dabbing her eyes with her sleeve. 'The people who killed Abbie are the same ones who believe that the destruction of innocence in God's image provides them with the most power. You need to understand that the world isn't just this five-senses creation that you perceive. We're drenched in much more, much stronger forces. If that doesn't seem possible, within your limited perceptions, then you are already accepting the lie that's all around us.'

'Are you talking about a spiritual world?'

'Look around you. Look at the misery, the savagery. We're all so obsessed with paying the rent, with fears for our security, that we succumb to their control system. They won't let that change for a moment, not a second even, because there's a war on for our hearts and souls, and if that stops we might become aware of the chains and find some way to break them.'

'Who are you talking about?'

'Those that set the agenda. Have you looked at the news recently? What kind of mind do you think it takes to wage war on indefensible civilians? To have the blood of millions of innocents on your hands year after year, decade after decade, century after century? We are in the realm of perpetual bloodletting – their realm – our world is run by a death cult and there's no escaping it. The most wicked people are the ones right at the top – and they're the ones in a position to cover it all up.'

Jean wiped her sleeve over her eyes again and gave herself some time to settle down. She seemed convinced of what she was saying, but Valentine knew that little of the information pointed towards a cogent case.

'I need evidence,' he said.

'There's never any evidence, chief inspector, it's just accusations and claims. It's the words of children against the words of the people who hold all the power. I've never known them to leave bodies lying around, they're too clever for that, it's only finger pointing.'

'Is that why you've given up, Jean?'

'I realised some time ago that we've travelled too far from the Holy Spirit. We all have – man is more than flesh and blood; there is the soul too. We've lost our connection with our true selves, our inner beings. They all know that, and they know we are lost.'

'*Lost*?' The word startled him.

'There's only one true path, chief inspector.'

19

On the way back to the car Valentine tried to take the temperature of McCormack's mood. He wanted to know how she felt about what they had just witnessed with Jean Clark, but her look was inscrutable. He knew he could just ask her, and receive an honest response, but he was searching for something more, something deeper. He wanted to drill down to the layer of communication below words, where mute understanding was possible. Sometimes, in the interview room, an involuntary sigh or a sideways glance could be worth more than speech to the detective. As he took in the DI now, he searched her features carefully because he knew that his own understanding about the situation might be lurking there too.

'What?' said McCormack. 'Why are you looking at me like that?'

'Like what?'

'Like you just caught me doing sixty past a parked school bus.'

Valentine grinned. 'Clare calls it my "walk this way" face.'

'That's quite apt, yes, I'll give her that.'

'Sorry, I was just trying to pick your view on what we've just sat through.'

'You could have just asked.'

'A picture paints a thousand words: your face might have said something you left out.'

McCormack unlocked the car and walked round to the driver's side. Neither of them spoke until they were inside with the doors closed.

'She was speaking in tongues most of the time, which went right over my head, but she also seems completely genuine,' said McCormack. 'I mean, she's turned her whole life upside down as a result of her experience, that couldn't have been easy.'

'Facing up to reality wouldn't have been easy either. Perhaps running off to the coast was the easier option.'

'She went through a lot, which means she would have had a lot to bury if she'd stayed where she was. And she believes herself to be facing up to reality, I think she's brought her demons with her.'

'Well, she could be entirely sincere in her actions and still be completely nuts.'

'That would be logical. But didn't you tell me that slavishly following logic can create its own problems, something about reasoning oneself into jumping off a bridge.'

'Reason and logic have their limitations, especially when applied to human beings, who can have both or neither, sometimes at the same time.'

'Which is why I trust my gut. And I trust Jean Clark's testimony.'

Valentine turned back to gaze at the camper van. 'You've reached the same conclusion as me then. But this doesn't bring us any closer to finding a motive, a means or an opportunity.'

'So what now, sir?'

'Now we go to back to your old home town.'

'Glasgow?'

'The university, to be precise. I want to talk to this occult abuse expert, Dr Stephen Mason.'

'The guy that Davis mentioned in the briefing?'

'That's the one. Perhaps he can join a few more dots.'

McCormack turned the key in the ignition. 'Well, if he can do that, I'm guessing that the picture will emerge in the same stark relief as Jean Clark's.'

'I think you might be right, unfortunately.'

Valentine clipped in his seat belt and settled in with his elbow balancing on the edge of the window. The rain, stopped now, was still being blown about in the wind from the wet leaves on overhanging branches. As he glanced back to the bleak caravan park that Jean Clark had made her home the detective grimaced. Black clouds were sitting high in the sky, directly over the coastal heath; a threatening presence seemed to be lurking there. Even though he knew it was just his own mental projection, he couldn't shake the feeling that his thoughts had been disrupted. There was a new anger, one he had never known before, simmering inside him now.

As the car proceeded on the steep incline of the coast road, Abbie McGarvie's voice seemed to be whispering to Valentine on the rushing sea-grass breeze. He couldn't make out the words, or even be sure of hearing anything at all, but it didn't matter, because he knew exactly what she would say.

He turned front, and tried to steady his gaze on the wet blackness of the bitumen. There was no point wailing to

157

the heavens for answers. They would find them in good time, of that he had no doubts.

By Glasgow University the officers had tired themselves of McCormack's one CD: an early KT Tunstall collection, and bemoaned the downward slide in the quality of both local and national radio broadcasters. Valentine was stretching his legs out in the car park as the DI retrieved her coat from the back seat.

'Well, here's hoping,' said McCormack, fitting herself into her coat.

'Davis speaks highly of him.'

'Oh, does he now?'

'Am I supposed to take something from that remark?'

'I'd query Davis's verdict on the colour of orange juice.'

Valentine toyed with a response, perhaps a teasing dig at McCormack's disapproval of Farah trousers and moustaches, but resisted; cultivating division among the team was never a good idea.

The detectives presented themselves at a sliding window inside the front foyer, where a back-office clerk peered above her oversized glasses and directed them to a stairway and a room number where Dr Stephen Mason might be found. It was a narrow staircase, stuffy and cramped, with a covering of dust that was gathering in clumps in the corners of the steps. When they reached the top, and located the door, Valentine's thoughts were welling around recent events. He wondered what kind of a man ensconced himself in this world. He understood the drive to further knowledge, but it seemed a singularly unappealing choice of subject matter.

'Hello, can I help you?' Dr Mason was a short, stout man

with a dark beard and a lilting, almost singing accent that may have come from the Western Isles but was beyond the range of the detective's ear.

Valentine introduced himself and the DI. 'I hope we've caught you at a good time.'

'Yes, as I said on the phone, I'm happy to help in any way I can.'

Mason offered the officers coffee and directed them to a well-worn Chesterfield in the corner of his study. The room was cramped, overstuffed with books and manuscripts, and had a musty air that seemed to be mimicking the stairwell.

'You mentioned your research,' said Valentine. 'I'm interested in some of the consistencies you've noticed in the cases you've studied of occultic child abuse.'

Mason leaned back, lacing his fingers over his chest. He seemed, if not comfortable with the subject, at least confident of his knowledge. 'It's a very consistent pattern that emerges in these cases. All the research, both at an investigative level and the medical analyses, show broadbrush similarities. Would you like me to detail the pattern?'

'As you see it, yes. That would be useful.'

'It's exactly the same story, over and over again. The child's induction generally begins between the ages of three and six, sometimes later, but generally speaking there's psychological imperatives for getting them young.'

'Imperatives?'

'Trauma bonding, essentially, that's the predominant control mechanism they use on the children.'

'I've heard a little about this; it's about breaking the child's personality by exposing them to stressful events.'

'That's part of it, the trauma aspect if you like. The bonding is the truly insidious part – it relies upon the child becoming so removed from the reality they've known that they'll do anything to return to normality.'

'How do they inflict the trauma?'

'The children are tied up, caged, beaten. Sometimes they're burned with cigarettes, whipped on the soles of their feet. They can be made to sleep in dark basements or on bare floorboards or even outdoors. Some are forced to eat from dirty dog bowls and only allowed to defecate outside. The means vary, but they are all degraded and forced to confront fears. The degradation can be quite horrific by normal standards.' Mason stopped talking and glanced over to the officers. 'Are you sure you want me to go on?'

'We need to hear this. Tell us about the trauma aspect.'

'When the child is fully controlled, they see their life resting in their controller's hands. The child's whole life then becomes about one thing, and one thing alone: seeking their controller's approval. I've seen children who could, quite literally, be controlled by the snapping of fingers, or with a whistle. It's that powerful, these methods have been perfected over generations.'

Valentine looked at McCormack, who peered back disconsolately. 'We're uncovering more of this world than we might want to see, but we don't have the option to look away,' she said.

'I've spoken to police about this sort of thing in the past, and even the most experienced find the details shocking. I don't know if you're aware but an extremely high proportion of police officers who infiltrate these Luciferian paedophile sects become suicides.'

The DCI shook his head. 'I didn't know that, Dr Mason. Though we just spoke to a social worker who, I think it's fair to say, hasn't processed her exposure well. She claimed that the object of the abuse was to breed children for flesh and blood sacrifices. Can she be taken seriously?'

Dr Mason nodded slowly, two or three times in succession, and then stared ahead reflectively. 'There was a serial killer in America called Jeffrey Dahmer who used to drill holes in his victims' heads and pour in hydrochloric acid. He was trying to keep the victims alive so he could sodomise their bodies without their objections. Dahmer wanted to create zombies he could abuse freely – he was a psychopath and these people exist everywhere, chief inspector. This kind of abuse is very real. It's my speciality, and I'm not alone in making a career out of it. Doesn't that tell you something about the scale of the problem?'

'I'm forming that kind of picture, yes.'

'The victims of these dark occultists are exposed to the worst kind of depravity imaginable. I've personally interviewed victims who have detailed being raped nightly in group sex sessions with upwards of ten or twenty people. Some have been involved in ritual ceremonies where they have been raped by thirty people. The numbers vary, and the depravity varies, but one thing that doesn't change is the purpose: these girls are breeding children for child sacrifice.'

Valentine watched as Dr Mason retrieved his coffee cup from a side table. He balanced the cup on the flat of his thigh as he sat stiffly, watching the officers for a response. After a moment, when he seemed to have assessed the detectives, he spoke again. 'I know this must be hard to digest, but I've examined hundreds of these cases and the similarities are consistent. These girls are breeders, they're kept constantly pregnant, some from as early as the age of eleven.'

'You're right, I am struggling to digest this,' said Valentine.

'My research has brought me into contact with many of these people. I heard about a high priest at one coven who it was estimated had impregnated more than a hundred such child breeders. None of the children that were produced were ever registered with the authorities, so no one ever knew about any of them. It's those children, more than a hundred of them, that were sacrificed.'

'That word, sacrificed, it doesn't do justice to what we're talking about. This is murder, cold-blooded and brutal murder on a massive scale. I can't get along with the word sacrifice, I'm afraid.'

'If you think about it rationally,' Dr Mason said, 'it shouldn't be so hard to comprehend. Human sacrifice has been a part of our story since the time of Sumeria, where priests sacrificed children to purify society. The ancient Egyptians, the Aztecs, the pagans were all at it. In your parlance, we've got form for it.'

'That didn't exactly go on in our own back yard though.'

'Really? In the cradle of Western civilisation, Greece, there was no shortage of sacrifice. If you remember, Aeschylus began *The Oresteia* with Agamemnon sacrificing his daughter to the gods. If you look hard enough at our Pagan and Judeo-Christian heritage, you'll find blood purification and sacrifice isn't as uncommon as you might think.'

162

'But surely we've progressed since then.'

'Progressed, really? Do you think because we can summon the knowledge of the world on a smartphone that we've actually progressed? I doubt it. My experience tells me that technology is really masking our true decay as a people. We haven't progressed at all. You must know as well as anyone, chief inspector, that evil is a living, breathing entity that has always been with us and always will be.'

Valentine cleared his throat, coughing into his fist. It seemed like a stalling motion, a diversion from what had just been said that allowed him to file away the academic's statement and move beyond it. 'Why? That's the part I struggle with,' he said.

'You might call it a sect, or a cult belief. They call it their religion. They believe themselves to be the sons and daughters, not of God, but of Lucifer.'

'They openly worship evil?'

'They don't see it that way. They believe God imprisoned Adam and Eve in the Garden of Eden and Lucifer, through the Forbidden Fruit, gave them intellect which set them free. This intellect, they believe, will give them the power to conquer nature and ascend to the power of gods themselves. I'm paraphrasing their beliefs, but essentially they're on a power trip.'

'You seem to be confirming my worst fears, Dr Mason.'

'You have entered the battlefield of the soul, detective. I advise you put on all the armour you can get.'

2016

He says he's my Keeper and that we have a blood covenant, but I don't know what that is.

'It's the power to rule you, Abbie,' he says.

'Why me?'

'Because you're mine and I know all the works of darkness.'

He tells me that the Master himself is his keeper and there is no power he cannot summon. I don't know what he means. I really don't know what any of this is about. It scares me so I try to think of Mummy and wish I was far away, at home or in another place completely, but he sees me looking away and I think he knows.

'No one can save you.'

'No one?'

'Not even your mother. You know I can summon her death in an instant. I want you to think about that, Abbie.'

'I don't want to.'

'Do it. Now, see your mother's death. See her blood running. I can do that, I can kill her.'

'No, don't say that.'

'But I can kill her, in any number of ways.'

'No.'

'See your mother, imagine her engulfed in flames. Her hair evaporating in the heat, her flesh peeling and liquefying before your very eyes. See her, Abbie, I can do that at any time I want. I can kill your mother.'

'No, I won't do it.'

'You will, Abbie. Maybe not right now but later tonight when you're alone, in bed, curled up with only the tick, tick, tick of the clock for company. Then you'll remember, then you'll see that image of your mother with her throat cut ... or burning on a stake.'

'I won't.'

'Oh, but you will.' He laughs as he leaves and I watch to see where he goes, just in case he really has any special powers like he says. I don't want to believe him because I want to believe that Mummy can still come and save me. I want to know she can stop everything, at any moment, but I don't want to test my Keeper.

What if he's right?

What if he really can do these things?

I start to think about Mummy and my little brother, and I wonder what might happen to them. I want them to be safe and I don't want to be the one that brings any harm to them.

The next day my Keeper brings me some pictures of children.

One photo is of a little girl, she has no clothes on and she's covered in thick, dark blood from her head to her toes. Her hair is so long but I can't tell what colour it is because it's been flattened to her head by all the thick, wet blood.

'Do you see her eyes?'

Her eyes are wide, staring out like they are too big for her head. I think they're going to pop. 'Why are they like that?'

'She has taken the Master inside her, her soul is more powerful because she has pleased the darkest power of them all.'

My Keeper takes me by the hand and we walk to the grove. The altar is the same one I saw inside the school when they took away Paige's baby. I see the same people in gowns and they have the silver cups that they filled with Paige's baby's blood. I know it's the same people and I know some of their names and their faces, but there are others too and I don't know who they are.

My Keeper tells me to strip, it's very cold and I get goose pimples and then I start to shiver, but all I can think of is Mummy and my little brother and how I don't ever want to do anything that might make them unhappy.

There's chanting now, and people reading from books, but I don't hear the words. I feel like my heart is going to burst out and I can hardly make my breath go in. When I do manage to take a breath it makes me tremble all over. I want to run and scream and tell someone but I know that there's nobody that can save me.

He lifts me onto the altar and tells me what to say.

'My mind, body and soul belongs to the Master,' I repeat the words.

I still think that someone will come to save me, that Mummy will appear and chase them all away, but it doesn't happen. No one is here except for me and the people in gowns, chanting and reading and carrying the cups.

There's hands all over me.

Some are holding me down.

I don't move because I'm frozen still.

Someone holds my head and forces me to face the sky but I can still move my eyes.

My hands are taken and pinned back and that's when I hear the baby crying. It's so loud that I know it must be very near.

The crying and the chanting and the reading make me feel sick, and I'm so dizzy that everything is spinning.

When the pain starts I try to scream but a hand is pressed over my mouth. It's like a hot knife stabbing inside me and I struggle to get away, but it's no good, it only makes the pain worse.

I know it's my Keeper because I see his face beneath the dark hood and I hear him say we have a blood covenant again. I try to kick and I try to struggle but the hands stop me and then something warm starts to pour all over my bare skin.

I try to see what is happening but I can't move my head.

The warm liquid spreads and spills over me and I can feel it pooling underneath me on the altar. I struggle and struggle but I can't see what's pouring over me, and then I realise the baby has stopped crying, and I feel like something has thumped into my heart.

I stop struggling and I let them hold me down.

The hands soon go away and they all leave me be.

The chanting and the reading stop too.

Only the sound of my Keeper is left, grunting and heaving over me.

I let my hand fall and feel beneath me to the altar and that's when I turn to see my fingers are dripping with the baby's warm blood.

20

Valentine stood in the hallway, peering into the small gap in the doorway to his daughter's bedroom and watching her sleeping. The first hint of a pale morning light was filtering through the blinds, suffusing the room with its dim glow. Chloe was sound asleep, her head resting peacefully on the pillow. There couldn't have been a bad thought basking beneath that beautiful face, he thought. The mere idea that there was the possibility of such a thing struck the detective as abhorrent.

As he gazed, he saw her eyes moving beneath their tightly closed lids. Was she dreaming? What would those dreams be? He remembered when she was born; he was just out of uniform and working the craziest hours imaginable. Whenever he managed to get to the hospital Chloe was sleeping, a small bundle wrapped in white that seemed so precious he didn't want to touch it. He would peer over the cradle and watch her every breath being taken. That she was there at all seemed like a miracle, something akin to magic; she was beyond precious to him. He was part of her, part of her being, part of her creation. He remembered thinking: could she be real?

As he kept his gaze on his daughter, through the narrow

gap in her bedroom door, Valentine felt his thoughts shift-
ing. All those aspects of his pride that Chloe had kindled,
all those feelings of joy and warmth and love were being
challenged now. He wondered what he had brought her
to. Was he still able to keep her safe? Had he ever had that
ability?

The world had always been a mystery to Valentine, an
endless confrontation of good and bad, but he had never
doubted the predominance of the good. Now he wondered, though. He no longer felt that assurance he once
had that the world was profoundly good. He felt helpless
and pessimistic for a world he now cared so very little for,
but worse, worried how his children would fare in it.

Valentine closed the door to his daughter's bedroom and
started for the stairs. In the kitchen he heard his father's
radio playing and knocked on the door of the extension.
The old man answered promptly, presenting himself,
shaved and showered, a familiar dark-crimson tie poking
above his V-neck jumper.

'Oh, good morning,' he said. 'You're up early, aren't
you?'

'I had a difficult night. I don't seem to have the same
need for sleep these days. I'm up with the larks whether I
like it or not.'

His father laughed. 'You're getting on, that's what it is.'

'Probably. Coffee?'

'Yes. Let me switch this wireless off and I'll be right
with you.'

The cupboard revealed the instant coffee jar to be empty,
which forced Valentine to tackle the cafetière, another of
Clare's designer purchases. She wasn't a coffee snob, but

some of her friends who came round might be, so of course it wouldn't do to have anything less to hand. He found himself checking the price on the label automatically and following on with the usual frowns and head-shaking.

'Something wrong?' said his dad, appearing from the extension and taking a seat.

'I don't know about you, but I feel a bit undeserving of Clare's £12 coffee.'

'She likes to keep up with the Joneses, that's just her way.'

'I know. I'm just being my usual, unreasonable self, I suppose.'

'I wouldn't go that far.'

Valentine delivered the cafetière and cups to the table and sat down. There was a lull in the conversation and then he spoke again. 'Maybe you're right, Dad. Maybe it's not me that's in the wrong, maybe it's the rest of the world.'

'Oh, you're feeling like that today, are you?'

'I never get this way. I try to just keep on keeping on. I'm not one for tackling the big questions.'

'Sometimes you can't help it. I just heard on the radio that the term "Ladies and Gentleman" is being outlawed on train station announcements now. What are we if we're not ladies and gentlemen any more? When I look at the world these days, I quite often want to just ask to get off. You're not alone, son; it's not unnatural.'

'I know, everything natural's being turned into the unnatural. We're in a crazy state of affairs. I wonder what's behind it. Have you ever felt that there's something bigger than us, bigger than all of us, in play here?'

His father had his coffee cup half way to his mouth but lowered it. 'What do you mean?'

'I don't know. I think it might just be this case; it's wearing me down. I can't help but think there's something wicked out there, something evil, gleefully so, revelling in the diabolical nature of itself.'

'The job never usually gets to you, son. I've only ever seen you thrive on the challenges. I don't quite understand how you can do that, but you always do.'

'Not this time. This is different; something's changed in me, Dad. I can't quite put my finger on it, but it's like I've stared into the abyss and everything else is tinged as a result. I can't explain it, but I have this sense of something older than time, bigger than life and death, or good and evil. Does that make any sense?'

His father reached out and gripped Valentine's arm. 'I know exactly what you mean, son. You'd have to be a fool in this day and age not to think that.'

DCI Valentine was seated in front of the chief superintendent as she forced the blade into the skin of the Cox's Orange Pippin and started to peel a long, looping spiral. She managed to talk over the sideshow, dangling the peel ever upwards above the desk, until finally dropping the lank helix over the waste-paper basket. The CS seemed pleased with her effort, smiling to herself as she returned the knife to the top drawer of her desk, slamming it shut.

'So, Bob, what you're telling me is that you have nothing concrete, except this scrote Frizzle's breach of an existing probation order?'

Valentine drew his gaze back from the waste-paper basket. 'I have a lot going on. The squad's following several lines of inquiry.'

'Oh, please, spare me the media speak – it's me you're talking to.' She bit into the apple and reclined in her chair, admiring the extent of her bite, which had cut to the core.

'We now know there's absolutely no question that Abbie McGarvie was being abused. The post-mortem confirmed that, and the pregnancy might tie her to a perpetrator in due course.'

'If you can find one.'

'Well, we're working on that.'

CS Martin swung her chair round to the front and started peering over the open blue folder that held the case notes. 'The post-mortem rules out the father, Alex McGarvie, who was the original accused in the first case.'

'Yes, I saw that had come in this morning. Wrighty said the girl had multiple abusers, and the experts I've spoken to since tend to confirm this pattern in such cases.'

'Oh yes, the social worker and the academic.' She seemed to have tired of the apple now, placing it on top of the folder and reclining in her chair once again. 'None of that builds a case, Bob. You realise how shaky all of this looks, especially since nothing's come out of those searches on the Sutherland estate.'

'I wouldn't say nothing came of the searches, we have the indicators of some unusual activity in the outbuilding ...'

The CS cut in. 'A good brief could explain that away as typical farm activity.'

'It's not a farm. Sutherland doesn't keep pigs, so why are

buckets of pigs' blood covering the floor of his outbuilding? I'm not saying that on its own this proves a thing, but coupled with the teenage trespassers' testimony and the rope ladder with Malky Frizzle's prints all over it, I have my suspicions that something very odd has gone on there.'

'Be careful where you tread, Bob. Remember this victim has already caught our attention once before. If you uncover the same themes emerging again then you had better make sure that you have a watertight case, do you understand me?'

'I do. Which is why I've left it as late as possible to put the difficult questions to Alex McGarvie and David Sutherland.'

CS Martin tapped her finger on the blue folder. 'The file says McGarvie's been interviewed by DI Davis.'

'Yes, he came in last night. I haven't caught up with Davis yet, but I'm assuming there were no explosive revelations, otherwise he'd have been on the blower.'

'And Sutherland?'

'He has a formal invitation to attend the station.'

'Tread carefully, like I say. I can't imagine a man of his means will give us much room for manoeuvre.'

Valentine got to his feet. 'Agreed. I'll get Davis to drop in the notes on the Alex McGarvie interview.'

'How are you finding Davis – fitting into the team okay?'

'Overall, yes. I suppose it helps that he's single, and happy to work all the hours God sends.'

'Single? No, he's married with three kids.'

'*What*? He told me he lived alone, with no ties.'

'No. Ian Davis is a family man like yourself, Bob. Are you sure you haven't mixed him up with someone else?'

Valentine felt his face prickling. 'I'm quite sure I haven't got the wrong end of the stick. Perhaps I'll need to have a word with him about this now.'

'Fair enough.' The CS picked up the blue folder, closed it over and flung it at Valentine. 'Back to the mill with you!'

21

Valentine closed his hand around the file and held it beneath his arm. It was still there, held in place by simmering anger, when he slammed the door to his own office. A band was tightening around his chest now, as he slapped the blue folder down on his desk and paced towards the window. He remembered the doctor's advice he'd once received about his breathing in such situations. It was a variant on the counting to ten method: taking a breath and stretching it out was a way of slowing the escalation in heart rate. It had seemed to work, at first, but he was too aware of the trick now for it to do anything other than constrict his breathing. He looked out to the sky, grey as ever, the uniformity separated only by a white smear of low-hanging cloud. The darkening horizon indicated there would be rain soon, and likely blown on the back of gales that were already worrying the streets below.

The DCI fell into distraction, watching a bin lorry inching along the road. A bin man – it still seemed safe to assign gender to such a lowly position – was following the lorry with a green wheelie-bin dragging behind him. If Valentine had his way DI Davis would soon be eyeing refuse-worker status as something to aspire to. The thought pulled him out of his anger. Davis was a family man – he had three children, according to the chief super – why would he deny the fact so brazenly?

Valentine gazed out at the approaching gloom that covered the street vista. The rooftops were already incurring a waxy sheen from the dimming sun and any hope of a turnaround seemed forlorn. The bin lorry had reached the end of the road now, was turning and heading out of sight. He imagined another row of green wheelie-bins lined up, perhaps miles on end, that needed to be collected. Was the work really so different from his own? It was just cleaning up the mess of others. He made a low grunting laugh and headed back to the incident room with his head somewhat cooler, if not any clearer.

The door's hinges sung out as the DCI entered the incident room. There was little recognition of Valentine's arrival – the squad was too deeply involved in the case by this stage – and few acknowledged him. He stood in the doorway's blunt shade, swaying a little as he scanned the room for Davis, who he quickly picked out. The DI was standing before the board, scratching the edge of his nose. Davis grew dimly aware that he was being observed and, turning towards his watcher, lost several shades of colour from his face.

For a few moments Valentine returned Davis's solemn stare, until he was interrupted by the sound of quick footsteps in the corridor behind him. 'Ah, you're back,' said DI McCormack.

'I was in with Dino.'

'Oh dear. Still, at least you're all in one piece.'

Valentine turned away from McCormack to see if

Davis was still watching him. The DI's stare sunk away, and he returned to the board. 'Was there something you wanted?'

'Yes, I've just burned an audio copy of the Alex McGarvie interview Davis conducted last night, I thought we could go through it.'

Valentine made a show of checking his watch, tapping the face. 'Give me ten minutes. I need to have a word with Ian – alone.'

'Sounds ominous. Is there something I should know?'

'Ask me again in ten minutes.' He peered round the DI and started to move towards the other end of the room.

'Okay. I'll see you in ten, then,' said McCormack, hoisting up her shoulders into a perplexed shrug.

At the door to the glassed-off little corner office, Valentine grabbed the handle and took a step inside. He still had Davis's attention and didn't need to do any more than motion him with a nod to follow. When the DI entered behind him, Valentine turned back to the door and closed the Venetian blinds – more for the effect of unnerving Davis than the maintenance of privacy. If he was going to deliver a carpeting, it could serve as a public warning to anyone else considering lying openly to the boss.

'Take a seat, Ian,' he said.

Davis pulled out the one chair facing the desk and sat down. 'Is everything all right?'

'Well that depends.'

'On what?'

'On what you tell me, Ian.'

Valentine was leaning on the window ledge, his arms folded, as he faced the back of DI Davis's head.

Davis turned. 'What's this about?'

'Guess where I was this morning, Ian?'

'You were going over the Abbie McGarvie case with the chief super, weren't you?'

'That's right. I can't say I'm normally a fan of such gatherings but on the odd occasion I do uncover some very interesting snippets.'

'I'm sorry, you've lost me.'

Valentine unfolded his arms and started to twiddle his wedding ring. 'Is there something, anything, that you think you might have misled me about, Ian?'

'No. Nothing.'

'Are you very sure about that?' He smacked his hands together. 'Because much as I take a dim view of my officers lying to me, I take an even dimmer view of them trying to cover it up.'

Davis's brows settled into a frown, his whole face seemed to tighten and firm. 'I'm quite sure. Perhaps you should just come out with whatever grievance you imagine that you have with me.'

'You told me that you were single, Ian. I distinctly recall the exact conversation, and a second conversation with DI McCormack who said you had confirmed the same to her. But, today I discover from CS Martin that you are in actual fact a married father of three.'

His features relaxed. 'I am single.'

'What?'

'I am a single man. And I live alone, I don't think I've lied to you at all.'

'So, are you saying that CS Martin has lied to me?'

Davis touched his forehead and sighed. 'I suppose you

could say, on paper, that I am married. But I've left all that behind.'

'You've separated from your wife?'

'No. Not in any official sense. We just don't communicate.'

Valentine pushed himself from the ledge and took a step towards the seated Davis. 'And the children?'

'Yes, those too.'

'You don't have access?'

'No.'

'Have you sought access?'

'No.'

'Ian, you have three children and a wife. You're telling me that you have effectively abandoned your family.'

DI Davis remained still, his face stonily unresponsive. He didn't reply.

Valentine tried to disinter an emotion from the DI's expression but couldn't find any. His own emotions were telling him to grab the detective by the shoulders and shake him until he saw sense, but it didn't seem to be an option. It was beyond his remit to inquire about the circumstances of Davis's decision, no matter how much it offended his moral sensibilities. He found his focus primarily on the children. Surely that's what we were all living for, surely that's what the job was about: securing a safe place for them to grow up in? As his thoughts spiralled Valentine realised he was attributing his own attitude to Davis, and he couldn't hope to get anywhere near the truth that way.

'Okay, Ian, let's leave it at that,' said Valentine. 'But I don't want to see you misrepresenting the truth to me again. And I mean even *your* version of the truth. I demand loyalty from my squad, and that means I won't tolerate fudging of facts, playing semantics, or bloody well being *economic with the actualité*. Is that understood?'

'Yes, perfectly.'

There was a knock at the door. Valentine nodded to Davis, who let in DI McCormack on his way out. She made a show of closing the door behind her.

'Jesus, what's up with Ian?' said McCormack.

'Good question.'

'He walked out that door like he was carrying the weight of the world on his shoulders.'

'Maybe he is. Certainly it's no weight I'd like to carry.'

'Perhaps you should tell me more.' She walked in front of the DCI and waited for a response, her head lilting towards her shoulder. The expression suggested she felt left out on new and useful information and she wasn't going to let it slide.

'Sit down, Sylvia.' Valentine walked around the desk and dragged out his chair, the castors squealing. 'I know you've expressed concern about Davis in the past.'

'I think *concern* is a bit strong. His work's been sound, better than that even, it's just on an interpersonal level I've found him a little … *odd*.'

'We're on the same page, at least we were until I spoke to Dino about him earlier.' Valentine detailed his talk with the chief super and the response from DI Davis. He kept the exchange factual, trying not to let his anger at the betrayal influence McCormack's own reaction.

'Wow. I'm a bit lost for words,' said the DI. 'Why would he do that?'

'I've no idea. It seems such an unnatural course of

180

action to me. Even if the situation had become difficult, as obviously these things can be, it still seems a very extreme course to take.'

'Did he seem in any way regretful, or doubting of his actions?'

Valentine shook his head. 'Quite the opposite, he was very matter of fact, like this was the only sane thing to do.'

'I'd have to disagree. In fact, I'd have to say I think entirely cutting off your wife, and more importantly, your three kids, sounds utterly insane. I don't know what kind of cognitive gymnastics you'd have to put yourself through to make that sound rational, or even doable.'

'I've had rows with Clare, as you know, but even if we went our separate ways I wouldn't be able to simply flick a switch and pretend the past never happened. And as for my kids, the very idea that I might never see them again would finish me. I live for those girls, and I'd die before giving them up.'

McCormack's mouth tightened into a thin line; she seemed to be holding back uneasy doubts. 'I like your rationale a lot more than Ian's.'

'I think it suffices to say that our colleague is a very troubled man. Even more troubled than perhaps we already suspected.

22

Valentine opened the blinds in the corner office and tried to avoid making direct eye contact with DI Davis, or anyone else in the broader interview room. The level of activity he'd observed earlier seemed to be diminishing, though he conceded it might be the failing light outside that dimmed his perceptions. Either way, the thoughts now swirling inside his mind were certainly gloomier. He closed his eyes tightly and started to rub at his eyelids with the knuckles of his closed fists. For a moment the darkness was a welcome distraction – a leavening escape from the outside horrors that were building everywhere. But when he returned to the realities of the room, to the clicking of the mouse DI McCormack was working at the PC, he knew real darkness was inescapable. It was all around him, a tightening grip that wouldn't leave until he had a young girl's killer in custody.

'Right, I've set up the Alex McGarvie interview audio on your PC,' said McCormack, turning to face the DCI and making a mocking, open-mouthed expression. 'God, have you looked in a mirror, Bob?'

'No. What is it?' He was weary, washed out. But no worse than usual.

'The last time I saw black circles like that under some-one's eyes was at Edinburgh Zoo's panda enclosure.'

'The compliments are flying today. You'll get a better response with sugar than vinegar.'

'Not where I come from. Have you seen the diabetes figures for Glasgow?' She made a reassuring smile. 'Look, we can go through the interview later if you want to take a break.'

'I'm fine.'

'I'm only thinking about, y'know.' She patted her chest, on the left side, to indicate the location of the heart.

'The stabbing was some time ago. I'm fine, really. I'd probably do even better if people stopped fussing over me.'

'It's just, well, I know you haven't been sleeping and we're both taking on new roles so that can't make your lot any easier.'

Valentine wondered why she hadn't mentioned the wor-ries over his wife's debts too, she seemed to be piling his troubles so high. 'I appreciate the concern, but really, I'm fine. I'll try to get a few more early nights. Now, let's get on with listening to this interview.'

'I should get Davis in too. Unless that's going to be too uncomfortable after your little chat.'

'We need him in here to highlight the non-verbal cues,' said Valentine. 'The other stuff needs to go on the back burner anyway – where, hopefully, it won't boil over.'

'Okay, boss.' McCormack headed for the door, leaning out into the interview room and calling DI Davis. For a brief moment he had the pleased look of a dog who's just heard its name, and then he put down his pen and eased out from his desk. When he reached the end office the DI stood outside for a moment, pensively easing onto his toes, before taking two loping strides that put him directly in front of the DCI.

'We're going to go over the Alex McGarvie interview,' said Valentine.

'Of course. I was hoping to talk to you about that.'

'Oh, yes ...'

'The acknowledgement you thought you'd witnessed, between McGarvie and Frizzle on the station steps, well, you were on the money, sir.'

'They know each other?'

'It would be impossible not to, given that McGarvie hired Frizzle to work at Finlayson.'

Valentine looked at McCormack, who was already positioned to return his gaze. 'Play the audio, let's hear what McGarvie has to say for himself.'

The first few minutes of the recording were an odd preamble by McGarvie, detailing how he had already been declared innocent by the previous investigation. His plaintive tone dipped into self-pity when he started to talk about Abbie's death, but he seemed to go on the attack when Malcolm Frizzle was brought into the conversation.

Finlayson's heritage as a Christian school was heavily relied upon as justification for hiring Frizzle, a man with a record of abusing young girls. Everyone deserved forgiveness, claimed McGarvie, and there had been no indication that Frizzle had misplaced the trust shown in him by the school.

'Don't you think it's odd that Frizzle suddenly left his

post at Finlayson when the allegations of abuse arose?' said Davis.

A moment's hesitation followed before McGarvie replied. 'No. I think that given Mr Frizzle's previous experience with the authorities it's actually a perfectly rational explanation for his abrupt departure.'

'Maybe Frizzle actually had something to hide.'

'I'm not accountable for his thought processes, detective.'

'But then Malcolm Frizzle turned up at the Sutherland estate,' said Davis.

'This is news to me.'

'Are you familiar with the estate, Mr McGarvie?'

'No.'

'But you must be aware it's located adjacent to the road where Abbie met her unfortunate end.'

'If you say so.'

'It's not about my saying so, Mr McGarvie, it's a matter of fact. Your daughter died on the road next to the place where Mr Frizzle worked.'

McGarvie didn't reply. The empty silence stretched out until DI Davis posed another question. 'Don't you think that it's more than a bit odd, that Frizzle went from working for you to working within spitting distance of where your daughter died?'

'I'm not on trial here, detective,' snapped McGarvie, his voice rising. 'You're not my judge.'

'Answer the question, please.'

'No. I don't think it's odd really. Ayrshire's a pretty small place when you get down to it.'

Valentine reached out to the keyboard and paused the recording.

'He seems to be getting a bit agitated.'

'He was,' said Davis. 'I put it down to bourgeois pomposity at first, but as the interview wore on I got the distinct impression that he resented my presence utterly.'

'What do you mean?'

'What I mean is, and this is something I saw on the first case, it's like these people think they're bulletproof.'

'Bulletproof?'

'Yeah, like someone's got their back. Like we're just the police and ultimately their fate will be decided by much higher forces.'

'We'll see about that … Press play again.'

The audio recording continued where it had left off, with DI Davis posing another question for McGarvie.

'Your daughter was the victim of some very serious and sustained sexual abuse, Mr McGarvie. The post-mortem report revealed this in detail.'

'Abbie was a very wilful child.'

'Excuse me?' said Davis. 'I'm not quite sure what you're saying.'

'She mixed in many circles that I'm sure I was unaware of. I couldn't be with my teenage daughter twenty-four seven. No one would expect that, surely.'

'But sexual abuse, Mr McGarvie. You don't seem surprised?'

'We live in dark days, the nature of man is fallen – how can I be surprised?'

'It would seem to reverse the outcome of the previous investigation, don't you agree?'

'I don't see how, unless you can prove the two are related.'

186

'One thing that you won't be able to dismiss so easily is the fact that the post-mortem revealed your daughter to be pregnant.'

'*Pregnant?*'

'Now you seem troubled.'

'Of course I am.'

'Why?'

'She was my daughter.'

'And she was pregnant. Which is incontrovertible proof that someone was abusing her.'

'Are you suggesting I'm more concerned by that fact than by the fact that my daughter was suffering?'

'If you don't mind, I'll ask the questions, Mr McGarvie.'

'This is absurd.' Chair legs started scraping on the floor.

'Sit down, please.'

'I've had enough of this ...'

'Mr McGarvie, I'm not finished.'

'Well, I am.'

'Mr McGarvie, do you have now, or have you ever had, any connection to a man called David Sutherland?'

'Who?' His voice dropped, became calmer. 'I've never heard that name before.'

'Are you sure?'

'Yes, quite sure.'

The audio stretched into a silent gap, which ended with DI Davis shutting down the recording and turning to face the others. He sat back, in front of the PC, and tucked his hands behind his neck. For a few seconds no one spoke, and then Davis made a half-smile and said, 'Well, what do you think?'

McCormack was first to respond. 'Cagey, to say the

least. Especially for a man who has just lost a daughter. I'd expect some more compassion.'

'I cut him some slack for having been through this whole process once already,' said Davis, 'but not a great deal.'

'I'm not cutting him any,' said Valentine. 'The only time he showed any level of concern, in the entire interview, was when you mentioned that the post-mortem revealed Abbie was pregnant.'

'And why might that be?' said Davis.

'I'd suggest it's because if we can match a suspect to Abbie's child then they will have nowhere to hide.'

'I think you're onto something, boss,' said Davis. He sprang forward, easing out of his chair and heading towards the door. 'Wait a minute, I've got something to show you.'

As Davis left, returning to his desk, Valentine turned to McCormack. 'What's all this about?'

'I've no idea. Davis kind of does his own thing.'

The DI came back into the office, closing the door behind him. He held a blue folder in front of him, which he placed on the desk. The officers huddled round a photocopied map that Davis pointed to with the eraser end of a pencil.

'Look at this,' he said. 'I've been checking a few old Ordnance Survey maps for the Sutherland estate and I think this is very interesting.'

'What are we looking at here?' said Valentine.

'This is the main house and the grounds.'

'Very interesting, Ian, but what's the relevance to the case?'

'Look at this. It's the outbuilding where we found the salt and blood.'

'The cow shed,' said McCormack.

'What we thought was a cow shed, which may actually have been used as such for some time, but it's not.'

'Well, what is it then?'

'This map points out something interesting, look here ...' He pointed with the pencil again, to a little black cross marked on the map.

'A cross?'

'That indicates that it was once a chapel.'

'And?'

Davis's enthusiasm started to show as colour in his cheeks. 'Ancient chapels like this are important because they were originally built on ley lines. These geographical markers are regarded as significant energy points by occultists, they're seen as having a power that's desirable for their rituals.'

'And there's a ley line running right through Sutherland's estate?'

'Yes, there is. And given what we found there, we're certainly not the only ones aware of the significance of this.'

'No, we definitely are not.'

23

Kevin Rickards was sitting in the furthest corner of the
booth, bending a Tennent's beer mat between his fingers
and the tabletop as Valentine walked in. O'Briens bar
was the last pub in the town with privacy booths, an
appeasement to nostalgia on the part of the owners. When
Valentine appeared in the doorway, Rickards nodded
towards him and indicated the chair in front. Rickards
had a calm air, and the look of a man who had learned
to pick his fights well. His broad shoulders, perched on
a broader chest, indicated a tensed stock of energy that
probably hadn't been given vent in some time. He looked
formidable, or as Valentine was fond of saying in a strong
Ayrshire lilt, not to be messed with.

'Thanks for coming,' said the DCI.

Rickards reclined in his chair, tipping his head so far
back that it rested on the booth's dark-panelled wall. He
eyed the detective cautiously. 'Save the gratitude till you've
got something to thank me for.'

'Can I begin the process with a pint?'

He nodded. 'Make mine a heavy.'

As Valentine went to the bar he tried to recall if he'd ever
met Rickards outside of the Tulliallan training academy.

He couldn't be sure, but he did remember many protracted poker matches in smoky dorms, with bawdy cracks and unedited, manly mockery. They were different times; today's recruits were far more testosterone deprived. The detective was still holding the thought when he returned to the booth with their pints.

'Makes a nice change to see a cop who isn't a green tea drinker,' said Valentine.

'Ex-cop. But I get the point, there's still a few of us around.'

Valentine immediately sensed a thawing. 'You'll remember Jim Prentice.'

'Jim "the Gas". How could I forget him?'

'He showed me a picture in the paper today of one of our blokes, a uniform officer, in six-inch-high red heels. Apparently it was some PR stunt for the media unit. I honestly can't tell whether they're working for us or against us at this point.'

'We must have the scrotes terrified – we're not going to get too many collars chasing them in stilettos.'

Valentine laughed. 'It does seem like the powers that be are more concerned with promoting a PC image than improving the clear-up rates.'

'They've precisely no interest in clear-up rates, unless it fits their political agenda. They'll tip millions into chasing people who post wrong-think on Facebook about one thousand four hundred girls being raped in Rotherham, but don't dare suggest we actually go after bloody criminals. It's too screwed up for words. I'm glad to be out of it to be honest.'

Valentine sipped his pint as Rickards continued towards

a rant about the state of the police force and the betrayal of the communities it served. Law and order had already been sacrificed, it seemed, in favour of an anarcho-tyranny operated by a corrupted elite and a fawning political class who wanted nothing less than a complete collapse of the West. Which he predicted was coming, sooner than anyone dared to think.

'Is that why you left, Kev?' said Valentine.

'Who told you I had any choice?'

'What do you mean?'

'You know how this works, Bob. In any line of policing that you show an aptitude for, you get promoted, except child trafficking – there you get your funding cut, suspended and ultimately booted out the door. And that's if you play nice.'

'What's going on there, I mean, why do that?'

'Because the tentacles reach all the way up, all the way to the very top of the pyramid.'

Valentine put down his pint and watched the white foam descending inside the glass. Rickards was touching on just the points that had been occupying his own thoughts. 'What did you find that upset them?'

'Kids being pimped out, that would be the main thing. That's hard enough to handle; you never get your mind around the six-year-old child prostitutes with scabies and cysts, or HIV.' A strong undercurrent of resentment ran through his voice. 'I've seen girls that age, on the game, passed around and addicted to class A drugs, servicing suited-up clients right under the noses of social services, who just do not want to know; that's the killer – nobody wants to know.'

192

'I've heard similar stories recently, from one of their own.'

Rickards' hard grey eyes wandered. 'Jean Clark told me you'd called.'

'I found her revelations difficult to take.'

'You would, at first.'

'Are you saying there's worse to come?'

'Jean comes from the care system, which is a paedophiles' playground, but that's just the tip of the iceberg. It's who the care system's covering for that you need to really worry about.' A moment's trepidation stalled his speech. 'I need your assurance, Bob, that anything I tell you will remain confidential. Between you and me alone.'

Rickards' statement killed the conversation. The sound of late-afternoon traffic fell around them. A weak, amber-tinted sunlight forced its way through the window of the booth as they sat facing each other through the silence.

Valentine tapped a blunt finger on the table. 'I think you know that having my confidence goes without saying, Kev.'

'We're just two old-school coppers having a chat,' he said, his voice brusque now. 'But certain things have happened to me over the years that made me question everything.'

'I understand. I've found myself questioning the very nature of reality since I took on this Abbie McGarvie case. I don't know where I'd be without your old wingman.'

'Ian Davis is a good bloke, he's had it tough too.'

'Do you mean his marriage?'

Rickards stayed silent for a moment, then picked up his drink. He seemed to be choosing his response carefully.

'I can't speak for anyone else but I can speak for what happened to me when I got too close to Abbie McGarvie's abusers.'

'Go on.'

'My boss brought me in, told me to close the door, and warned me that if I didn't drop the case it was over for me.'

'What was over?'

'Everything. He threatened to break me, suspension, gross misconduct, sacking. None of it worked. I called in HR and do you know what happened? He repeated the lot, right in front of the HR chief. Nothing scared him, except me upsetting paedophiles in suits. Eventually, I went to corruption command and that's where it got interesting, that's when the real threats started.'

'Real threats?'

'I'd worked under my boss for more than seventeen years, he'd been to my daughter's wedding, and do you know what that bastard did? He threatened to have my little granddaughter taken into care. She was three years old, Bob, could you imagine how I took that? I've seen first hand what happens to kids in care. I wasn't going to let that happen.'

Valentine watched the emotion welling in Rickards' eyes and gave him a moment to compose himself. When enough time had passed for the DCI to continue his questioning he spoke again. 'These paedophiles in suits, who are they?'

'They're a death cult.' He swallowed, and tried to divert his gaze. 'Psychopaths, a coven of evil. Does it matter what we call them? We all know who they are, they're the ones we see every day, everywhere.'

'Everywhere?'

'They rule us, Bob. They're the ones with all the power and they recruit from their own. Think about this, why wouldn't they? They want psychopaths whose lineage has deleted the very parts of the mind that you and I hold most precious, most dear – the love we have for our children, and by extension our wider family, our fellow man.'

'Wait a minute, you're saying they prey on their own?'

'They kill the empathy in their young by trauma control, that's what the abuse is, a means of passing power and the means of maintaining it from one generation to another.'

'But the other children,' Valentine said, understanding, 'the ones on the street and in the care system, that just makes them fodder for these rituals.'

'Blood sacrifices are all part of it, the goal is to induct their own into their occult ways. They want our future rulers to have no empathy so that they can act cruelly without thought or conscience. At the top of our society, you need to understand, is a complete inversion of everything. Good is bad, ugly is beauty, pain is pleasure. Their genetics have deleted empathy for their fellow man, and their occult religion has created a system of cruelty that's utterly unimaginable to the likes of you and me.'

Valentine ran his fingers through his hair, grabbing a bunch at the base of his skull. His temples had started to throb, a low persistent pulsing echoing in his eardrums. He slumped back in his chair and tried to take in the information that Rickards had just dispensed, but it didn't seem to register. His world was listing, all previously held beliefs swaying with the dark depths of a murky new reality.

'I see this strikes a chord,' said Rickards. 'Of course it does, you're a thinking man, Bob, but most don't want to believe. Most want to hide, to turn on the telly and take that false reality as the gospel. Even when they know, when they sense that something isn't right, that our world is awash with injustice and evil, they'd sooner believe all the propaganda that we've never had it so good. There's whole industries dedicated to dumbing us down and numbing our senses to all of this. It takes a strong soul to rebel against the programming.'

'I don't have a choice any more. I have a young girl lying on a mortuary slab to consider.'

'Think about this, then: just look at the world today and you know what I'm saying makes sense. Think about how nothing seems right, how everything is upside down, how the people we're supposed to look up to simply repulse us. Look at our world, the endless wars, the state of the country we call home, the depravity and degeneracy that's being pushed twenty-four seven. Trust your gut, Bob; you know it's telling you that something's up. Think about the way those in charge whitewash everything that contradicts their hellish narrative and ask yourself who is really behind the curtain?'

'I know what you're saying makes sense, it's just that I really don't *want* to believe it.'

'You need to break free of the programming. There's no sense in this world, everything is mad but you have to become mad too to understand the problems we're facing. If you don't face up to that, there's no hope.' Rickards reached forward and put his hands, palms down, on the table. 'Everyone is against us; you have to come to terms with that fact right now. These people don't even want us to have the possibility to think like this, and they will do anything they can to stop it. What was it Orwell said? The image of the future is a boot stamping on a human face for ever. No, it's much worse than that. Think about what you've already seen and imagine how it might become. They hate us, they hate our children, and they would sacrifice all of us for what they believe. This is nothing less than the very definition of evil.'

24

At the pier-end sat a small lighthouse. It was disused, had long since stopped emitting any light. Over the years the exterior of the lighthouse had been left to deteriorate, the white paint, now flaking, replaced with sprayed-on graffiti slogans. At its extreme point, facing the sea and adjacent to the harbour mouth of the port of Ayr, the lighthouse still held a prominent position, but it was a sad and fallen symbol. It was possible to buy postcards of the landmark, pictured in better days, but nobody in the town regarded the lighthouse as anything other than a remnant of lost glory. A sorry, sad image of decline and deracination.

Valentine looked up at the thick swirls of concentric glass plates, where the magnified rays of light were once sent over the waves and rocks. He thought about the passage of time, about childhood. He'd once helped his daughter make a lighthouse for a school project, a pathetic cardboard and plasticine effort with a tiny torch bulb on top. He'd wired the rough model up to a battery and he smiled now to remember the look on Fiona's face when she first saw the bulb light up. He felt another glow in his heart forming, just to recall the precious memory.

'You're miles away,' said Rickards. 'What's on your mind?'

Valentine smirked. 'Would you believe, my own daughter?'

'Yes, I would. It's only natural. I went through the very same justification process. It's alien to you to believe that there are people out there who will do these things. You think of your own family and how you feel about your daughters and you can't imagine anyone ever feeling any differently towards their own offspring.'

'That's what I've been going through. I'm struggling to understand that it's possible to behave this way.'

'Like I said, it's natural. I felt like that. But, you have to get over it, Bob, you have to give yourself the freedom to believe that your outlook is only one way of seeing the world and there are others who don't share that outlook. Their view is different, very different.'

They set off round the base of the lighthouse, seeking the sheltered lee, out of the wind. The sound of the sea lapping at the rocks below was interspersed with the occasional spray of a larger breaker and, once in a while, a wave would breach the pier completely and splash loudly on the surface flags, calling attention to the sullen climate.

'Run through how this works, then,' said Valentine.

'It's a complex process, until you understand it, and then it becomes incredibly simplistic,' Rickards told him. 'The ultimate objective is to create something known as a control file.'

'A control file?'

'A blackmail file might be more apt. Think of a politician, in any country of the world, that a criminal cabal might seek to control, how would they go about achieving that end?'

'You've already answered your question: blackmail, bribery.'

'There's those. But what if they don't go for that, or what if it ceases to have the desired effect? That's when a little more creativity is required. In the past, you might have noticed a disproportionate number of our politicians were homosexuals; that wasn't a coincidence, it was because they were easy to blackmail back then. Today there's a disproportionate number of paedophiles in power, because it's the ultimate taboo, and the ultimate blackmailable transgression.'

'You're saying paedophiles are actually sought out and manoeuvred into positions of power because they are easy to blackmail?'

'You must have heard of the dossier that was handed to the Tory government in 1984, and subsequently went missing.'

'I saw it made the news cycle for quite some time.'

'When a political paedophile scandal makes the news it tends to follow a familiar pattern of disinformation. The accusers are discredited and the perpetrators are excused, unless there's a deceased paedophile who can be thrown under the bus to let the living ones carry on regardless.'

'Sounds familiar.'

'It's an international issue, Bob. I've seen cases involving a former prime minister, a president of the United States and even a member of the royal family. I've also seen evidence that there's been more than a hundred cases similar to the one in that dossier that have been scattered to the four winds.'

'What have you seen in those files?'

'You might call it a modus operandi. They locate a mark, an ambitious politician or diplomat they want to influence, and they target them. Sometimes it's a simple honey trap, other times it's a more complicated brownstoning set-up.'

'Brownstoning?'

'Yeah,' Rickards said, 'it's a term they use. It involves exposing the mark to a hedonistic party lifestyle, getting them in bed with young women, or boys if that's their thing, and gradually introducing younger and younger girls or boys until you have the mark in bed with a child. The event is filmed and there you have your control file. It's documented evidence of wrongdoing used for the purpose of blackmail.'

'And this is common practice?'

'Bob, this is common practice at the milder end of the scale. Some of the information I've been exposed to would make this look like a mild misdemeanour. We're talking about a Luciferian cabal who take their beliefs and practices very seriously. This is why we're dealing with such high levels of secrecy; this is the reason for the shutdown of my investigation. Any one of these cases has the potential to fell giants. To be frank with you, Bob, and you must know this by now, there's no way they're going to let you get close to the truth.'

'Going on what you've told me so far, I'm surprised I haven't been pressured already.'

'You haven't got close enough yet. There's only so much you can uncover in a week, but once you get close to that third rail, you'll feel the heat. These occultists operate at the pinnacle of our society; it's a criminal gang and how they draw in those outside the gang is through blackmail. Those that are brought in will display all the enthusiasms of the convert, because it's in their interest to.

'And those that don't?'

'They're not given a choice. They either join and progress, or they die.'

'Killed?' Valentine asked, already knowing the answer.

'Of course. This is standard operating practice in all criminal fraternities, you must know that.'

'I've heard of drug gangs demanding new recruits carry out a murder to show their loyalty.'

'The very same thing, though in this instance the recruits won't be asked to tattoo a teardrop beneath their eye. This criminal gang guards its privacy fiercely; if they were exposed then the fallout would be felt in every area of our society.'

A low gust, a westerly, blew around the base of the lighthouse, bringing a sandy effluvium whipping at Valentine's shoes. For a moment he watched the miniature sandstorm swirling, until it finally settled in a sloping, granular buttress against the pier wall. A rusty Pepsi can was dislodged from its hiding place in the next burst of wind and started to rattle along the concrete path. The sound, sharp and jangling, was an outrage the detective couldn't handle and he pointed back towards the town.

'Let's get out of here,' he said.

'It's getting a bit blowy, I suppose.'

The two men walked silently until the end of the pier, ducking the threat of the hovering gulls overhead. The darkening sky was descending, like a low smoke haze that threatened to engulf them completely. There would be a greyer, dimmer sequence of events to unfold in the heavens, thought Valentine, as he withdrew his gaze to the ground beneath him.

'Tell me more,' he said, bitterly.

'What would you like to know?'

'It's hard to say that I'd like to know any of this really.'

'I understand that, too.'

'But given I still have unfettered access to this investigation, I need to be able to continue digging while I can.'

'Has any of what I've told you rang any bells – with your investigation, I mean?'

Valentine peered closely. 'Some.'

'I can get into specifics, make assessments, if you like. But, I'm not sure how you'd feel about exposing the actual case files of an ongoing investigation to a cop who's been kicked off the force.'

'This case has stretched my moral fibre to just about snapping point. I wouldn't rule anything out, if I don't get the result I want.'

Rickards hesitated. 'Well, the offer stands. But in the meantime, why don't you just hit me with anything that's causing you particular concern.'

Valentine gathered his thoughts before he spoke. 'There is something. It bothered me right from the start and I haven't been able to come up with any explanation for it whatsoever. Even listening to you today, there's nothing in what you've said that hints at reasoning for it.'

'Go on.'

'When we found the girl, Abbie, she was naked, all except for a pair of tennis shoes on her feet. The shoes had clearly been put on in the normal fashion – they were laced up, not rushed into, or just thrown on.'

'This struck you as strange, right?'

'Yes. Like, she'd been given a get-out, or a chance to escape by her attacker, but why would anyone do that? There's no reason I can comprehend.'

Rickards turned to the sky, and his face became conscience-stricken. There seemed to be a thought process forming in him, a conflicted set of emotions vying for prominence with each other. 'This could be worse than I thought.'

'What do you mean?' said Valentine.

'Some cases, like the ones I detailed to you earlier, are simple enough to untangle because they have a clear motive. But, this is different.'

'In what way?'

'Bob, I don't think you're dealing with a straightforward case of occult abuse, or a control file blackmailing. I think you're dealing with something bigger than that, if my understanding of what you've just told me is correct.'

'And this is based on the tennis shoes?'

'What you've described is a situation I've never actually come across before, but it's something I've heard of. You won't be aware of a phenomenon known as the most dangerous game.'

'No. I'm not.'

'This is an undertaking of a particular section of the elite that like to push the boundaries of their occult rituals. It's strictly for those at the very pinnacle of the cabal, those that take an extremely perverse interest in the suffering of their victims.'

'I'm struggling to see how what you've already told me could be any worse, but go on.'

204

And so Rickards went on. 'There's an adrenal gland in the neck that secretes a particular chemical called adrenochrome. This gland produces the substance under one set of circumstances alone: fear. When a human being is exposed to the very limit of terror, the gland's production is believed to be a delicacy by the highest order of the elite.'

'This shouldn't shock me, after learning of the child sacrifices and the blood drinking and flesh eating, but somehow it does.'

'Could it be because you see where I'm going with this?'

'I want to know what this dangerous game is, Kev.'

'Not any game, the most dangerous. In its most simple term, for people like you and me, it's hunting. We're talking about putting another human being through the same torment and torture that animals are subjected to for perverted pleasure.'

'Hunting people?'

'That doesn't do it justice. Remember, Abbie McGarvie was a child. If you found her the way you did, I'd wager she'd been stripped, abused, and was limbering up to be sacrificed in the most terrifying of occult practices.'

'Who would do this?'

'Someone with a taste for adrenochrome. Someone who, in my experience, would most definitely know exactly what they were doing. Those people aren't bottom feeders; they're the ones holding up the keystone. I've never heard of a victim of the most dangerous game to have been found. If you have a victim's corpse to prove this practice took place then you can be guaranteed that something went very, very wrong.'

205

2017

I don't like to talk to anyone at school now. The playground's noisy, all the silly kids running around and screaming. They don't have a single thing to scream about. I want to scream back at them, tell them to stop, but they're only little kids. You can't harm little kids, I could never do that. Not ever.

I turn up the cuffs of my sleeves and try to put them over my ears, but the noise doesn't go away.

I can still hear everything. All the running, all the screaming.

I turn to face the wall and try to look away, but it doesn't help. I'm still here. I'm still me, there's nothing in the world that can change that and it makes me sad inside.

There's all kinds of pictures moving through my head. I scrunch up my eyes and try not to see them, but they're still there. They never go away.

I see blood and babies. I hear the baby wailing. There's a man in a hood. He has little white hairs poking out of his chin, and his teeth are cracked and dirty. I push him away but I'm not strong enough.

'No ... No.'

I know I'm mumbling. I talk to myself all the time now and sometimes people hear me.

My teachers say: 'Stop that at once!'

But sometimes I can't. Sometimes I can't stop anything. I wonder, is there a thing in the whole world I can control? One thing. Just one thing that I can keep from hurting me.

The baby cries again. It's bleeding, blood spilling everywhere.

'Stop. Please stop. Please go away.'

I want to cry now, but I know that I can't. If I cried then somebody would see me do it and that would only make things worse. I can't make things worse, I can't bring any more attention to me. I've been warned so many times that one day I'll be made to really suffer. I have to get my mind right, that's what they tell me.

'Stop all this behaviour, or you will suffer for it.'

'Stop it, at once.'

'Do you hear me, Abbie? Do you want to bring more pain upon your soul?'

The noise is starting to get louder and louder now.

Kids running, everywhere.

I'm starting to tremble, that sometimes happens, and my breath gets heavy. I try to catch my breath but I can't, I just can't.

Nothing helps.

I gasp and gasp.

But nothing helps.

Everything goes dizzy, and I feel hot then cold.

The air's all stuffy, even though it's chilly out.

My knees wobble and then give way. The ground beneath me seems to slip and I'm falling, falling into a deep hole.

I see clouds above, white fluffy clouds, on a pale blue sky.

There's a loud thud, like a bang, behind me.

My head hurts. I scream out.

It hurts.

Really hurts.

But I can't see anything.

'Abbie ... Abbie ...'

There's two dark, round eyes over me. I try to focus on them and soon I see a full face.

'She's fine,' says Mrs Thompson, and she eases away.

'Where am I?'

'You're in my office.'

I look around and see my feet tucked up on the couch. There's a blanket over my legs and a cold, damp facecloth on my head.

'What happened?'

'You had a dizzy spell. Don't worry, it's nothing to concern yourself with.'

She says she has to go; she's got a class to teach. She steps away and puts her hands on her hips, she's staring at me and shaking her head as she speaks again. 'What in the world are we going to do with you, Abbie McGarvie?'

I bite into my lip. I don't know what to say.

'Oh, don't make that face. Your father would be ashamed of you.'

'Why?' I want to take the word back but it's too late, it just popped out.

'Because you are causing nothing but trouble for every-one.' Her voice has a kind of angry echo and I look away. I think she's seen my face, and knows what I'm thinking, and that's when she starts to smack the pillows, pumping all the dust into the air.

I start to cough and then she stops. There's more words from her but I don't listen. I'm starting to get sleepy and it's like I cannot even fight it as my eyelids start to close.

I dream about the babies. I always dream about them now.

The only dreams I have are about babies or men in dark hoods with spiky little hairs on their chins. Sometimes the babies bleed and sometimes they cry and once a baby cried out for the Master.

I dream and dream, and even though I want to wake up I can't. It's like I'm trapped here in my dreams, just like in real life. There's no way out, no escape at all. And all I can do is suffer.

'Abbie.' It's a man's voice. 'Wake up.'

His hands are on me, under the blanket. When I look up I pull my legs away from his sweaty hands, but he only smiles.

'Hello.'

'Who are you?'

'I'm Malcolm. You can call me Malky.'

I've seen him before, around the school. He wears one of those mustard-coloured coats like the janitors, but I don't think he is one of them. He does something else.

'What do you want?' I pull up the blanket to my chin.

'Just to be friends.'

I shake my head.

'I was friends with Paige.'

'What?' I haven't seen Paige since she was taken away. I miss her, I really do. It makes me sad to think of Paige and where she might be now, or what might have happened to her.

'She used to come to my parties.'

'What parties?'

'Didn't Paige tell you? I'm the party man.'

I don't know what he's talking about and he makes me feel queasy. His hand slowly starts to work its way under the blanket again and soon I feel it touching my leg, rubbing and stroking.

'No,' I say.

'It's all right, don't be nervous.'

I let him touch me. His hand goes all the way up my skirt and into my knickers. I want to pull away, but he watches me to make sure I don't. He has the eyes that tell me, one false move and I'll hit you. I don't want to be hurt, so I stay still as he puts his fingers where he wants to.

'There, see,' he says. 'I told you it was all right.'

I hear people outside the door, walking in the corridor. He hears them too and looks over his shoulder. The noise troubles him and he yanks his hand from under the blanket. When he stands up his mouth is twitching, curling down at the corners and showing his bottom row of teeth. He looks angry, but only for a few seconds, and then he turns back to me and starts to smile again.

'So, do you want to come to my party?' he says.

I shrug. 'Will Paige be there?'

He laughs out. 'No, I'm afraid Paige's partying days are over.'

I don't know what he means. 'Where is the party?'

'I don't know if I should tell you.' He moves his head from side to side, then starts to rub at the back of his neck.

I know he's only teasing me now. 'It's in a big old house, out in the country. Do you like the sound of that?'

I shrug. 'I don't know.'

'Do you like planes? This house is next to an airport, you'll be close enough to see them landing.'

'I'm not interested in planes.'

'Well, what about dressing up? Do you like fancy dresses?'

'Tell me about Paige.'

He looks away and I can see him rolling his eyes. 'She's gone, right.'

'Where's she gone?' I really want to know where she is.

He starts to get angry with me again. 'Stop asking about that stupid bloody girl!'

'Okay.'

'You won't see her again, ever.' He pulls away the blanket and starts to wave his hand. 'Up, c'mon. Get up. You're coming with me.'

'Where?'

'I told you, didn't I?'

'To the party?'

'That's right, yes. To the party in the country.'

'But it's a school day.'

'Don't worry about that.'

'What about my dad?'

He tips back his head and laughs. 'Your dad's the one that sent me, Abbie. Now, come on, hurry up, we've got plans for you tonight.'

25

Clare was sitting with her feet up on the couch, flicking channels on the television. A slight curl played on her lip as her husband walked in the room, but there was little else by way of an acknowledgement. She settled on a show he'd never heard of, it seemed to be a re-run from daytime television. A stout woman in pink was lambasting another so-called celebrity about her choice of words; it was all false, the same propagating of political correctness he'd heard a million times before.

Valentine looked at his wife – she was smiling now, laying down the remote control, content with her choice of entertainment. He looked towards the window and stared into the garden at the thick shrubbery and the carefully pruned trees. He wondered what it was all about. Was he only working to maintain an illusion? Playing happy families just to signal virtue to the outside world? An outside world he was growing to hold in contempt. He retreated back through the door and closed it behind him.

In the kitchen he listened out for movement in his father's room but couldn't hear anything. Knocking on the door, he opened up and peered round the jamb.

'Hello, Dad.' The old man was seated at a green-baize

card table, the deck in front of him laid out in a game of patience.

'Oh, hello.'

'Mind if I join you? Clare's watching *Loose Women*.'

'That sounds like your kind of thing.'

'It's a very deceptive title.'

Valentine walked in and joined his father at the card table.

'You fancy a game of whist? Or maybe rummy?'

'Whatever. You choose.'

His father started collecting up the deck. 'How was your day?'

'I wouldn't know where to begin answering that.'

'No improvement?'

He shook his head: how should he reply? Their last conversation, that morning, had been a comfort to him – they always were – but he didn't like leaning on the old man. At his time of life he should have been beyond sorting out his son's troubles. But there was nobody else he could turn to. 'I caught a member of my team lying to me.'

'Oh, dear. Did they have a good reason?'

'I'm not sure.'

'Should I ask what the lie was about? Feel free to ignore me if I'm being a nosy old bugger.'

'It's fine.' Valentine picked up the cards his father had dealt him. 'He's new to the team, and he'd told me he was a single man, but I found out he actually has a wife and three children that he's estranged from.'

'That's a tricky one. In my time, there was some shame attached to that sort of thing, but I wouldn't have said that was much of a factor today.'

213

'There's a void where shame used to be in our lives.'

'It's a concept that's been cut from our vocabulary.' His father's eyes wandered from the cards in his hand. He appeared to be deep in reverie for a moment, a subtle warmth emanating from him.

'It made me think. A lot of things have been making me do that lately.'

'The passage of time does that. Don't despair; things have a habit of changing, good principles can quickly come around again.'

'But, I can hardly process how everything I see around me has changed already. In my brief lifetime. Goodness knows how you must feel.'

'Hey, you cheeky swine!' He smiled. 'I'm not that old.'

'Sorry, I didn't mean ...'

'I'm only teasing you. When I think about the world today, son ...' The faraway look returned. 'I do wonder what my own father, and his generation, would make of the mess we've created.'

'What do you think he'd say?'

'That we'd grown weak, that we'd confused comfort with civilisation, something like that. He didn't mince his words; he might have only been a miner but he was still a learned man. He had a good eye for the truth of the matter; I think the war taught him what people were capable of. There's one thing I can say for sure that he would have said: the war he fought wasn't for this mess. He always said he thought his generation had been sold a pup, but he'd be bloody horrified watching the news today, even the sanitised version of events we get.' The card game seemed to have been abandoned. 'My late father would be sickened by the stories you bring home time and again.'

Valentine doubted that sharing his work had been a good idea. 'Don't worry yourself, Dad.'

'Oh I don't.' His response was sharp. 'I'll be shuffling off soon enough, and without a care for this bloody place. It's those girls of yours I worry about. They're the ones my heart goes out to.'

Clare appeared at the doorway holding the cordless phone. She balanced her free hand on her jutting hip, her elbow poking out to the side as she spoke. 'You have a call. It's your lady friend.'

'What lady friend?'

'The one you spent the night with on Arran.' She had the tact to cover the mouthpiece as she spoke.

'Clare, please.' He rose from the card table and took the phone but kept a hard stare on his wife. 'Hello ...'

'Oh, hello, boss.' DI McCormack's voice was emotionless and he immediately recognised the formal police tone, it was always used to mask seriousness.

'What is it?'

'I'm afraid it's not good news.'

'Go on.'

'Phil's on his way to the hospital. There's been an incident.'

'What happened?'

'He was trailing Malcolm Frizzle, sir. Something appears to have gone wrong, there was an altercation in a car park behind some hotels on the beachfront.'

'A fight between Phil and Malky?'

'It's all a bit confused at the moment, sir. All I can

215

confirm is that we have Phil en route to hospital and, I'm afraid, we also have a deceased person at the scene.'

'Dead?'

'It's Malcolm Frizzle.' She paused. 'I can send a car for you, if you like.'

'No, don't do that. I'll make my way there now. Meet me at the scene, I'll follow my nose.'

As he hung up Valentine felt a surge in his blood. The ground beneath him swayed slightly as he headed for the door, snatching his jacket from the hall-stand.

'Are you going out again?' yelled Clare.

He didn't reply. By the time he reached the car, his thoughts had settled into a torrid rhythm, beating on the inside of his skull. The idea that an officer of DI Donnelly's standing would be stupid enough to confront a scrote like Frizzle was preposterous. But confrontations happened all the time, they were part of the job. And he had a scar as thick as his index finger running the length of his chest to prove it.

He slid behind the wheel and slammed the door. He drove in a daze, getting stuck behind a blue Toyota whose driver seemed lost, alternating between slowing and speeding with no apparent reason. At the beachfront he followed his own instinctual directions, first down a narrow, cobbled street and then a broader road that was lined with Victorian villas, all converted into guesthouses.

In the rear car park Valentine was waved through a taped-off cordon by a uniformed officer holding a flashlight. More uniforms and a smaller number of white-suited SOCOs were already in position, darting beneath the ten-foot-high poles supporting the lighting fixtures, which cast ghoulish shadows on the wet tarmac.

White canvas, draped over a boxy skeleton, flapped in the wind as he approached the scene. 'Hello, sir,' said DI Davis. He was emerging from the top of a low embankment where dark shrubbery masked a thick copse of trees.

'What's that you have there?' said Valentine.

Davis held up a clear plastic evidence bag. Inside was a small dark shape that, even in the dim light, couldn't be mistaken for anything other than a handgun. 'Automatic, boss. It's a SIG Sauer.'

'McCormack didn't say anything about a firearm.'

'She wouldn't have, I only just found it.'

'Has it been used?'

Davis folded over the evidence bag and put the gun in his jacket pocket. 'I take it you haven't heard how Frizzle copped it?'

'Shot?'

'Two bullets in the back of the head. Routine execution style, don't you think?'

'Christ almighty. Get it checked for prints and run the serial number; it probably won't give us anything more than a point of manufacture, but you never know.'

'I don't know if this is of any consequence, but I'm pretty sure the SIG is a favourite with the intelligence service.'

'If it is, it's of no consequence to me. You know I don't like coincidences; I prefer to deal with hard facts. That gun belonged to somebody, we don't know who, but it's now our job to find out.' Valentine turned back to the parking bays, just as DI McCormack's car was pulling up. She spotted the officers and started jogging towards the embankment.

'Phil's been taken into emergency surgery,' she said as

she pulled a stray clutch of hair from her eyes, turning to the DCI. 'I didn't know when I called, sir, but it's a gunshot wound.'

Valentine looked at Davis. 'Have you checked the magazine?'

'It's a match: three bullets missing.'

'We have the gun?' said McCormack.

'Ian found it, in the bushes.' Valentine started walking towards the white tent the SOCOs had erected. He motioned the others to follow as he went.

'Boss, are you saying the murder weapon was disposed of a few yards away from the scene?'

'Yes, so what's your point?'

'Frizzle's been taken out, mafia-style, and then the gunman flees without the gun. Something's not right here.'

'He also shot Phil before fleeing. I don't know what happened in between then and now, but I do know Phil was supposed to be shadowing Malky. If Phil stumbled across something he wasn't supposed to see then there could be any number of reasons why we have an officer down, a dead scrote and an assailant on the run. Until we've looked more closely at the situation, we can't make any assumptions.'

Valentine flung back the flap of the tent and ducked down. A SOCO was perched over the corpse, collecting residue on a wooden taper; he looked up and removed his blue face mask as the officers entered. 'Shoe guards, please, I don't want my scene contaminated!'

'It's my scene, actually,' said the DCI. 'So just keep your wig on and tell me if you found anything lying around.'

The SOCO's tone softened. 'Some skull fragments, brain matter ... Nothing I wouldn't expect, sir.'

Valentine looked at the face of Malcolm Frizzle, wide-mouthed and open-eyed, a dark red-to-black swathe painted down one side. The victim's expression, on the whole, didn't look too different to the way it had when Valentine had last seen him: the impassioned fear was still there, as was a nervous assumption of impending doom. Someone had gotten to Malky, but that had happened long before he came to rest in a dark and wet car park on the edge of Ayr.

The crouching SOCO stood up and presented the officers with a small box containing blue shoe covers. 'If you're staying, please put these on.'

The DCI waved down the offer and turned back towards the tent's opening. As he stomped out, Davis and McCormack followed.

'Sylvia, you wait here for the fiscal,' he said.

'I get all the fun jobs.'

'Well, when the merry-go-round stops, head out to the hospital and stay there until Phil comes around.'

Her head drooped. 'Yes, boss.'

'I want to know what happened here tonight and hopefully Phil will come round and shed some light on that.'

'I'll let him know we're praying for him,' said McCormack.

Valentine nodded, turning to Davis. 'You can come with me. I think we need to have a very thorough look at Malky's living conditions, and if he's left anything lying around that might give us a clue as to why someone would want to blow his brains out so abruptly.'

26

Valentine was hunched over his PC, his index finger resting on the mouse-wheel, scrolling up and down. The email containing the report from the technical team didn't make any sense to him. He clicked on the little cross in the corner of the screen and shut the file; there was no point rereading it, the facts weren't going to change.

He rubbed his face, massaging his eyes. It had been a long night. The search of Malcolm Frizzle's harbour-side flat had yielded nothing, except the victim's antipathy towards housekeeping, and a laptop with a missing hard drive. There had been no reason to assume the laptop had been tampered with by anyone other than Malky – sex offenders were prone to disposing of hard drives the second police showed an interest in their activities – but this morning's email from the lab raised more doubts.

A new load of worries had arrived, out of nowhere. As he slumped in his chair his face was inches from the screen. He eased back, exhaling loudly, and smoothed his palms over the desk. He was trying to figure all the new angles of the case that had presented themselves when he spotted DI McCormack coming through the door of the incident room. She was hanging up her coat as Valentine leaned out of his office and called her in.

'Good morning, sir,' she said.

'Morning ... How did it go last night?'

'It was a late one, I didn't want to disturb you.'

'You wouldn't have, I didn't really sleep.'

'I'd have disturbed your wife.'

'Clare doesn't need any help on that front, but I appreciate the consideration.'

McCormack crossed her arms, and eased onto the edge of the desk. The turn of her mouth indicated a change was coming to the choice of conversation. 'Phil came round last night, sir.'

'I was about to ask how he was.'

'The doctors say he's likely to pull through, but he's had a narrow escape.'

'Another one of us to add to the list.'

She nodded. 'Let's hope he's the last.'

Valentine returned to his chair. 'Did Phil give us anything to go on?'

'He said he was following Malky, as per usual, and that he was heading back to his flat down the harbour.'

'Taking the standard route?'

'Yes. The same way he always went. But this time, there was someone waiting for him in a black car, possibly a Lexus, definitely a saloon of some sort.'

'Where was Phil at this stage?'

'Quite a distance behind. He said he had no indication that anything was amiss until the gunman emerged from the car. The rest was a blur – he ran towards the man, there was a scuffle, gunfire, and Phil gave chase.'

'And the gunman got away?'

'Phil says he didn't actually realise he'd been shot, he heard the gun go off but in the struggle he thought the gunman had simply struck him. He continued in pursuit but the gunman reached the car, and that's when Phil realised he was losing blood.'

'Christ almighty. That explains how the gun got left behind, anyway.'

'If nothing else.'

The incident room was starting to fill up now. Bodies slotted in behind desks and began to contribute to the hum of activity. In the corner, next to the photocopier and a filing cabinet, where a tray of cups stood, DI Davis was eyeing a trip to fill up the kettle.

'There's Ian, call him in,' said Valentine.

McCormack knocked on the glass and beckoned the detective. He returned a green mug to the tray and nodded. His movements seemed stiff and edgy as he walked towards the other end of the room.

'You wanted to see me?' said Davis.

'In you come.' The DCI leaned forward. 'Looks like Phil's going to pull through.'

'Well, that's a relief.' Davis shrugged, seeking more of an explanation.

When McCormack had relayed her hospital report again, the officers faced each other over the desk with grim fears growing all around them.

'So what now?' said McCormack.

'Our search of Malky's flat didn't yield anything, except for a laptop that someone had stripped the hard drive from.'

'And quite a few empty Stella tins,' said Davis.

Valentine nodded. 'I had an interesting mail from the techies this morning. Apparently, Malky's online activity over the last twenty-four hours has been unusual.'

'Really?'

'Yes. All social media deleted. And, very interestingly, his Google drive – pictures and documents – all scrubbed.'

'Why would he do that?' said McCormack.

'Don't assume it was him. It could be someone who is trying to hide something that they don't want us to see.'

'Like what?'

'Well, your guess is as good as mine, but it would have to be something incriminating. We're trying to recover everything now, but it's going to take some time.'

Davis leaned a hand on the wall. 'Malky did make a lot of claims about what he'd seen out at the Sutherland place – remember what he told those girls that he picked up at the bus stop in Monkton.'

'That's where my thoughts were heading, too,' said Valentine. 'Ian, can you remember the name of the gym Malky was heading to on the day we showed up at Sutherland's?'

'It was the one out at Whittlet's, the big one next to the roundabout.'

The DCI got up from where he was sitting; he picked his jacket from the back of the chair and headed towards the door. 'Then we should pay them a visit, right away.'

'What are you thinking, sir?' said McCormack.

'I'm thinking, if Malky was a member, he'll have a locker. And there might very well be something interesting inside it.'

*

The gym was an ugly slab of post-modernism. Poured concrete and PVC window frames, with a revolving door as centrepiece. The hallway was an obstacle course of fitness-class flyers and glass cabinets stuffed with swimming goggles and Lycra wear. Valentine felt exhausted just navigating the stairwell; he wondered how anyone could enjoy visiting somewhere so soulless.

'Who comes to these places?' said the DCI. 'I feel like I'm in a casting call for *The Stepford Wives*.'

McCormack and Davis halted behind him, the recently promoted DI answering, 'There's a drop-box for your personality next to the yucca plant.'

'I don't doubt it.'

'Can I help you?' The girl behind the counter was permatanned, her solid black hair sprayed into an immoveable force.

Valentine opened his mouth, conjured voice, and decided not to bother. 'You deal with this, Sylvia.'

McCormack took the floor and, after displaying her warrant card and introducing the officers, was met by a bulky manager in a shiny grey suit and white, starched collar. He studied the team for a moment then retreated into his office and returned with a bunch of keys on a blue lanyard.

'The members' lockers are down at the rear of the changing rooms,' he said, indicating a swing door. The officers followed him through.

'Do you recall Malcolm Frizzle?' said Valentine.

The manager nodded, his head lolling on thick shoulders. 'Yes, there was a little bit of trouble.'

'Trouble?'

'I shouldn't really be relaying this – client confidentiality and all that.'

'Remember you're talking to the police.'

'That sounds ominous.'

Valentine caught the manager's gaze. 'There was a murder last night. If I thought you were withholding information, I'd have to take you down to the station and question you under caution. How does that sound?'

'Okay, I'm not trying to be difficult.' He raised his palms, rattling the lanyard.

'What trouble did Frizzle cause you?'

'There was some funny business with one of the younger members around the pool – the young girl's father took exception.'

'Did it get nasty?'

'Raised voices, that was all. I warned him, of course.'

'It doesn't sound like anything out of the ordinary for Frizzle. We're definitely talking about the same man.'

They'd reached the locker room. The manager walked straight to where the number corresponded to the key in his hand. As he reached out with the key, he tapped at the blue-fronted steel door. 'Here we are.'

The key inserted, the locker sprung open, and the door was eased wide.

Valentine reached in and removed a sweat top, shaking it out before dropping it on the ground. There were a few more items, an unopened packet of spearmint chewing gum and a dog-eared Gideon's Bible.

He picked up the bible. 'Malky didn't look the religious type to me.'

'Maybe he'd seen something recently that pushed him over,' said McCormack.

Valentine returned the bible to the locker and latched

on to another item, it was a small digital camera with a flat screen on the back.

'Did you ever see him with this?' he said.

The manager shook his head. 'Cameras aren't allowed in the changing rooms, we don't even like to see people with smartphones back here.'

Valentine turned over the camera and tried the on/off switch at the side: a dim orange bulb started to glow then grew even dimmer. 'Looks like the battery's flat.'

Davis reached in to the locker and withdrew a cable. 'Might be worth charging it up, sir.'

'Oh, I think it's definitely worth charging it up.'

27

A long yellow slant of early sunlight sat across the car windscreen. The bright light highlighted the weathered railings that skirted the car park, divvying up the vehicles. From inside the heat-seared Audi, Valentine lowered the moistening windows a few inches and reclined in his seat, sighing. His eyes darted to the dashboard, and then back to the fading paintwork, before settling on DI McCormack. 'No sign of life?'

'It takes a while.' She picked up the camera and inspected the cable. It was still attached to the car's cigarette-lighter socket.

'What's that green light now?'

'Oh, it's on.' McCormack slid the side switch again and an icon appeared on the screen. 'Booting up now.'

DI Davis tried to join in the front-seat huddle, leaning over the armrest and handbrake and peering into the small screen on the back of the camera. The initial photographic offering was much as expected: lots of pink flesh, in swimming suits, and all belonging to girls no older than fourteen.

'What a bloody creep,' said McCormack.

'You weren't expecting bowls of fruit, were you?' Valentine shook his head as the DI flicked through the photo cache. She continued her tirade about the girls' ages, and state of undress, until the screen-shot abruptly altered. 'Oh, hold on ...'

'What's that now?'

McCormack turned up the camera, trying to discern the new set of shapes from another angle. 'Don't know, looks like an interior. I see a light.'

'Electric?'

'I think it's a flame, candle likely.'

She pressed on through the new pictures, they were all blurred and only odd snatches appeared in focus. In one, a whole hand appeared; in another a shadowy figure. McCormack was flicking quickly when one photograph finally jumped out; its content couldn't be confused.

'Oh my God,' she said.

'Is that what I think it is?' said Valentine.

'If you think it's a little girl being abused, I'm afraid the answer's yes.' She handed over the camera to the DCI.

Valentine looked over the remaining images of men in dark robes with a young girl laid out on a stone altar, like a sacrificial offering. He couldn't see her face, and some of the men were in masks, but others were revealing their identities. None of them appeared to be aware that their images were being captured.

'Hold on,' said the DCI, 'I know this one.' He held up the camera.

'Who is he?' said Davis.

'I think his name's Rosenthal: he's a member of the European Parliament, don't ask me for any more details, but it's definitely him, I'd know that smarm-merchant anywhere.'

'Holy God.'

The detective returned to scrolling through the images, finally the girl on the altar came into focus. 'It's Abbie McGarvie.'

'Are you sure?'

'I'm certain.' He viewed more images. 'Not only have we Abbie in here, but this picture will require you both to put your seat belts on right away.' He passed the camera to McCormack.

'David Sutherland,' she said. 'I told you we should have taken him in.'

'Well, we're taking him in now.' Valentine turned the key in the ignition and engaged the clutch.

As they drove, McCormack delivered the news that there were more incriminating pictures still to come from the camera. 'Boss, I think I've found another political figure. Closer to home this time.' She held up an image of a portly man, stripped to the waist, in the same pose as the others.

'Miller, I'm sure he's been around since the fag-end of New Labour.'

'Oh, Jesus, there's more yet.' McCormack put down the camera and handed it to Davis on the back seat. 'I can't look. I just can't look at any more.'

As he took the camera the DI's eyes started to grow round. He was gritting his jaws as he spoke again. 'This is grotesque. And Malky had this, all the time. It would have turned us away from him and onto the ones in the pictures. Why didn't he bloody well hand it over?'

'Because he was a Renfield,' said Valentine.

'A what?' McCormack turned, squinting towards the DCI.

'Malky didn't carry out this sort of thing – he was strictly a low-grade nonce, violent occult practice was beyond him. But he wasn't beyond supplying those that did like it – that's why I called him a Renfield; remember who that was? The depraved one who went out rounding up the victims for Dracula, so the vampire could keep his hands clean.'

Davis grunted. 'These bastards were too busy pretending to be solid, upstanding citizens. And there's only so many of their own daughters they could initiate into their sick ways before they started running out.'

'They're all too busy hiding in plain sight. Malky was their cover. The pictures were obviously his insurance policy, or maybe he wanted out when he saw the real truth of what was going on, but they wouldn't let him out by that stage. Either way, he wasn't about to bring the pictures to us and implicate himself, especially when we were investigating Abbie's death and she was in the pictures too.'

The car thundered down the bypass, overtaking a row of slow-lane hatchbacks. By the turn-off for Monkton, Valentine was gripping the steering wheel with spongy, wet palms. He dabbed the flat of his hand on top of his trousers and then repeated the motion. He was starting to lurch forward, crouching over the wheel like a gargoyle. His mind was racing now, all thoughts converging in a rhythmic pounding behind his forehead.

The DCI envisioned a dramatic scene at the doorway as they appeared, perhaps some kind of intervention on behalf of Sutherland's security staff. It crossed his thoughts to call ahead for backup, perhaps a wagon full of uniforms to close off access to the airstrip. As the thoughts played he decided against any strong-arming and, after all, Sutherland was capable of shutting the DCI down without anything more elaborate than a telephone call. Valentine knew he would need to be careful, because he was walking a tightrope, with the case balanced on one end of the pole, and his career on the other.

As he pulled in through the gate on the airport road, the detective felt the tyres start to slide away on top of the loose scree. He sat up, steering into the slight skid, and brought the vehicle in line with the property wall. The green, rolling lawn was tilting gently alongside, the pond water casting up bright gleams. The picture was of almost perfect stillness until the Audi's brakes screeched haltingly outside the main door of the impressive property.

For a moment, Valentine sat breathlessly, listening to the steady beating in his chest. Stepping out, he was a little unsteady on his feat. An old instinct was warning him to calm down, to keep his impulsive thoughts at bay. There was an angry discourse setting up inside him, and he wanted answers to the questions he'd collected. He knew Sutherland would be in no hurry to provide useful responses, however, and any uncouth prodding could have the opposite effect to the one he craved.

McCormack approached from the other side of the car. 'You okay, boss?'

'Yes, fine.'

'You look a little wobbly.'

'I'm just gathering my thoughts, and more importantly, my emotions.'

'It's not easy, I know. After seeing those pictures I just want to lock him up and throw away the key.'

231

'Well, that's my intention.'

'Something tells me it might not be as easy as that, sir.'

Valentine made for the stairs. 'We have to start some-where.'

The bell-pull made an elaborate call to attention. There was no movement inside the property for some moments and then a dark shadow passed over the windows that ran either side of the door. Opening up, David Sutherland stood in his stocking feet, a hand louchely tucked inside the pocket of his baggy corduroys. For a second he appeared not to have registered the officers' presence and then he directed his gaze at the DCI.

'Have you come to replace the wisteria your mob tram-pled to death?' said Sutherland.

'I'm concerned with a far more serious death than that,' said Valentine, dropping a solemn accent on the word death.

'What on earth are you on about?'

'All will be explained in due course, Mr Sutherland. Right now, I think you should get some shoes and a coat because you're coming with me to answer a few questions in the far less congenial environs of King Street station.'

Valentine stood outside the interview room and waited for DI McCormack to return. The DI had taken it upon herself to supervise the printing of the pictures from Malcolm Frizzle's camera personally. The station's only functioning colour printer was three floors up and on the opposite end of the building. The break in proceedings had allowed the DCI to compose himself and take a moment to plot the direction his questioning should take, but from Sutherland's reaction he sensed trouble.

DI Davis appeared in the corridor, reeking of cigarette smoke and twitching nervously. 'Hello, sir.'

'What's up with you?' said Valentine. 'You look like you've seen a ghost.'

'It's just my way, I get pensive when it's a cert.'

'We're well positioned, but pretty far from a cert.' The logic escaped the detective. 'Why do you get pensive?'

'Suppose it's because there's everything to lose.'

Valentine didn't like this unforeseen turn of events. Davis was right about one thing, though: the result was theirs to lose, and he wasn't about to throw it away. 'You can leave this to Sylvia and me,' he said.

'But it's been my case, from the very start.'

'You've done well, son. Now go and iron things out upstairs.'

'But it's my case.'

'It's my case, Ian.' He dropped some gravel in his voice, the conciliatory tone obviously proving futile.

'Oh, come on, that's not fair.'

'There's no fair hairs on a monkey's arse, you know that. Now get up to the incident room and make sure we have a solid showing for when Dino appears.'

Davis moved his head and his eyes started to darken. When he turned back to face the DCI his forehead was sheened with sweat. He was holding in a tirade, but only just.

'Do you hear me, Ian?'

'Yes, boss.'

As Davis turned for the stairwell, DI McCormack was

coming in the door. She nearly dropped the blue folder she was carrying and a couple of glossy A4 printouts fluttered to the ground.

'Hey, watch where you're going,' she yelped.

'Leave it,' said Valentine, bending down to retrieve the prints.

'What's got his goat?'

'Me.'

'What do you mean?'

'I put him on the bench.'

McCormack straightened the pictures. 'Why?'

'You just saw why – he's a time-bomb.'

'That guy's got issues, I mean it.'

'You've noticed that, too?'

The officers headed towards the interview room and went inside. Sutherland was sitting, arms folded, on one side of a standard-issue office desk. He ran his fingers through his hair and crossed his legs as the detectives sat down opposite him, but he refused to acknowledge them.

'Why do you have me in this place?' snapped Sutherland.

'I'll be asking the questions, not you,' said Valentine.

'Oh, is that how it's going to be, is it?'

'You heard me.'

Valentine looked over the man in front of him. It was the same man that he had earlier spotted in the horrendous images he'd found on Malky's camera. It didn't lower the DCI's opinion of Sutherland to know that he kept company with sick perverts because he had never had a high opinion of him in the first place. Neither did it give him any satisfaction to know that he had found such incriminating evidence, because there were young girls who had suffered

234

terribly. And one in particular, who had died because of her involvement with him.

'Why didn't you come in to see me when you had the opportunity?' said Valentine.

'I don't do everything I'm asked,' said Sutherland.

'I would have thought an invitation like that, from a senior police officer, might prompt a different response.'

'Really? Well, I'm not generally in the habit of jumping to attention at the behest of low-grade civil servants, no matter who they think they are.'

Sutherland was being unduly combative; it could have been a trait of his class, or a misplaced sense of security. Only the latter worried Valentine, but just a little. Sutherland might have once believed he was in a stronger position than he was, but the photographs in the blue folder sitting between them now said otherwise.

'Tell me how you came to know Malcolm Frizzle?'

'Who?'

'Don't play dumb.'

'I employ quite a number of people, you do realise that.'

'Like I said, don't play dumb.' Valentine leaned forward, balancing on his elbows as he spoke softly in Sutherland's direction. 'I've had a dead pervert taken out, professionally, but perhaps not as professionally as his executors think. So, unless you want me to get very angry, very early on in this chat, I'd start answering some of my questions.'

'Most of my staff come from an employment agency.' His tone lowered a little, like he was prepared to play nice to better his predicament quickly.

'Did Frizzle?'

'I'd have to check.'

'Perhaps he was recommended to you by someone, a friend or colleague maybe? Someone like the deputy head of Finlyson School, Alex McGarvie?'

Sutherland's gaze thinned. 'I don't recall.'

'Frizzle's dead now.'

'Is he?' The response was timid.

'You say that like a dish towel blew off the line.'

'We weren't well acquainted.'

'I don't suppose you have to be particularly well acquainted with all your suppliers.' Valentine let the last word sting a little. 'I say suppliers, meaning, of course, suppliers of flesh.'

'I-I'm not following you.'

'Oh, I think you are.'

The DCI turned to McCormack and nodded – she opened the blue folder and started to lay out photographs, one by one, in front of Sutherland. He watched, as the images mounted up before him. None of the horrific sights of young girls being abused, the occult practices or the clearly identifiable faces, including his own, made any impact until one.

'I'm not saying another word until I have my QC with me,' blurted Sutherland, wide-eyed, pushing the prints away.

Valentine gathered the photographs towards him and selected one. He held it up, next to his face, as he spoke. 'Simon James Rosenthal sits in the European Parliament, a very powerful man overseeing billions of pounds worth of annual subsidy. I must confess, I didn't know that much about him but I've had a closer look at his portfolio since he cropped up in my investigation.'

Sutherland made a sideways glance at the officers but kept his lips tightly shut.

'Of course, it's not Mr Rosenthal's multi-billion-pound portfolio that we're concerned with here. I'm far more interested in his predilection for little girls. No comment, Mr Sutherland?'

'I want my lawyer now.'

'Nothing to say about your friend, Mr Rosenthal, here? You're obviously well connected; you appear to be in some kind of club, tell me about those robes, and the masks.'

'I'm not saying another word until my lawyer is present.' Sutherland was breathing hard, exhaling downward through compressed nostrils.

'You're entitled to legal representation, in due course.'

'Now!' He turned on the officers, slamming his palms down on the desk.

Valentine held still; he kept his composure until Sutherland retreated into his chair and seethed to himself. When he judged the moment to be right the DCI calmly collected up the photographs and put them in the folder. He rose and walked out with the folder under his arm, DI McCormack following.

Outside the interview room McCormack was the first to speak.

'Wow. Just wow,' she said.

'Did you see his face?'

'I didn't think people actually spoke through gritted teeth.'

'David Sutherland clearly does.' The officers started to walk towards the stairwell. 'And to think this is all thanks to Malky Frizzle. I could almost thank him.'

'Don't get too carried away.'

'Do you think Malky put the rope ladder out for Abbie?'

Valentine shrugged. 'We'll never know. It's possible, he was working a number on them, that's for sure.'

'Do you think it's possible Malky thought these sickos were going beyond even his limits?'

'I'd be cautious about measuring Malky for a halo quite yet. He was a scrote and a perv, and this is how that type always gets brought down. Some people call it hubris, I call it the law of stupid.'

'The law of stupid, sir?'

'You get enough psychopaths together in one place they'll start to screw each other over for power, because that's what they do. Someone made a mistake bringing in Malky Frizzle to such a sophisticated set-up, but that one mistake has turned out to be our greatest asset.'

28

As Valentine and McCormack walked through the door of the main incident room they were met with spontaneous applause. McCormack raised the blue folder containing the pictures over her head and smiled, but she promptly corrected herself when she noticed the DCI's expression. For a moment, the group continued to applaud, a few banging on desktops and whistling to add to the air of jubilation. The entire room seemed overwhelmed, elated with the news that Sutherland was in custody and, given the new evidence, more of his associates would be joining him soon.

As the tumult died away, Valentine found himself the focus of every pair of eyes around him. He knew what they were expecting to see, but he would have to disappoint them. The uneasy tension setting up in his gut insisted there was only one way to break the spell: directly.

'Okay,' he said, 'now, let's not get carried away.' He flagged his palms at the group.

'Come on, boss, you've got a result,' said one of the cocky uniforms.

'No, we're far from over the line, actually.' His voice had grown hoarse; he didn't like delivering bad news to such a motivated group.

DI Davis pressed to the front of the gathering. 'What happened in the interview with Sutherland?'

'He's playing coy.'

'But we've got his mug on film!'

'That's not a confession to any crime, Ian. And it's certainly not a confession to how Abbie McGarvie came to be cold on the tarmac outside his estate.'

A palpable fatigue settled into the room; it were as if the earlier enthusiasm had been siphoned off through the valve of a deflating balloon. Valentine waved the group back to their positions and they returned to stare disconsolately at computer screens. Only DI Davis resisted the call, leaning over a desk and shaking his head – he looked close to bawling.

'Ian, join myself and DI McCormack in my office, when you're ready.' The officers traipsed through the unusually silent incident room towards the office. Inside the door, Valentine headed straight to his desk, where he noticed a number of post-it notes had been stuck in his absence.

'Are you redecorating with those?' said McCormack.

'One, two ... there's five messages all from Kevin Rickards,' he said.

'The cop?'

'Ex-cop.'

'What does he want?'

'I've no idea, apart from that I'm to call him back.'

'You should do that, it might be important.'

Valentine dialled the number but before the call connected he spotted the chief super stomping towards him, eyes ablaze, through the incident room. He put down the receiver and nodded in her direction. 'What's up with her?'

McCormack turned and commented, 'She's like a scalded cat.'

'I know that look and you're not far off.'

DI Davis was outside the door, reaching a hand towards the handle. He jerked backwards as CS Martin entered.

'Bob, my office right away.'

'Can I get a clue what it's about?'

'No you bloody cannot. Get moving, now.' She directed a painted thumbnail over her shoulder then turned on her stiletto heels and marched back the way she had just came. Outside the swinging door, Davis was open-mouthed. He followed the super's definitive movements, and the bobbing heads that accompanied them, and then he turned back to the office and puffed out his cheeks.

'I have a bad feeling about this,' said McCormack.

'Me too,' said Valentine, turning towards her and noticing she was staring out the window, and appeared to be talking about something else entirely. He walked over to the window. 'What is it?'

'Somehow, I don't think they're selling double glazing.' The DI was pointing to a group of men, four in total, dressed in dark suits, who were exiting a black saloon at the front of the station.

'What the hell?'

'My thoughts entirely.'

Valentine dashed back to his desk and picked up the phone, he pressed the speed-dial button for the front desk. Jim Prentice answered on the third ring.

'Jim, what's the story with the new arrivals?' said the DCI.

'Oh, you mean the Men in Black?'

'Stop messing around.'

The desk sergeant's voice grew weary. 'That's another group just in, there were some more earlier.'

'Who are they?'

'Nobody's told me, which can only mean one thing: I'm not on the "need to know" list.'

Valentine sighed. 'I get the impression I'm about to be gelded.'

'That sounds painful, old son.'

'You don't know the half of it.'

DI McCormack and DI Davis had gathered around the desk; they stood pensively before Valentine as he drummed his fingers on the top of the telephone.

'Well?'

'It looks like Special Branch.'

Davis lashed out at the desk with his foot. 'No! I'm not letting them do this to me again.'

'Calm down, Ian.'

'Bollocks to that.' He kicked out again, this time a wooden panel split in the desk.

'Ian!'

DI Davis stood squarely, gripping fists, and then lurched violently for the exit. He grabbed the handle and yanked the door, smacking it off the wall and dislodging the Venetian blinds, which slid into a heap on the floor. In the incident room he snatched up his jacket so roughly that the chair trailed him a few steps, before falling and being abandoned in the middle of the floor.

McCormack and Valentine stared in disbelief, the scene picking up an open-mouthed audience.

'God, he's flipped,' said McCormack.

'You're not kidding.'

'Should I go after him?'

'And do what? Tell him there'll be other cases. I don't think that's going to fly with Ian.'

'But we should do something, he's clearly gone off the deep end.'

The DCI felt too much of his own anger swelling inside him to deal with Davis at this moment. He rubbed the base of his skull and tried to ease out the growing tension there – it wasn't working. He was close to an explosion all of his own.

'Ian's a big boy, he'll have to figure this out for himself,' he said.

Valentine made for the door, leaving McCormack alone in the office. By the mid-point of the incident room he already had the feeling of being dragged away from the investigation by undercurrents beyond his control. He saw Abbie McGarvie's face in his mind, her cold eyes staring right into him again. There was nothing that he could do, and he wanted to tell her so. He felt the vision of the girl again, pressuring him to fight for her, to help.

'Please, there's no one else,' she was calling to him.

He tried to look away but the cold eyes followed.

He scrunched up his own eyes and took a deep breath, but she was still there. Would she never stop? Would she now be trapped on the Bridge of Souls like Hugh Crosbie had said?

Valentine forced his way through the door and marched down the corridor towards the chief super's office. He was burning up, part anger and part tension swelling inside him – a fight or flight scenario he couldn't avoid if he wanted to.

He stood beyond the door, trying to find some calm

anywhere inside him, and failing. His legs were thick and heavy, the muscles of his calves tensing and constricting. He brushed his shirtfronts with the flat of his hand and straightened his cuffs, but these acts didn't alter his appearance any more than his mood.

He turned away from the door, took two steps, then spun round and walked straight in.

'You wanted to see me?' he said.

'Sit.' She pointed to the chair in front of her desk. CS Martin was hunched over her blotter, her shoulders so tense her head seemed ready to snap off. She pinched her mouth into a tight knot, then spoke in a reedy whine. 'Where have you been today?'

'Are you asking for a timetable of my movements?'

'I think you know what I'm referring to.' She drew in her cheeks, her stare intensified. 'And to whom.'

'This is about Sutherland, right?'

'David Sutherland, you picked him up.'

'Yes. I had good reason, and evidence.'

'I don't give a shit if you had a signed statement from Queen Elizabeth II herself to back up your actions – you took him in without my bloody say-so!'

Valentine felt the hostility rising at him in rays. 'It's my investigation.'

Martin wet her lips with the tip of her tongue and spoke slowly and firmly. 'Not any more.'

'What are you saying?'

She turned away and crossed her legs behind the desk. 'Cast your mind back to a conversation we had a few days ago, when a young girl had been found splattered on the road. What did I say to you then, Bob?'

244

'You gave me the authority to re-investigate the Abbie McGarvie case that had already been thrown out by the courts.'

'No!' She pointed her finger, a red fingernail jabbing the air. 'I said you have my authority to investigate the original case *only* if you found a connection to Abbie McGarvie's death.'

'I believe I have sufficient evidence to justify that.'

'But what else did I say?'

'Look, I can't remember every detail of every conversation I've ever had, it is nearly a week ago.'

'Well, you should have been paying closer attention.'

'Is this leading anywhere?'

'It certainly is, now. Let me repeat for you again. I told you to investigate quietly, very quietly, and that I didn't want anyone outside the station to get wind of your activities, even if you found anything. Now not only do I have it on good authority that you have been liaising with a disgraced former police officer but you've dropped the hammer on David Sutherland.'

Valentine saw where this was leading; there was no point in defending his actions now because the decision had already been made. 'So, Kevin Rickards is to be smeared now too. It's not enough he was thrown off the force for getting too close to the corridors of power.'

'Leave it, Bob.'

'That's what this is about, isn't it?'

'I said, let it go. You're off the investigation and the case will be taken up by a specialist unit who have been monitoring the situation for quite some time. I'd like you to prepare a full handover, including all your evidence and case notes.'

'It's a joke, right?'

'Do I look like I'm laughing?'

It was Valentine's turn to point the finger. 'You've thrown me under the bus. And what about Sutherland?'

'He'll be released.'

'*What*? I have him on film assaulting a child.'

'He's already out the door. And another word, Bob, and you will be too. I don't think you fancy paying off that big holiday on half-pay, so I'd shut up and march, now.'

Valentine jumped to his feet, the blood racing in his veins. 'That girl, that poor bloody girl.'

'Empty the incident room and disband the squad.'

'Who speaks for Abbie McGarvie now?'

'I'm warning you, Bob.'

'I have an officer in the hospital. He was shot, for what? To throw all our work out and let a pack of dark-suited nonces carry on regardless.'

'Right, that's it. Turn in your warrant card. I'm suspending you, effective immediately.'

'You can do what you bloody well like,' he raged, marching for the door.

29

Valentine ran down the stairs, powered by fiery resentment. At the entrance to the cells he pushed the door with such force that it rebounded noisily off the wall. The sergeant on the counter stood up and gazed at the DCI, struggling for the right words to greet him.

'Where's Sutherland?' said the detective.

'Gone. You just missed him – his lawyer came and picked him up.'

Valentine smashed the heel of his hand on the wall and turned for the door. In the stairwell he pushed open the emergency fire doors that led to the car park. He strained his eyes in the low, late-afternoon sunlight, and caught the glinting movement of a car. As he set off running the scene swam into focus. He knew what he was doing wasn't going to help the situation, but he didn't care.

The burgundy Jaguar screeched to a halt as Valentine stood in the road, right hand aloft like a halt sign. He watched the driver get out and start walking towards him, berating him in a threat-laden legalese, but he didn't return the man's gaze. He turned for the passenger: David Sutherland.

Valentine's movements were purposeful and swift,

latching first on the door handle and next on Sutherland's collars, pulling him out of the car in one smooth jerk and slamming him against the side window.

'You must think you're very smart, Sutherland,' he growled.

'Get your hands off me.' His words were backed by a conscience-stricken gaze. 'I'm warning you.'

'You've nothing left to threaten me with.'

'Get off me.'

Valentine bundled him closer to the car, shoving hard. 'You might think you're going to get away with this a second time, and bumping off Malky, but you're not. I've got your number, and all your big friends too. There's no one left to save you. You can all go down together.'

The lawyer started to peel at Valentine's arms, belching platitudes about assault charges and official complaints. The detective ignored him, continuing his rant.

'Do you hear me? You've got nowhere to run this time. I'm coming for you, one way or another; from now on you'll spend your days looking back over your shoulder for me.'

Sutherland looked defeated, the colour draining from his face. He didn't reply to the threats now, merely curling himself as far from the DCI as he could get, turning his face away. Valentine's arms ached and a tight band encircled his chest. He released Sutherland and pushed him away, sending him sliding towards the ground.

The lawyer stood in front of Valentine, anger clearly swelling up inside him. 'I'll be calling for your dismissal for this!'

Valentine grinned. 'You'll have to join the queue for that.'

As he walked back to the station, he felt the tension surging in his arms and shoulders. He had achieved nothing with his actions, but something close to satisfaction was forming inside him. There would be a point, in the not too distant future, when he would regret what he had just done – he knew that – but it didn't matter. His cares were for the young girl who had died, and what she had been through. Someone had to care about Abbie McGarvie's death, and it gored him, more than he could express, that he was perhaps the only one who really did.

Valentine knew what had occurred was a travesty, and he should fight it, but he didn't know how. Other officers had tried and paid a dear price for it – one losing his livelihood and another just about losing his mind. There had to be a way to find proper justice, to expose what was going on, but now that he was off the case, and off the force, he didn't have the answer to that quandary. But he wasn't giving up, for Abbie, and also because he'd just promised Sutherland that he wasn't going to stop until he and all his horrific clique were behind bars.

In the station foyer Jim Prentice called out from behind the front desk, but Valentine flagged him down. There was a remark about being a sour puss, and rising in the ranks clearly not suiting him, but he resisted the goading. It was a welcome amusement to the detective that the latest news about his position hadn't been picked up by the station's top gossip yet.

The DCI was half way up the stairs when his mobile rang.

'Hello,' he snapped.

'Bob, finally got you.' It was Kevin Rickards. 'I've been ringing all day.'

'It's been a busy one.'

'For me too. Look, I need to have a chat with you in person, and the sooner the better.'

Valentine stopped ascending the stairs and balanced a hand on the rail. 'What's up?'

'I can't talk on the phone. You understand that, don't you?'

'Yes, I understand.'

'How about where we met the last time?'

'I know where you mean. I can be there in an hour.'

'Okay, that's good. Thanks, Bob. You won't regret it, I can assure you of that.'

He hung up and continued to the office, wondering what it was he wouldn't regret – his mind bristling with curiosity but also doubts. At the top of the stairs he noticed DI McCormack leaning in the doorway of the main incident room; when she spotted the DCI she broke into a brisk jog in his direction.

'Where have you been?' she said. 'I've been like a first-time father on a maternity ward.'

'I had a dust-up in the car park.'

'*What*? Who with?'

'Sutherland.'

She grinned. 'Yeah, right.'

'I wish I was joking.' Valentine eased past the DI. 'You better come in. I need to talk to the squad, and right away.'

It felt warm in the packed room, compared to the windy car park. He loosened his collar and started to roll up his shirtsleeves. There was no point trying to compose his thoughts, to present a clear and cohesive explanation for why the lead detective on the investigation was being told

250

to stand down, because he didn't posses such a thing. It was one of those situations where it was best to detonate the explosives and retreat – the fallout was something they would have to deal with individually.

After only a minute or two in the incident room the detective was already aware of a crowd forming around him. He strode to the front of the whiteboard and motioned for a huddle. DI McCormack was among the first to push to the front and place herself in a prominent position by his side.

'Okay, if everyone's here, I have an important announcement to make,' said Valentine. 'I've just come from a meeting with the chief super and, effective immediately, the Abbie McGarvie case is being taken over by special investigations.'

'*What*?' said DI McCormack. A low susurration of hushed voices spread around the room.

Valentine nodded slowly, two or three times in succession. 'I know it's not what you want to hear, but it's out of my hands now.'

'Boss, we have an officer who was shot in the course of this investigation,' said McCormack.

'I have made that point too, I'm afraid it fell on fallow ground.'

'This is beyond the pale.'

'And, it gets worse.' He motioned the group to quieten down. 'Also, effective immediately, is my suspension from active duty.'

'Are you serious?'

'I'm not going to mess about with a topic like that, Sylvia.'

'But why?'

'It's probably better I don't go into details.' He stepped away from the board. 'DI McCormack will be in charge of the handover of the case; if you could give her your complete cooperation, please, that would be appreciated.'

As the detective passed through the crowd of chattering, unhappy faces, DI McCormack bailed him up outside his office door. 'Am I to get any more information or are we all going to be abandoned in the dark on this?'

'Come in here.' He nodded towards the door.

'Well?'

'Sutherland's movements were obviously being monitored when we brought him in. Either that or he made a call on the bat-phone while we were waiting for him to put on his coat and shoes.'

'I don't understand.'

'He's protected.'

'Meaning?'

Valentine rounded up his jacket and briefcase. 'The man's not entertaining members of the highest political office because he likes their company. He's running a sophisticated brownstoning ring under our noses. The airport, the estate, the Luciferian rites – it's how the elites roll. Sutherland's job is to facilitate it and record it so that no one gets out once they're in the group's clutches.'

'And we have to just sit on this?'

'What do you think would happen if we didn't?'

'You mean, what would the public do if they found out they were ruled over by psychopathic paedophiles?'

'That's what I'm asking you.'

'There'd be a revolution by the morning.'

'Of course there would.'

'So that's your answer, we sweep it under the carpet?'

Valentine put his coat on and closed up his briefcase. 'Look, Sylvia, I've just been suspended and Dino is trembling like a constipated greyhound through there. I'm not any happier about this than you are. I don't know what to say to you right now, but I might just know a man who does.'

She stepped aside from the door. 'Who might that be?'

'Kevin Rickards. I'm going to meet him now. I can't recommend you follow me, because that is likely to see you suspended too if anyone was to find out, but I'll understand if your blood is running as hot as mine.'

'Lead the way.'

The shops and offices of Ayr had already emptied out, some of their staff making their way to O'Briens pub at the top of the town. The bar was busy, but not bustling. The days of workers seeking rowdy oblivion on the sounding of the shift's close were largely a thing of the past. Mostly, men with pints were propped on stools, but a cocktail promotion had attracted some smartly dressed women from the professional set. The crowd looked content, happy, blissfully ignorant of the heinous crimes unfolding in their midst. Valentine looked over the gathering and wondered just how much success he'd have explaining what he'd learned in the last week to them. He realised none of them had a clue of the real nature of certain elements of their species, the most prominent members, but he couldn't judge them for it. Their entire existence – the ruled and their rulers – depended on the tightest lid being kept on everything that went on.

'Bob, over here,' called Rickards.

Valentine and McCormack moved over to the booth. As he stepped inside he noticed DI Davis sitting in the corner, crouched and pensive.

'Hello, Ian,' said the DCI. He didn't know Davis was still maintaining regular contact with his former boss and the revelation seemed like another of his betrayals to add to a long list.

'I'm sorry about earlier, y'know, kicking your desk. I'll get it fixed,' said Davis.

'Don't worry about it, turns out I won't be needing it for a while.'

They sat down around the table.

'Why's that?' said Rickards. 'Has something happened?'

'I've been suspended.'

'Jesus.' Rickards shook his head over the table, when he looked up again his eyes were shining. 'I heard about the investigation being pulled.'

Valentine stared at Davis, who looked away. The DCI didn't like leaks on his squad, even if the information channel was facing the right way, and it burned inside him.

'So they're going by the play-book,' said Rickards.

'You could have predicted it, I suppose.'

'Based on my experience, it was never going to play out any other way.'

Davis cut in, 'Where's Sutherland?'

'Last I saw him he was being driven away by a smarmy QC.'

'He'll be at home now, sprucing the place up for tonight.'

254

'What are you on about?'

Rickards' tongue prowled his top lip as he measured his response. 'That's why I called you here. To talk in private.' His gaze was on McCormack.

'You can trust Sylvia, she knows as much as I do.'

'Okay. If you're sure, Bob.'

'I'm sure.'

McCormack spoke up. 'I've not been suspended, I'm still on the force, but we're all on the same page.'

'I see. I think you must know by now that both Davis and myself never stopped investigating the original Abbie McGarvie case.'

'I was coming to that conclusion,' said Valentine. 'It must have seemed like a stroke of luck when you were dropped into my team, Ian.'

Davis nodded, a weak grin forcing up the tip of his moustache.

'I've been in contact with some sources today,' said Rickards, 'and I've received some interesting information about the imminent arrival of a high-flier.'

'You're talking about Prestwick Airport?'

He nodded. 'I don't have a name, but it's top-tier; they're laying on the full diplomatic security detail.'

'If this has been on the cards then I can see why my case has been shut down so abruptly.'

'That would have happened anyway, but yes, some serious organisation has gone into this, and Sutherland's fun park is the main attraction.'

Valentine turned to McCormack. She was holding herself in a tense manner, clearly as confused by the emerging information as the detective was.

'I'm not sure I see where you're going with all of this, Kevin,' said Valentine.

Davis sparked up, getting out of his seat. 'You don't? *Christ*, don't you get it yet?'

'Calm down, Ian.' Rickards patted Davis on the arm, then gripped his fingers round his shoulder, forcing him to sit down again. 'Bob, there's only one way we're going to get a result here, you must see that.'

'We can't just walk in and scoop them up. I've done that already today and Sutherland was promptly released.'

'But I will have to make arrests if I see anything that breaks the law,' said McCormack. 'I won't just turn a blind eye because you've both been stonewalled already.'

'I'm not talking about taking them in.' Rickards' strong features sat rigid.

'Well, what are you talking about?' said Valentine.

'Catching them in the act. If we can turn the tables on them, get them on film, then we can blow this whole operation wide open in the media.'

'You must be mad,' Valentine bridled. 'If Sutherland's people are as strong as we think, then what makes you think the press would even touch it?'

'They won't have a choice!' snapped Davis. 'The print media's on its last legs, there's an alternative media online that will lap this up.'

'He's right,' said Rickards. 'The dam's breaking online. If the old media won't run with the story, the new lot will. I know just where to take this. Trust me, people are ready to hear the truth.'

Valentine sat facing the two men, letting the new thought turn over in his mind. There was a time when he would have dismissed the proposal out of hand. It was dangerously close to vigilante action, to putting his head on the block – and everyone else's – but he had nothing to lose now.

He wanted justice for Abbie, and for all the other damaged girls she had brought to him. He closed his eyes and weighed up the dwindling list of options.

Six Days Ago

All the way into the country I wonder why Dad has sent this man for me. He says his name is Malky and I don't like it because it sounds like a rough person's name. I'm not supposed to talk to people like that, Mum says so, but so does Dad. The man yabbers the whole time about silly stuff, he sings along to songs on the radio and he squeezes my knee whenever I take my eyes off him. I think he's a little bit mad. I don't like him one bit.

'Your lot think you're something,' he says.

'Who?'

'You know, your lot, bloody snobs.'

I don't think I'm a snob. 'I'm not like that.'

'Your old man is, thinks he's the dog's bollocks because he has a few bloody letters after his name and a few quid in the bank.'

'Oh.'

'*Oh*, you say. Oh, right. You know what I mean.'

I don't say anything to that and he lights another cigarette. I think he doesn't like me after all, but it doesn't really matter because since Paige went I don't think anyone likes me anyway. Anyone except my mum and my brother, but I hardly get to see them now.

I think about my family, about Papa even, and I start to wonder if I'll ever see any of them again. I don't know why I think like this but the thought comes into my head and I start to feel a tingle deep inside my chest that makes me want to cry.

I love them, but nobody else. Not anyone.

'I hear you're a bit of a wild one,' he says. He flicks his cigarette in a little tray in the dashboard and white ash goes all over my knees.

'I don't know what you mean.'

'All the wild ones end up at the party, that's why Paige was taken.'

'*Taken?*' The word sounds wrong, scary.

'Oh, yes. She was a wild one, so they said. But not any more.'

'What do you mean?'

'I mean she went running.'

'Running?' He starts to laugh and his voice breaks into a hacking cough. He's almost choking himself but he can't stop laughing. It's all a great big joke to him.

'Tell me about Paige.'

'No!' He snarls now, and he looks angry again. 'Shut up about her.'

We're outside a big gate, a metal one that's painted black with no other marks at all. He has a little controller, like we have for the telly, and he points it at the gate – it starts to open up, very slowly, and we drive through.

'Bloody big shots,' he says, looking all around us. 'What do you think, is it a palace?'

'It's very palatial, yes.'

He sneers and parrots me, *'It's very palatial.'* I can tell

I've annoyed him. He's starting to frighten me. I wonder what all this is about – the party and the running. I wonder what he means when he goes on about Paige. I start to see her face in my mind, her lovely soft hair and her pale blue eyes. I can even hear her voice; it always makes me feel calm and happy, but not today.

'These posh bastards think they're something,' he says, 'but I know what they really are.'

'What?'

He grins, and taps the side of his nose. 'Bloody scum of the earth. The worst there is.'

'Why?'

'They look down at me, they think I'm filth, but I'm not anything like as bad as them. I know there's a line.'

'Why are you saying these things?'

His face is very red now, little white lines at the side of his mouth and eyes are standing out on the dark flesh. He looks like an imp from a picture book, a fairy tale or one of those folk stories about little goblins that live underground.

He stops the car and grabs my arm, his fingernails dig into my flesh. 'Ouch, you're hurting me.'

'Shut up, just listen for a minute, will you?' He jerks me closer to him, his face is right next to mine. 'These people are freaks. They think they have me over a barrel, but I have a few tricks up my sleeve too.'

'That hurts.'

'Will you just listen?' He throws my arm down.

'I'm listening.'

'They're going to take you to the old cow shed later, down there.' He points to a shabby old building on the edge of the long lawn. I can only see one side and a part of the roof. 'They'll make you run, they'll say if you can run far and fast enough they'll set you free, but they won't ever let you go.'

I'm scared now. 'No, don't tell me this.'

'Listen, we don't have much time. Behind the building there's a path – you have to run right to the bottom of the path and head for the biggest tree. I've put a rope ladder there, if you can reach it you can go over the wall. There's no other way out.'

'Why? Why are you telling me this?'

'Because they'll kill you if you don't! Are you so bloody stupid? These people are freaks, it's what they get off on. Christ, listen to what I'm telling you.' He punches his fists into the rim of the steering wheel.

'But why would you help me?' I don't trust him, and I don't want to believe that any of this is happening.

'Because if you get out, I get out. I'll have something on them too, not just the other way around.'

I start to tremble. I feel the tears on my cheeks. 'Is this what happened to Paige?'

'Paige was unbreakable, just like you. They make sport of the girls they can't control.'

'What happened to Paige?'

'They hunted her down and killed her.'

I cry. My head droops and tears fall onto my school skirt, little dark drops on the grey cloth.

'Oh, Paige.'

'It's too late for her, but not for you, or me. Just do what I tell you and we can get away. Trust me.'

'Okay. I will.'

'You'll run for the big tree, and the ladder?'

'Yes, I will.'

'Good. I'll wait for you on the other side of the wall. If everything goes to plan, we'll have an interesting story to tell, and one or two pictures as well.'

'Pictures?'

'Never mind, that's something for me to worry about. You just worry about getting over that wall.'

30

Valentine and McCormack walked over to the Odeon car park in Burns Statue Square. It was still early evening but there were fewer cars about, most being merely a blur of tail-lights on the road out of town. The solid block of the cinema building, sitting in the full sweep of the road, was an ugly blemish on the skyline that pitched the officers into shade as they walked. Ahead of them, a shabby drunk yawed from side to side on the pavement, making an unwelcome obstacle for them to avoid. As they stepped out, McCormack's quick footsteps made a stabbing noise on the tarmac and then came a gasp as she momentarily lost balance.

'Are you all right?' said Valentine, grabbing her arm and holding her up.

'Just lost my footing.'

He watched the drunk stagger on, unawares. When he returned his gaze to the DI he noticed the loose folds of skin sitting beneath her eyes. A whorl of hair unfurled itself from her head and was forced back into place.

'You look a little rattled. Are you sure you're okay?'

'Yes,' she nodded briskly.

Valentine released her arm and she stumbled again. 'Okay, let's get you into the car.'

'I'm sorry, I don't know what's wrong with me.'

When they were seated inside the Audi, Valentine put the heater on and turned to face the DI. 'Something's up. You can't kid a kidder.'

'It's just... I was never one of the cool kids at school.'

'What do you mean by that?'

'I mean, I worked bloody hard to get where I am.'

'I know, that's why I promoted you.'

She made a weak smile. 'I was always the kid with the homework handed in first. I never forgot my PE kit once. I was one of the swotty ones, not the cool kids, like I said. So all this meeting behind the bike sheds makes me nervous.'

Valentine smirked. 'I understand, and it's natural. But I wouldn't ask you to risk your career doing anything you didn't want to do.'

'It's not that. Not at all. I know I have to do this because the other way has already failed.'

'You see that, do you?'

McCormack paused, her drowsy eyes flickered. 'This investigation has changed me, awoken something in me that I didn't know was there.'

'Meaning?'

'Do you remember when we opened Malky's locker and found that bible?'

'Yes.'

'That shocked me. It was like he'd felt the same thing, like there was a battle going on between good and evil. I must sound ridiculous, but it's what this case has made me feel – that there's more out there than us versus them. There's a real, palpable evil among us.'

Valentine looked away. 'I know what you're getting at.'

264

'You feel it too?'

'We all do. Can't you see it in Kevin and Ian's faces?'

She sat in silence for a few seconds and then replied. 'Yes, I do see it. It's everywhere. Don't you think it's strange, though?'

'In what way?'

'Well, at any other time we'd all be happy with collaring a nonce like Malcolm Frizzle, and here we are going after his enemies in exactly the same manner.'

'We can't know what Malky's motives were.'

'No. Of course, but I certainly don't think they were pure.'

'He never had a pure thought in his life. Look, don't go equating us with that dirtbag – we're not descending to his level – we're merely baiting the hook to catch the fish.'

'That's agreed, but my point is, sir, that it didn't work out for Malky, so why should it work out for us?'

The inky twilight came down around them on the small copse. Davis, crouched over and perching on a large tree-stump, cupped a lit cigarette in his hand. As the others sheltered behind him his skin appeared waxy and pale, his face jutting like a solid cleft of rock. Valentine watched as Davis pressed the cigarette to his lips, time and again, patting the filter like a child's comforter. He was ill at ease, jumpy.

'Why don't you come back here, Ian?' said Valentine. 'No one can get into the outbuilding unless they come through the front door. We'll see them in good time.'

'I'd sooner stay here and watch.'

'But there's nothing to be gained, Ian,' said Rickards.

'I said, I'll wait!' he bit.

'Okay, Ian. Stay calm.'

He spun round. 'I am bloody calm!'

Valentine gazed into Rickards' eyes. A mutual understanding was passed between them. There was no point in riling Davis any more than he already was. They had a simple enough task to do, and it was in no one's benefit to isolate one of the small group's members and single them out for censure.

The others kept clear of the gathering gales and watched the property. Sutherland's house had a row of six Georgian-style windows running along the top floor. On the ground level were four windows, two either side of the stately entrance that was flanked by Doric pillars. It was an impressive property, but the large windows afforded very little view of the interior. The lower windows were occluded by wooden shutters and the upper, though exposed to the outside, showed no more than a well-lit, but empty, interior.

Occasionally, a small, bunched-up woman with timid movements would appear on the front steps and throw out what looked like handfuls of salt. She appeared to be part of the wider group, a participant of some description, but it was unclear what she was actually doing.

The airport party had arrived in a motorcade of three black saloons, and were met by a thin, angular man with outsized hands who ushered them in. None of the important new arrivals had appeared again since. All was quiet inside Sutherland's mansion, almost painfully so to those observing the goings-on.

266

Valentine turned to Sylvia. 'You OK?'

'Fine. How about you?'

'Cold, it's brass monkeys out here.'

'What about the ... ?' She ran a finger up and down her sternum.

'I wish people would stop asking about my heart.'

'Sorry.'

The conversation had been picked up by Rickards. 'I heard about that at the time. A stabbing in the heart, vicious.'

'It wasn't one of my better days.'

'It can't have been an easy recovery.'

'I take so many pills I rattle now.'

'You're better off out the force with that hanging over you – less stress – with any luck they'll just pension you off.'

'I'm not ready for the knacker's yard.'

Davis picked up the gist of the conversation. 'Why not?'

'Sorry?' said Valentine.

'The knacker's yard. It sounds okay to me.'

'You're only a young man, Ian. Aren't you being a bit nihilistic?'

He tutted. 'Is that what you think?'

Valentine noticed Rickards drawing his attention, making a cut-off gesture with his hand and shaking his head. The DCI conceded to someone who knew Davis better than him and kept quiet.

'Hold up, here she is again,' said Davis. 'Salt lady ... and she's not alone this time.'

The others gathered behind Davis at his vantage point and watched as the thin man came out first, carrying a burning torch.

'This is it.'

A group of men in dark, hooded robes started to trail from the mansion house in a slow procession. The single-file trail gave way to a group of four, carrying a girl, naked and splayed, on their shoulders. A further group of torch-bearers came up behind them and the entire collective made its way towards the now darkened woodlands.

'Okay, let's get into position,' said Valentine.

'Yes, let's get going,' said Rickards. 'Everybody know their stations?'

A chorus of replies came from everyone but Davis.

'Ian, did you hear me?'

He didn't answer again, instead slipping down from the tree stump and disappearing into the dark of the wood.

'Jesus, what's wrong with him?' said Valentine.

'Leave him,' said Rickards, checking the battery pack on the camera was still charged. 'He'll be fine. Just remember if anything goes off, and McCormack has to intervene, the rest of us have to regroup.'

'Are you okay with that, Sylvia?'

She nodded. 'Yes, fine.'

'We won't leave you stranded, or in danger.'

'I know.'

'Then, okay. Let's do this.'

Valentine and McCormack made for the stone outbuilding and positioned themselves below the line of the window ledge on the back wall. The ground was moist, squelching underfoot, and the entire area was in complete blackness. Valentine heard Rickards making his way to the other side of the building, pressing through the undergrowth, old, fallen twigs snapping as he went. The detective tried to discern

Davis's whereabouts, but he couldn't hear any more movement or see further than a few feet in front of him.

There were some moments of silence. Complete stillness in the wood where the only sound was the rustling of the wind among the branches. Valentine looked up to see the sky through the patchy canopy – it was streaked with the moon's reflected glow – and then he settled in to gaze upon the eternal emptiness.

When the group from the house neared, their torch-glow began to illuminate the outbuilding. Long shadows stretched along the ground, and then crawled slowly up the stone walls. It made an eerie setting, even before the robed bodies came into view, with the bright flames contrasting starkly against the darkness of the woods.

When the door was pushed open, the interior of the building was illuminated by shooting amber slats of light. A stooping man in dark robes moved to the middle of the room where a heavy iron grate was suspended from the roof beams. Around the grate's edges were black candles, which the man set about lighting with the flame of his torch. When his task was complete the naked girl was laid upon the grate and the others gathered round.

Outside, Valentine watched the goings-on with a growing sense of dread. The girl seemed barely conscious, her head lolling from side to side; occasionally she would try to reach for the side of the grate, to sit up, but would be pushed down. She'd been drugged, that was clear. What was less clear was her fate.

'I can't see their faces,' said McCormack.

'How's Rickards going to get any pictures?' said Valentine.

'That's my point.'

'I won't leave her lying there in that state.'

McCormack made to rise and Valentine grabbed her arm. 'Hold on, just keep your powder dry. Nothing's happened yet.'

'Look at her, she's in and out of consciousness.'

'I won't let any harm come to her, I promise. But we need to get some evidence too, we need Rickards to get some pictures.'

The men in robes started to move around the grate, like it was an altar they were worshipping at. They chanted together, but the words were not distinguishable. The girl's distress only seemed to grow now; she turned from side to side, thrashing her arms like she was in the grip of nightmares.

At the height of the girl's agony, two of the robed men grabbed her legs and another man pinned down her arms. She screamed out, but it was as if no one heard her. As she writhed, the small, bunched-up woman appeared. She was holding something under her robes; as she lowered her hood, the others followed. Her next action was to hoist up her arm: a long-bladed dagger was in her hand, catching the candlelight and casting its reflection to the walls.

'Oh, no ...' said Valentine.

'What?'

'Under her robes!' He ran into the darkness.

'God no.'

As Valentine went he heard McCormack's feet pounding the earth behind him. He heard another sound, a louder thudding, and then there were shouts and screams.

'We're too late!' yelled McCormack.

Valentine didn't reply, he kept pushing through the undergrowth, batting back the low-hanging branches. The shouting intensified, changed tone completely.

'Something's not right,' he bellowed.

They were screams of terror now, but soon silenced by a louder, more definitive, and final, horror.

As a gunshot rang out Valentine halted in the darkness of the woods. Standing still, he heard nothing more – no screams, no panic. Not a voice, or a whisper.

He held steady, his heart pumping so loudly he could hear it in his ears. His spine was rigid, his whole body frozen.

Then another shot came. And another.

The detective tightened his eyes.

A final shot.

Nothing seemed real. The entire moment was marked with the utter unreality of dreams. He couldn't process where he was, or what had happened. For several seconds he stayed still, and then, as if responding to prodding, he ran for the door of the outbuilding.

Valentine arrived at the open entrance a few seconds before Rickards and McCormack.

'Oh, Jesus, what have you done?' he said.

McCormack put her hand over her eyes and turned away.

Rickards was the first to enter the building, as he moved, the baby in the old crone's hands began to cry. The sound of the screaming child sent McCormack rushing in, snatching up the infant.

'Ian, what have you done?' Valentine said.

Davis stood over the fallen and bloodied corpses with

271

the handgun still held in front of him. The smell of gunpowder and a smoke haze hung in the air around him. He was a pale phantom of himself, but somehow calmer than Valentine ever remembered him to be.

'Ian ... give me the gun.'

Davis knelt down and started to remove his victims' hoods. There was Sutherland, with a large portion of his frontal lobe missing. The MEP, Rosenthal, he was dead too. The Labour member of parliament, Jonathan Miller, executed at point-blank range. And Abbie McGarvie's father, Alex McGarvie, dead.

'Ian, please.'

Davis rose and looked straight through Valentine, ignoring his request. He called out to Rickards.

'Tell my wife and kids, I had no choice.'

'No, Ian ...'

He raised the gun to his temple and pulled the trigger.

'No, Ian ...'

There was a brief flash from the muzzle of the SIG Sauer and DI Davis's head jerked sharply sidewards. He fell quickly, onto the bloodied heap of bodies that now covered the earthen floor of the old, stone outbuilding.

'Have nothing to do with the fruitless deeds of darkness, but rather expose them.'

– Ephesians 5:11

Epilogue

Lately Valentine had lost the knack of early starts. The morning coffee had been coming later and later – it would soon be a mid-day affair. He could understand how those with time on their hands became different people. It was possible to change completely, alter your outlook on life. He knew some who had become slobs, couch contents. There were others who became obsessively fastidious, like over-grooming parrots who plucked away their plumage.

It was strange how people changed. He knew he had. There was a time when he thought he wouldn't be able to live without the force, because he believed it was his life. He was wrong, of course. It had never been that. It had never been more than a part of his life – there was more to Bob Valentine, and there was so much more to life.

'Are you sure you don't want me to come?' said Clare.

'No, I have to do this by myself.'

'You know I'm there to support you, whatever you do, Bob.'

He reached out to brush her arm. 'I know that.'

Clare smiled, an easy gesture, like a child's. 'Look at your shoes,' she said, 'you could see your face in them.'

He laughed. 'Dad did them for me. He's not at all bad with the shoe-brush.'

'He's some man.' She leaned over and pressed her lips to his cheek. 'You're quite the chip off the old block, Bob.'

He watched his wife walk back into the house and he headed out to the car. The Hyundai Getz wasn't a match for the Audi, but if he put down the seats he could get his golf clubs in the back, and he certainly wasn't in any danger of a speeding ticket.

As he headed into Ayr, Valentine tried to prepare himself for what was ahead. He hadn't seen any members of the squad, or even any colleagues, save the odd uniform on the High Street, since he'd been suspended. There had been no shame attached to his departure. At first, he wondered why, but later he found he simply didn't care. His only concern was for the way his team might be affected – he didn't especially want DI McCormack to suffer unduly for her part in what had happened. He'd had his career, and she still deserved hers, if that's what she wanted.

He parked outside the gates of the cemetery and made his way into the open gathering. The wind raked his hair as he walked, stirring up old thoughts about Ian Davis on the day of his internment. Valentine would never know what had driven Davis over the edge, but he could, in retrospect, follow some of the trail there. It was pointless, of course, to do that now. Davis was gone, but raking over his actions could be left to others.

He spied McCormack with some officers from the station, and made his way to her side. As the ceremony began the wind picked up, worrying the priest's cassocks and the spray of roses on top of the coffin. Clouds crossed the sky and some weak sunrays were lowered over the cemetery, scattering a bouncing light. The mood was sombre, perhaps more than any other time he could remember.

When the ceremony was over, and the coffin lowered into the ground, a woman in black came forward with three children, the oldest couldn't have been more than six. As he watched the children scattering soil on their father's remains, it seemed like the image of true sadness. As they turned to leave he watched them go, sidling past a floral tribute spelling the word 'Daddy'.

'It breaks your heart, doesn't it?' said McCormack.

'In ways I never imagined possible,' said Valentine.

'I've been thinking about what Dr Mason said about the suicide rate among detectives on this sort of case.'

They started to walk back to the cemetery gates. A blackbird swooped over them and rested on a gravestone.

'What Dr Mason said was on my mind too. That and one or two other things.'

McCormack gathered her collars, squinting into the wind. 'I'd been thinking about the earlier shooting,' she said.

'You mean the shooting of Malcolm Frizzle?'

'And Phil Donnelly. We still have nothing to go on.'

'My conclusion is that Malky simply fell foul of the wrong people. Davis wouldn't shoot one of his own.'

'But if he hadn't found the gun at the scene, we might not be here today.'

'Perhaps. But here we are.'

McCormack looked around, doubts falling from her face. She changed the subject. 'I didn't see Kevin Rickards here, I thought he'd definitely show.'

'I spoke to Rickards, I don't think he wanted to upset Davis's wife by attending.'

'Oh, is there some kind of difficulty?'

Valentine turned to face McCormack, halting in the pathway. 'It was Rickards' idea for Davis to send away his wife and kids; he thought it was for the best, for their safety. Rickards had faced a lot of threats himself, but he never imagined for a moment that separating Davis from his family would be one of the things that pushed him over the edge like that.'

'How could he?'

'How could any of us?'

They'd reached the road.

'Such a horrible outcome,' said McCormack.

'So much heartbreak.'

She held out her hand. 'Goodbye, Bob.'